I0727365

MARLOW

BILLIONAIRE BAD BOYS & BLUE COLLAR MEN
BOOK TWO

EVIE RILEY

Marlow

Billionaire Bad Boys & Blue Collar Men
Book 2

Copyright © 2025 Evie Riley

ISBNs: 978-1-77357-768-5, 978-1-77357-769-2

Published by Naughty Nights Press LLC

Cover Art By CDG Cover Designs

Names, characters and incidents depicted in this book are products of the author's imagination or are used fictitiously. Any resemblance to actual events, locales, organizations, or persons, living or dead, is entirely coincidental and beyond the intent of the author.

No part of this book may be adapted, stored, copied, reproduced or transmitted in any form or by any means, electronic or mechanical, including photocopying, recording, or by any information storage and retrieval system, without permission in writing from the publisher.

Thank you for respecting the hard work of this author.

PROLOGUE

Marlow

"You're actually going through with it?" My best friend's straightforward tone, while normally charming to a fault, was beginning to grate on my ears.

Save for the fact of this being the third time he was bringing up the same subject, I was beginning to wonder how many times it would take for me to repeat myself before Silas finally gave up and accepted the fact that I was doing this.

Coming from his perspective, I supposed I could understand the bewilderment to a certain extent. After all, sitting behind a desk while staring at numbers on a screen all day, every day, wasn't exactly screaming extreme sports enthusiast.

I was a fit man and took care of my health as much as I could given my work schedule, but even that had its drawbacks. There were only so many trails in Ellington Heights I could run before I began to go stir crazy.

Hence the need for a change.

"For the millionth time, *yes*. Can you get off my dick about it?"

On the other end of the phone, Silas scoffed. "You can't expect me not to worry about you. You're going to a fucking wilderness camp where there's mountain lions and bears around. It would be shitty of me *not* to worry about you."

While he had a point, his loud opinion about it certainly wasn't what I wanted to hear. This year, I was on a mission to better my health—to get myself into the best shape of my life and have fun doing it. As wild of a concept as it was to do just that at a wilderness camp, I didn't care.

Not if it kept me from keeling over like my late pops.

"Thank you for caring about me," I said.

The zipper to my bag only barely stayed

together, the opposite side of it bulging with how much stuff I'd managed to cram into the small carry-on sized case. In the welcome packet that had been sent to me a week prior, there were hardly any specifics on what I was supposed to be bringing along with me, outside of the basic toiletries.

Which left liberty for creative freedom.

"Wow, try not to sound like you're being held at gunpoint next time."

"Don't you have lives to save? An organ to stitch back together perhaps?"

"Nope." He let out a grunt that slowly morphed into a deep sigh. "Got the next forty-eight hours off. Lucky me."

Was it really luck if he'd been on a nine-day rotation before this?

While I admired Silas's work and his chosen career path, the life of a surgeon typically sounded like torture to me. Even on the good days where he got to brag about attaching some kid's limb back onto their body.

"Though, I'm sure you'll be calling me your first night there," he said, his tone slipping from that usual nonchalant tone to one that never failed to instigate me. "You'll see one bug bite on your skin and end up losing your mind because you'll convince yourself it was a snake bite instead."

What the hell was with the stray balls?

I got that he was pissy I was leaving him for six weeks, but damn, he didn't have to go for my jugular like that. At least Avery had the decency to sound happy for me, even if he, too, didn't get my decision to go.

I wasn't looking for understanding, I was looking for support. Simple as that.

"How much?" I said.

"What?"

"How much are we betting? Seeing as you're *so* confident I'm going to come crying to you on day one."

"Night one," he corrected. "And you definitely will. Or at least, in the first week."

"How. Much," I gritted through my teeth.

The other end of the phone was silent for a moment, allowing me to finish the rest of my packing while he continued to devise what was probably a very diabolical punishment for me if I was to actually lose this.

Ironic, seeing as how my toxic trait was being competitive as fuck. Turning it into a superpower for my job was the ultimate fuck you to the universe and subsequently everyone else who dared to think they'd be good enough to win against me.

Finances were a game played on a massive scale where the stakes were the difference between buying a second vacation home or getting evicted and kicked out onto the streets. The potential to ruin someone else's life simply by making one wrong move was thrilling if not downright boner inducing.

But I digress.

"It's an IOU," he finally said.

Raising my brow, I repeated. "IOU?"

"You remember what it stands for?"

If only I could reach through the phone and strangle him. The worst part is that he'd probably like it.

"What are the parameters of this IOU?"

"The usual. One favor at any time, any place, anywhere. Winner gets to choose the timeline on when the favor needs to be redeemed by."

"Fine," I said, hauling my bag off of my bed in order to swing it around and dump it next to my door. "You've got yourself a deal. I look forward to proving you wrong."

"Me too. Though, I doubt you will."

Oh, he was so lucky he wasn't standing right next to me. "Goodbye, Silas."

"Call me before you lose service. So I know where to send the forest rangers when they have to come rescue you."

Rolling my eyes, I slammed my thumb down on the 'end' icon and tossed my phone onto my bed.

What was it with surgeons and being giant asswipes?

It had to have been taught somewhere in medical school: 'how to be a douche 101'.

Or maybe it was an upper level class. A real 304.

Whatever. I wasn't about to let him get in my head about this. I'd made my decision weeks ago when I'd signed up and sent in my yearly physical for medical approval. Surviving a wilderness camp for the next six weeks was going to be fine.

I was going to be fine.

All that I'd walk out of there with was probably a mild case of poison ivy and a whole favor richer.

Ah, I could taste the sweet victory lap I'd be doing now while Silas got to eat his words—both metaphorically and physically, because the second I got back from this trip, I was going to make him write down his doubts and then force feed it to him.

A real, put your money where your mouth is type scenario.

Cruel?

Maybe, but he started it.

Good thing I was happy to end it.

My phone chimed with my alarm, reminding me that I needed to get in my car and head over to the pickup site, pronto.

Grabbing my phone and my bag up off the floor, I slung it over my shoulder and gave my bedroom one last cursory glance before shutting off the light and leaving it, and the rest of my problems, behind for the next six weeks.

CHAPTER 1

MARLOW

WAKEFIELD WAS as lush as it was mountainous with the small town about an hour outside of Ellington Heights. Remote and nestled right in the valley of Mt. Craigleith's incredible and towering peak, it was a hidden gem that not many tourists were familiar with, leaving it withstanding the test of time and its annoying insistence on constant change.

Charming brick shops were woven between the narrow streets of Wakefield's downtown district, making it hard for our travel bus to cruise through the budding traffic that was already starting to congest the main drag. Aside from the early hour, there were plenty of residents wandering the sidewalks, coming and going from businesses that were just beginning to open their doors.

This town seemed to have the kind of Hallmark charm that my own possessed without any of the snotty rich folk who tended to meander the well-kept streets with their designer clothes and over the top attitudes.

Although a bit hypocritical on my part, considering I was *also* of the wealthy majority of assholes back in Ellington Heights, I liked to see myself as not *quite* part of the pretentious lot that were obsessed with going to country clubs on the weekends and bothering the poor drink cart girls while shooting birdies with my five thousand dollar club set.

My brand of fun was in the form of dragging my friends to lounge clubs and getting a taste of whatever hot piece of ass came waltzing by with a tight set of jeans on and a drink order already waiting on the tip of their tongue.

Or so it went before Avery had to go and get himself hitched on us. Don't get me wrong, I was happy for the guy because out of the three of us, he deserved to find his happiness the most, but damn did it kill what little time Silas and I had barely gotten back from him after his self-imposed exile to the city.

Despite that, I wasn't one to look down on him for it—avoiding Ellington Heights at all costs. As someone who had a hard time staying in one place myself, what was the point in coming back to old stomping grounds you'd far outgrown?

Unless, of course, it was in the form of a cute little mechanic catching your eye.

Funny enough, getting the phone call late one afternoon by a nervous sounding Avery, pestering me to come down to a local hole-in-the-wall restaurant over in Edgewood sounded like some kind of weird scheme to get back at me for the hangover I'd inflicted on him last time we went out together.

However, the moment I'd stepped into that restaurant, I knew things were changing. Avery's life had undoubtedly—and with no pun intended—become much more colorful since the last time I'd seen him.

All thanks to a humble mechanic from Edgewood.

It gave Silas and I plenty of fodder to poke fun at Avery for being such a late bloomer. Though, now with Avery off living his happily ever after and Silas buried in work like usual, I was ready for some kind of change of my own. Drastic enough to eat up all six weeks of my stored vacation in one go, along with packing over a grand and half's worth of gear tucked safely inside my weekender.

Having never been the type to sit idly while my life continued to pass me by, I was confident that with these upcoming few weeks, I was going to change my life one way or another.

This was all a massively impulsive idea—one spurred by the slow ticking time bomb that I heard rattling off inside of my head every single morning I stared in the mirror while I brushed my teeth and contemplated if I was just seeing things or if there was in fact *another* wrinkle creasing my forehead.

At thirty-five, I was staring down the barrel of middle age and while I'd never had the idea of kids or a husband locked and loaded to pull the trigger on when I was good and ready, I was also starting to feel that weird, niggling of an annoyance that my life was passing me by while I had nothing to show for it.

Ridiculous, of course. I was a fucking millionaire.

But I digress.

Out the window, a rickety old wood sign was the first thing I spotted once the bus pulled off from the main drag and headed past a break in the tree line. The thick canopy of pines shaded us while my ass bruised from the potholes, the descent into what was going to be my home for the next month and a half ripe on the horizon.

My eagerness to prove Silas wrong was a burning pit in my stomach. Mainly because if I had any chance at putting that asshole in his place, I'd take it. We'd been friends for long enough at this point that any sort of competition placed before me on a silver platter would be taken with the utmost sincerity and treated as an official declaration of war.

Especially, when it could end with a big old 'fuck you'.

My stomach lurched with the bus's sudden slamming of the brakes once we reached our destination, bringing us all to a hard stop that had the couple behind me slamming against the back of my seat.

"All right, everyone!" a voice from the front called out. "Welcome to *Austin Adventures!* We're going to have you all stay in the general area until we can get beds assigned. Then you can get yourselves acclimated to the campgrounds before the welcome ceremony begins."

Excitement boiled inside me. A whole big shindig, guaranteed to get me connecting with the people I'd be spending the next six weeks with. Not to mention, it gave me the perfect opportunity to scope out whatever single hotties had come on this expedition like me.

I wasn't delusional to think all I'd be doing on my sabbatical was cruising for someone to fuck behind one of the pavilions, but it could be an added bonus. White water rafting and hiking didn't need to be the only things that would help blow off some pent up steam.

Who would I be to pass up on something like that if it were offered to me?

I grabbed my things and headed off the bus into the awaiting sunshine, my body relaxing the moment the crisp mountain air hit my face. Ellington Heights wasn't smoggy by any means, at least not as much as the city, yet out here the world felt different—alive and brighter than back home in a way that was hard to describe.

The sun beat down on my uncovered arms, the makings of a tan—or what would be the more likely case: a nice, roasted burn in my case —were already underway. Unfortunately, being locked inside of a financial building all day wasn't exactly doing wonders for my complexion, other than leaving me looking like a sickly Victorian child during the winter months.

I wasn't going to call Silas over it to complain. He'd take that as a marker under his column that he was winning.

"Morning, everyone! I'm going to start doing a headcount." A man around my age waved a tablet in the air. His medium length blond hair was pulled back from his face with a bandana headband.

He was a fit man, his body clearly used to the stress and strain of outdoor activities, outlined with under the thin material of his tight clothing that he'd no doubt be stripping off once noon hit along with the heat. He had that commanding way about him, a leader among the lost sheep he'd soon be guiding through the wilderness.

As his voice rattled off in the air, moving down the list, I let my gaze wander around the property.

We weren't the only group in attendance from what I could see. Aside from ours of around fifteen or so, there were more moving about the grounds in small clusters, some of them already fitting with gear to go out for the day while others were taking their time absorbing the place like I was.

Austin Adventures was a popular tourist destination from what I'd researched. Experts in the ways of wilderness exploring, river rafting, and tree top courses, among whatever else was buried under the tabs of options I'd grown bored of clicking through the last time I'd been on their website and had actually pulled the plug with signing myself over to their mercy.

Coming from a background of casual workouts to keep my body in shape and sitting behind a desk all day while only occasionally getting up to pace around my office while I convinced yet another client not to jump ship at the slightest drop in their stock value, I knew I was going to have plenty of sore nights ahead of me. Which is the exact reason I'd stuffed plenty of topical cream and a travel sized heating pad into my bag before I'd left.

"Marlow Knight?"

My head snapped back, my hand raising automatically like a first year school boy. "Present!"

A few people around me laughed to themselves, which only led to stroking my ego and shooting them a wink. I was used to being the life of the party, the class clown as it were, and proudly carried that title well into my adulthood while the rest of my peers were content with dampening their personalities in order to fit in with our homogeneous society.

I had a good chance at finding someone as high energy as me while I was here, and if not in my group, then among one of the several others.

How hard could it be to make friends among a bunch of outdoorsy extroverts?

"Thanks, everyone," the man addressed us again. "Make sure to stick with your partner during the first day. There's going to be a lot going on that you both will need to be present for before activities start tomorrow."

Around me, my group began to break off into pairs without any of them discussing the logistics behind picking their partner. Almost like it was all preplanned and I was simply that idiot who forgot to put his name down on the signup sheet.

Huh...

I flagged down our guide. "So, what happens if you *don't* have an assigned partner?"

"You didn't come with anyone?" he asked, his brow perked up over the rim of his aviators.

"Nope. Just little old me." My comment was meant as a joke, one I figured he'd appreciate considering it was going to make his job easier when assigning me to whatever group activities were available for any given day without the hassle of having to coordinate between two people's schedules.

However, he surprised me when a frown tugged at his lips. A well-manicured finger glided over the tablet, tapping a few times while bringing up some sort of list I couldn't quite see from where I was standing. It was long by the looks of it, extensive like my stock portfolios.

I could appreciate a man who was organized. Just as much as I could appreciate one willing to come undone once the bedroom door was locked.

"That's odd," he mumbled—more to himself than to me. "You were supposed to be paired off."

Paired off?

Aw, fuck.

Don't tell me this was some kind of couple's retreat weekend or whatever. "Can't say I got that memo."

All that came with my welcome packet was an extensive list on how to keep your food safe from bears while out hiking and camping, a reassurance that CPR training that was mandatory among the staff and was strongly encouraged to obtain before coming to *Austin Adventures* for any newcomers, and the type of safety equipment used for overnight stays outdoors.

There were probably other things I'd skimmed over, but nothing had told me a plus one was mandatory.

He sighed. "I'm going to have to call the director."

I had half a mind to joke about offering myself up for mercy to whatever crotchety director was about to come stomping down here from their air-conditioned office and ream me out for fucking up their program, but considering how stressed this guy suddenly seemed, I kept my lips sealed for the time being.

Even if I'd somehow caused a rift in their plans, or whatever the fuck, the ball was in my court. I'd paid handsomely to be here and anyone with half a brain and a hankering to keep my money from being yanked from their pockets was going to be encouraged to figure it out.

"Hey, Blake," the guy spoke into his walkie. "We've got a situation down at drop-off. You mind coming down for a sec?"

The other end crackled for a brief moment before another voice answered. "Yep. Be right there."

Now, a radio was nothing to go off of but to me, he at least sounded younger than fifty. A good sign.

"Sorry about this," the guy said. "You were booked for a different package in our system."

"Does that matter?"

"Well, the pay is different, for one." Not that I cared, I was swimming in more funds than I knew what to do with. "And two, the pre-selected activities all require a partner."

"Well, fuck me, huh?"

He winced. My casual tone was clearly not

helping his stress levels if the pinch between his brows was anything to go off of.

Whoops.

Would reeling it back matter at this point, though?

"You don't have any one-man kayaks or anything?"

He seemed to hesitate. "You didn't sign up for—"

"Talos!" a voice called out, the man in front of me turning to the sound of it.

A figure jogged through the camp, pushing his way past the crowds of people wandering down the midway. He was dressed in a pair of khaki-colored cargo shorts and a loose t-shirt that was half tucked, the other part of it billowing up just enough to show off an impressive six pack with each pounding of his foot against the hard dirt.

The keys at his hip jingled when he slowed, reaching us. "What's going on?"

I scanned him up and down. He was young—much younger than I was expecting.

His handsome face was sun-kissed with freckles that were scattered along the bridge of his nose and cheeks, only a shade darker than his tanned skin. His golden brown hair was parted in the middle with sun-bleached highlights woven throughout the thick strands, long enough to cover his ears and brush along his cheekbones to frame his face.

His arm muscles flexed when he rested his hands on his hips, showing off their impressive bulk.

No way was *this* the director of the entire place.

How old was he?

Definitely not my age. He looked fresh out of college.

"So, he's with the deluxe package but doesn't have anyone with him," the man, Talos, explained. "And there's no one else we've got to pair him up with in the group."

"Oh!" The director glanced over at me. The sun caught his eyes, turning the brown pools into liquid amber. "Your plus one couldn't make it?"

I flashed him a smile. "Something like that."

God, he's cute.

"Would it be such a bad thing if I was riding solo?"

"Mmm, not necessarily."

What was his name, again?

Blake?

"But you wouldn't be getting your money's worth."

He snagged the tablet from Talos's hands, a single finger dragging along the surface of it while he flicked through whatever lists were pulled up. My gaze was unfortunately glued to the slight crook in the digit, an old break that never quite healed right from the looks of it. A by-product of working a job like this, I imagined.

"Is this your way of nicely kicking me off the property?"

Blake fixed his attention to me for a second. "No, of course not."

"I guess this is the part where I get to tell you I don't really care how much I paid for the package and that I just clicked on one randomly when I signed up."

Silas would accuse me of being too impulsive for my own good but I liked to see it as my free-spirited nature letting the universe take its course. Whatever direction I was meant to be ushered toward, I'd take it.

No questions asked. After all, who was I to question divine energy?

He blinked a few times. "You at least read through the welcome packet, right?"

"Yeah, of course. It was something about bears right?"

He was fighting a smile, I could tell. "Among other things."

Talos cleared his throat. "Should we, uh, put him in a solo cabin?"

"He can take the one we were going to assign to him originally." As Blake handed the tablet back over, he shot me a knowing look. "Something tells me you won't mind the extra room."

I kicked the duffle at my feet. "It was the bag that gave me away, wasn't it? Look, I tried to cut down on the necessities, but one can never be too sure which facial cream to take out into the wilderness."

He merely shook his head at me, bringing a fist up to his face to cough into in order to cover up a very obvious laugh. The problem with being a shameless flirt was when people resisted the charm no matter how thick I was laying it on. Don't get me wrong, I loved a good chase, but only if by the end of it I finally caught up to my prey.

Blake was a hard one to read. He'd thrown

me off with how young he was—or at least *seemed*, because who knew what kind of skincare routine the man had that gave him such a youthful glow—and coupled with his good looks, I was riding on half-assumptions here.

"So, does this mean that solo kayak thing is a go?" I lifted my bag off of the ground, slipping the strap over my shoulder.

"Feel free to take up whatever activities you want in between what was planned on the itinerary. I'll figure something out for you in the meantime. You've got a hike up to the waterfall in the morning, right?"

I shrugged, earning me another glowering look. Oh, it was too easy. Blake was a fun thing to poke at, especially when it was obvious he was trying so desperately not to fall victim to my charms. I doubted the poor man swung my way, but resisting the urge to tickle any sort of reaction out of him was just too enticing to ignore.

Talos cleared his throat again. "Yes, waterfall hike starts at eight."

I grinned. "Sounds fun."

Blake nodded at the both of us. "Good. Talos will walk you to your cabin. Please make yourself at home. The welcome ceremony is right at noon, so head over once you're done unpacking and getting settled. There will be some important information that our staff will be going over so don't miss it like you did your packet. After that, the rest of the day is yours."

A laugh escaped me at the subtle dig. "Thanks, Mr. Director. Promise I won't skimp out on this one."

This time, he did smile. "I look forward to quizzing you in the morning."

CHAPTER 2

MARLOW

"Wow, you survived your first night. Color me surprised."

I rolled my eyes at my own reflection, my toothbrush sticking out between my lips while I wrestled for my phone from where I'd tossed it onto the counter the second the other line had picked up.

I knew he'd still be awake despite the ungodly hour I was calling at. Even on his off days, Silas was bound to his horribly short sleep schedules.

"Fuck off," I garbled before leaning over and

spitting into the sink. "I even have a cabin all to myself."

I had to hand it to *Austin Adventures*, the place was fucking nice. The all-wood interior had the bedsheets and furniture seeped in the divine smell of cedar. There were two sets of bedrooms, both fitted with full-sized beds and a bathroom separating the walls from each other.

I had a small kitchenette with a water-stocked fridge and an entirely functioning stove unit, pots and pans having already been set next to it on the off chance I brought something back from the mess hall to cook.

There was an impressive stone fireplace that sat in the middle of the cabin, with pre-cut wood already in the log rack. Two sets of couches and a loveseat faced it, creating a cozy gathering place for the couples that were supposed to be staying here.

Lucky me that I got this entire place to myself.

"Who's dick did you suck to get that?" he shot back, tone mildly bored like he was flipping through TV channels.

"Can't it be chalked up to simply my luck?"

"Maybe with Avery. You? Not a chance."

"The jealousy in your voice is overwhelming."

All I got was a responding snort in return.

Finishing up my morning routine, I shut off the running faucet and headed back into my bedroom with my phone in hand. I tossed it onto the bed and grabbed my duffle, lifting the thing up onto the bed with a soft grunt.

I was curious to see how today would go. Mainly with how Blake was going to solve this little oopsie of mine. To his credit, he'd proven me wrong with my knee-jerk assumptions and had taken the problem—if you could even call it that—in stride. Whatever poor staff member he was going to be forcing onto this hike with me today, I'd pray for them.

If only because I was a beast at cardio.

"So, what wilderness adventure are you going on today?" Silas asked.

"Wow, he's actually curious?"

"I know. Crazy that I care."

Sometimes it was nice to have the reassurance, as stupid as it was to search for in the friends I'd had for more than a decade at this point. Against my better nature, there was still a small child-like part of me that craved praise, craved the positive attention I got from outside sources. I'd gone into finance for that specific reason, making sure that honing my craft would give me the end result I needed.

The paycheck was just an added bonus. What I actually wanted was that slap on the back and a good old '*atta boy.*

Pathologize that fucked up part of me as much as needed—my ID and my ego were on the best of terms. There was hardly anything I got embarrassed over anymore.

"I'm hiking to a waterfall today." Laying my clothes out flat on the bed, I turned to where I'd set my pair of sneakers and brand new hiking boots against the wall on the side facing the doorway.

The problem with last minute packing was now I was running into the fun little issue of having not broken in my footwear, a major misstep on my part. I knew better than to rawdog a three-hour hike and the uneven terrain that came with it.

Lucky me, I brought a fuck ton of socks.

"A waterfall?" He sounded skeptical. "Send a picture in the group chat."

"I will if I have service, but no promises."

The alarm on my phone chimed twice.

Shit.

I was late.

"Gotta go. I'll text you when I get back to camp."

Right as my thumb hovered over the 'end call' icon, Silas shot out a quick, "Don't get lost picking daisies."

I rolled my eyes before tossing my phone again. He'd eat his words. And I couldn't wait to be the one to force feed the shit to him with a smile on my face.

I PACKED LIGHTLY, throwing a small bag over my shoulders with two water bottles I'd stolen from the fridge, along with a spare change of clothes on the off chance that this gorgeous sunny day somehow turned into a downpour.

The worst part wouldn't be trying to trudge down a hiking trail with the slippery mud under my feet, but having to do it on top of being drenched to the bone in wet clothes. My second biggest pet peeve.

Number one?

Wet socks.

That shit drove me insane. There was nothing worse than a squelching shoe.

It didn't take me long to get from my cabin to the meet up spot, a small overlook right on the camp's lake. It mirrored the size of the one we had back in Ellington Heights that separated us from Edgewood, with crystal clear waters reflecting the blue skies above. There were only a few clouds dotting the horizon—and thankfully, all of them were white and fluffy.

"There he is," someone said when I slowed my jog.

"Uh oh. Don't tell me I'm *that* fashionably late." I slipped my thumbs under the straps of my bag, pulling just enough to alleviate some of the weight off my lower back.

Someone stepped away from the group to move closer to me—Blake, I realized once he slipped between a couple. He waved toward the front of the group, catching the attention of one of the staff members and shooting her a thumbs up to start moving our group onto the trailhead.

As Blake turned back to me, he said, "I was just about to send out a search party for you."

His dry tone tickled me, making my toes curl

inside of my shoes. I loved a man who could banter. It was a rare quality these days, unfortunately. Usually, men were quick to either grow dismissive of a conversation if there was no promise of sex at the end, or—in a straight man's case—the threat of emotional vulnerability was on the line.

There was probably some kind of pathology as to why I clung to Silas so heavily, considering he was the one that played with me the most. Avery was a touch on the sweet side, our emotional peach that needed to be handled tenderly in order to keep from bruising his pretty and delicate emotions.

I blamed that shit on his father, though. Getting beat down your entire childhood had to do wonders on the internal psyche.

The only silver lining was how well Brandon seemed equipped to cater to his boyfriend. That's what I liked about him the most.

"Hope you had a K9 unit on standby. I hear these woods can be quite tricky." I flashed Blake a grin.

His eyes narrowed slightly, the corners of his mouth fighting to remain flat. "I'm glad to hear you actually paid attention during the welcome ceremony."

"Would you believe me if I told you I took notes?"

He spun around on his heel. "Glad to hear you'll be passing my quiz, then. "

With the last couple finally heading up the trailhead, I had to wonder what that meant for me.

Were we waiting on another staff member to snag me and escort me up the trail themselves?

Or was I going to be put on something else entirely?

Not that I'd mind, but I was kind of looking forward to seeing that waterfall.

"While we walk, you can point out all of the plants you recognize. Especially the poisonous ones."

His answer had me stopping dead in my tracks. "Wait, *you're* coming?"

He glanced at me over his shoulder. "Yep. Come on, don't want to fall too far behind."

I forced my expression to remain neutral while I shifted into walking behind him.

Interesting.

I didn't hate the idea. Far from it, actually.

If Blake could entertain me until I found someone else to attach myself to for the rest of this vacation, why not lean into the offer?

He seemed more than willing to rib me in a weirdly professional way that kept me on my toes and my brain firing on all cylinders.

Out of anything, that was the one thing I missed about work. I was constantly challenged, forced to find new ways to beat the system all the while gambling with someone else's wealth that could cost me a pretty penny in replacing if I fucked up.

Finance had just enough gambling and strategy to it to satiate that addict side of my mind that craved *more, more, more* no matter how often I tried to feed it something healthy like puzzles and Sudoku.

The high that came with winning was unmatched in the worst of ways.

"Let's start with the poisonous plants." Blake's voice ripped me out of my thoughts.

"Oh, you were actually serious about that."

He whipped around to shoot me another look. "You ignored the welcome packet I painstakingly put together."

"My apologies, Mr. Director." I jogged up

the incline to catch up to him. My breathing picked up a bit from the action. I was used to running on a flat incline. Walking up something that had any kind of ascent was bound to get my heart pumping. "So, you actually own this whole place?"

He laughed, the sound flipping my stomach as he turned back around to face the trail. He didn't seem at all affected by the rapidly warming weather or the gradual ascent from where we'd started back on flat ground. Barely a hair was out of place on that pretty head of his. "My granddad did. I'm the lucky nepo-baby who inherited it."

"How old are you?"

"Twenty-eight."

Jesus, and I thought I was accomplished at a young age. To inherit such a large property and run it successfully—or at least from the looks of it, that's how it was doing—was a feat in itself. I'd had my fair share of accolades throughout the years, starting at the ripe old age of twelve when I'd won our private school's mathletes tournament for the first time. That was my first real taste of recognition over an accomplishment.

Since then, I'd been chasing that same high.

At this point, it was a wonder I wasn't some

kind of adrenaline junkie looking for the next insane thing to fire up those starved neurons in my brain that would most definitely kill me one day. But then again, the praise was the core crux of it all.

Without that, what was the point in accomplishing anything?

"You're avoiding the question, by the way," Blake prodded.

"Oh. Right. How could I forget my promise?" I held a fist up to my mouth and cleared my throat. "Let's see... the poison plant family. There's ivy and oak. Can't forget about their sister, hemlock."

"Wow, so he did pay attention."

"I wasn't kidding about the notes." I was, but he didn't need to know that little white lie. "Belladonna, cow parsnip. Queen Anne's lace if you're stupid enough to *eat* it."

Blake let out another laugh, causing my stomach to clench again.

It had to be the freckles, or the way his nose scrunched up slightly, that was doing it for me. I had a healthy, and albeit *robust,* sex life back home, so I couldn't exactly excuse myself with the whole '*I need to get laid*' lie that I was dying to lean into with how attracted to Blake I was growing.

There wasn't anything wrong with being attracted to a man like him, aside from the obvious of not knowing which team he swung for and causing all sorts of awkward issues because of that. He was hot, fit, and someone who was easy to keep up with during a conversation.

What more could you want?

The thing was, I wasn't looking to get involved with someone high up in the camp's echelon. Far from it, actually. A casual hookup here and there to spice up the day's activities were all fine and good, because at the end of the night, I'd be returning to my cabin alone. Just how I wanted it.

Getting involved with a staff member right off the bat was probably asking for my vacation to implode in on itself. And at that point, I'd only have myself to blame.

"I'm curious." His tone was light as he spoke. "Why'd you come to something like this alone?"

I shrugged, hooking my thumbs underneath my bag's straps again. "No reason. Wanted to try something new. Why?"

Blake shrugged right back. "Like I said, I was curious. We don't get many singletons unless they're a parent of one of our kids."

"Aw, you got little tikes running around? I didn't see any yesterday. They stay overnight, too?"

He huffed softly. "I should probably stop calling a bunch of teenagers 'kids'. They hate it. But I can't help it when I've had a lot of them since they were preteens."

"School program?" I wagered.

He shook his head. "At risk youth. Specifically LGBTQ identifying."

"Oh." That was... surprising. And not at all what I was expecting to come out of his mouth.

He eyed me from his peripheral. "Mhmm."

Oh, I knew that tone. It was the *'watch what the next thing out of your mouth is'* without outright asking me if I was going to be a bigoted asshole or not. Ironic in the best way, considering I felt like my preferences were made pretty clear upon opening my yawning trap of a mouth.

Though on the other hand, one could never be too sure these days. The freedom of expression knew no bounds, after all.

Who was I, or anyone else for that matter, to judge based on perceived inclinations?

Growing up in Switzerland during my formidable years was an experience I'll never forget. Being surrounded by my two best friends, day in and day out, who accepted me for whatever I wanted to be, had shaped me in a way no other outside force else ever could.

I was indebted to those times, much simpler now that I was in the thick of adulthood and could reminisce on how small my problems were back then.

"I see it now." I shot him a grin, elaborating when I received a brow raise in return. "You're a softie at heart."

His lips parted in surprise, lashes fluttering over those deep brown pools that were calling my name, begging me to stare into until I was lost within the dark depths. Suddenly, he drew a hand up to his face, partially covering it from view.

Too bad because I would've loved to revel in what shade of red he was currently turning. I bet it looked lovely against his tanned skin.

"Anyway." He cleared his throat, avoiding eye contact. "What do you do? Your job?"

"Nice segue. Very subtle." I preened at the look he shot me, basking in the attention once again. "Would it surprise you if I said I was in finance?"

"What kind of finance?"

"I'm a financial analyst. Mostly for investments. I get to play with rich people's money all day."

Blake slowly dropped his hand back down to his side. "Was that part of why you said you didn't really care you bought the wrong package with us?"

"Partly." It really wasn't my place to rub it in his face—no matter how unintentional—about my own wealth. Coming from money and then staying in it was a flex I wasn't often keen on putting on the table. Discussing jobs and finances was one thing, yet I found it distasteful to brag about what was currently floating around in the trust fund. Call me privileged, but it tended to do the opposite of what I wanted while in a conversation. "Think of the overage as a donation to your youth program. How about that?"

"How generous." His tone was dry but I could tell from the small smile trying to crawl across his face that he was happy to hear I wasn't looking for any sort of refund.

To me, a few hundred bucks was a drop in the bucket, but for a business like the one Blake was running, that could be the difference between buying an extra palette of food or trying to make due with chicken and rice for the third night in a row.

"Do you like it? Playing around with other's money?" he asked. "Seems kind of dangerous."

"Oh yeah. It's like gambling, I love it. Don't tell anyone that, though, they'll think I have a problem."

A laugh burst out of him. "He says as his eye is twitching."

Oh, I was riding high now. I'd earned myself a full-blown laugh *and* a jest. "Look, I can quit at any time."

Blake merely shook his head at me, his lips still twisted up in a half smile. "You know, I'll hold you to that. Six weeks out here will be a nice detox for you."

"Just don't try to get me into basket weaving. I can't afford bringing a hobby like that back home."

"I'll try to remember to keep you away from

the pavilion when Mara, our basket maker, starts doling out supplies next week."

I stopped short. "Wait, is that actually an activity you have here?" Man, I really needed to look up the damn itinerary.

To his credit, Blake gave me no answer, keeping me on my toes indefinitely. Instead, he simply nodded his head back toward the trail and said, "Come on, let's keep moving."

CHAPTER 3

Marlow Knight was... something else entirely.

A shameless flirt, for one. And an enigma wrapped up into a neat little package that was beginning to scream *'danger!'* every time I caught his eye with my own.

At first glance, Marlow was simply a friendly guy who liked to joke around and have a good time. The type of guy who'd be a good wingman out at the bar, but someone you'd hesitate to bring home to meet your parents. He was charming, funny, and a little bit reckless in the least threatening way possible.

Deep down, though, there was something else lying right beneath the surface. A kind of trickster energy that my own was feeding off of tenfold and I had no way of braking that train from careening off its tracks.

It'd been a while since I'd felt equal in a conversation—at least in terms of snappy back-and-forths that didn't end in the other person looking at me like I had ten heads or hurt because of something I quipped back with without dressing it up in a frilly little bow.

Whatever I threw at him, Marlow took with ease. An attribute I could admire in a man.

Taking over as his partner for the foreseeable future was a spontaneous decision on my part. One that was abruptly becoming clearer by the second how terrible of an idea it was. I was having too much fun being pulled away from my duties managing the camp's grounds, to the point where I'd left my radio back on the charger in my office intentionally before I'd even embarked on this hike.

That wasn't me. I was supposed to be more responsible than this. Not get caught up in some guy with charming dimples and a cheeky smile, whose tall and muscular body was as strong as it was nice to look at, who had a witty personality that had so easily won me over.

Keeping my well-oiled machine was a difficult task that didn't need to be derailed just because I'd suddenly caught interest in someone for once in my life.

My sisters would be beside themselves if they knew. I'd been badgered more times than I could count about burying myself in the campgrounds instead of going out there and actually socializing like any normal twenty-eight year old.

But what 'normal' twenty-eight year old was running a million dollar company, along with a non-profit on the side?

Not many. At least in this area.

"You good?"

Looking over to my left, I spotted Lydia walking over to me with a water bottle in her outstretched hand. Her shoulder-length blonde hair was pulled back in a high ponytail, slightly curled at the ends from the humidity, and that bounced with each step.

The hike up had been long but nice; a good kind of burn had settled into my legs not long after we'd reached the end of the trail and had come among Mt. Craigleith's twin waterfalls. The draft coming off of the water's spray was cool, as was the small area we had all settled in to rest and take photos of the water.

Marlow had wandered off not long after we arrived, leaving me to check in with the rest of our group, along with sending back a report to dispatch that we'd made it all in one piece.

"All good," I said, taking the water from her and cracking the top off. "Why?"

She shrugged, watching me toss back the bottle and drain half of it. "You looked lost in thought. Didn't know if something happened down at camp before we got up here."

Yeah, my libido suddenly rose from the dead.

"Nope, all good."

She eyed me carefully but kept her mouth shut once I had the cap back on the bottle. Lydia was a smart cookie, especially when it came to backing off on subjects that weren't any of her business. She was my survivalist expert, specializing in all things wilderness camping, hiking, and off trail exploring.

Coming out here was her bread and butter, and *technically*, I was encroaching on her territory. She was just nice enough not to say anything, or rather, was curious to find out *why* I'd volunteered myself when I should've been back at camp preparing for next week's batch of kids that were coming for the water obstacle course challenge contest we were hosting.

Ugh, I'm going to be up all night catching up on my planning...

"You look stressed, Blake."

I was. Especially now that I was out from under the umbrella spell that was Marlow fucking Knight. "Yeah..."

"You need anything? I can handle everyone if you want to head back."

My gaze darted over to Marlow immediately.

He had his phone out to record the spray coming off of the side of the cliff, his body moving slowly while he panned the lens to capture the entire beauty of this small slice of paradise. I'd overdone it volunteering for this activity. There was hardly any imminent danger that called for an extra pair of hands, not like belaying while rock climbing or camping out in the forest would call for.

Sighing, I ran my hand through my hair to

push the pieces falling over my forehead back. "You mind if I check in with Talos?"

Without another word, she unclipped the radio from her pack and handed it over to me, the frequency already tuned down to base camp.

"Talos," I said into the walkie.

There was a pause on the other end before a familiar voice responded. "Go for Talos."

"Can you switch to four?" Lydia stepped away to reconvene with the group as I tuned the radio to a private channel and waited for Talos to pop over onto it.

"*What's up?*"

"Everything okay down there?" A stupid question considering my second-in-command wouldn't delay in paging the ever-loving shit out of Lydia's walkie until I answered him. But I still asked anyway.

"All smooth sailing. How was the hike? You haven't been up there in a while."

Turning to face the water feature, it occurred to me how right he was mentioning that. There wasn't a particular reason *why* I never took the time to spend more than an hour or two outside nowadays, other than using the excuse that I was too busy. Since taking over after my granddad's retirement, I'd been crushed under the over-whelming need to fill his shoes.

A tall order, if I was being honest.

Having been in this position for a little less than five years, only now was I starting to feel like I was getting the ropes of it without default to calling my granddad to verify whether or not I was making the right decision.

And now I was being totally distracted. What ironic timing.

"Yeah, it was nice. Quick trip. I might come back early."

Talos chuckled. "You that out of shape?"

I rolled my eyes. "Funny. You need anything?"

"We're all good here. Take your time, Blake. Enjoy the fresh air for once. You're getting a little pale."

I looked down at my bare arm.

Was I?

"I'll see you at dinner."

"Call me if something happens."

"Yes, you worry wart. I will."

Switching back to the default channel, I let the walkie drop to my side to rub a hand over my face. Maybe Talos was right. Hell, Lydia too. I was cooping myself up too much in my office when what I really should've been doing was getting out and getting my hands dirty like the rest of my staff.

Paperwork could wait. We only had so much good weather before the bitterness of autumn hit and we were all forced indoors for a few agonizing months.

Why not get out and enjoy the good weather while I still could?

A nagging worry tickled at the back of my mind.

Sure, the paperwork wasn't going anywhere, but within six days, I'd have fifty teenagers showing up at the camp's drop-off zone, eager to be competing for this year's scholarship prize.

This was the first, of hopefully many more to come after this, annual event that was completely mine. From conception to the eventual execution. And I was definitely freaking out about it internally.

Not that I let anyone know that. If anything, they probably thought I was being way too lax about it—coming out here on a hike when I should be holed up in my office figuring out where the fuck to put all the kids and keep the adults that were already staying here out of their business.

Don't get me wrong, I enjoyed the money that we brought in from the buses full of outdoor enthusiasts, but my real passion was the youth groups. If I could somehow convert *Austin Adventures* into a strictly Youth Only destination without losing a fuckton of money, I'd do it in a heartbeat.

Those kids deserved their own spaces. Ones where they could *actually* explore the independent freedom that came with outdoor adventuring and not be bogged down by adults crushing them with their never-ending rules.

I hated that. I hated seeing such brilliant lights be sucked dry by society. Especially when they were LGBTQ. The world was a cruel place at times and if *Austin Adventures* was the only soft place for their poor heads to land, then I'd do whatever it took to make sure they were kept safe and happy.

"Everything all good?" Lydia asked, coming back over to me.

I tossed her walkie back to her. "Yeah, I'm going to head back. Just realized I've got a mountain of paperwork to go through."

She shook her head at me in a familiar way, reminding me a lot of my granddad. "Oh, Blake. Don't you get tired of pushing papers all day?"

Yup. But that's what came with the territory when you decided to take on a giant million dollar family business like this one.

I was damn proud of it, though. If paperwork was the price I had to pay to keep our doors open, then so be it. I'd welcome being the sacrificial lamb.

"Can you make sure Knight gets back down okay? He wasn't struggling coming up or anything, but I have a feeling he's the type to wander off and get himself lost."

Lydia turned to look over her shoulder at the same time that my gaze darted back to him. He was sitting on one of the logs where an old fire pit used to be, deeply engaged in some kind of animated conversation with a couple that was sitting on the logs opposite of him.

Marlow said something to the couple, causing them both to throw their heads back and laugh in unison. He was then offered half of their sandwich, a flourishing wave following as a thank you.

I truly was fascinated by him. Almost like he

was an exotic fish exhibit that I couldn't bear to tear my eyes from no matter how distorted my vision got from the warped glass.

"Yeah," Lydia drawled. "I'll keep him next to me. I'm sure he'll be more than happy to chat my ear off."

I hated to admit I was a little jealous, but quickly pushed those thoughts into the back of my mind. "Thanks. I appreciate it."

"No problem. Take your time getting back down there. I don't want to stumble upon you with a broken leg because you were rushing."

I threw her a chastised look. "I'm insulted you think I'd be so reckless when I was the one that taught *you* how to hike properly."

She smiled. "Guess my memory's a little fuzzy considering it's been so long.'

Point taken.

After next week, I'd *actually* follow her and Talos's advice and get out for once. It couldn't hurt to bake myself in the sun for a while, especially with the dig about my tan.

I just needed to get through next week. And then I'd be home free.

CHAPTER 4

M ARLOW

"I CAN'T BELIEVE my walking buddy ditched me," I said on our descent back to the camp-grounds.

Actually, I could, but I was trying not to hurt my own feelings over seeing Blake disappear down the trailhead at a quick jog, not even both-ering to come over to me to tell me something had come up and he was needed elsewhere.

I was choosing to believe at this point in time that a giant fire had broken out down at base camp and Blake was running to rescue the poor cooks trapped inside of the locked freezer. Only he knew the code to get in and people were on their hands and knees, frantically praying for an act from God to rescue their poor coworkers and would soon be crying out of joy once Blake showed up.

"Don't take it personally," my *new* walking buddy, Lydia, said. "He gets pulled in a hundred different directions all day."

I had half a mind to ask her *what* exactly had caused Blake to skip out on me like that. I highly doubted she'd get into it, though. Something about blah, blah, professional conduct or whatever.

Instead, I sighed and shook my head. "Don't tell me, that's just the excuse he gave you. It was because I smelled, wasn't it?"

Lydia's brows shot up, her face pinching into a confused and bewildered look. "No... he didn't mention anything about that. Don't worry."

Man, tough crowd.

"Phew! What a relief."

"There are toiletries down at Guest Services if you forgot to bring something with you. They've got deodorant, toothpaste, mouthwash, floss, extra socks, and whatnot."

Oh, sweet, sweet Lydia.

This was the time where I was supposed to be cooling down from my constant need to put my jester hat on and dance around the court until I was able to draw a laugh out of my audience. In any normal circumstance, I'd reel it back, read the crowd and find a better balance between continuing the bit like I wanted to and dumbing it down just enough so the other person could join in on the joke.

The unfortunate problem was that I was still riding that high of Blake *getting it* without me having to taper myself to a more *relaxed* kind of company.

And so therefore, my mouth was running way faster than my brain to be able to stop myself from saying, "No toothbrushes, though? Cheapskates."

Her eyes widened. "No, no. We have toothbrushes. Seriously, anything you need, we probably have. If we don't, we can send one of our councilors out to the Stop-and-Shop in town to grab something. It's no problem."

Regret hit instantly.

Aw, fuck. Now I was giving this poor girl something to worry about.

Coming from her perspective, I was some

wealthy shithead whining about not having something that was *most definitely* outlined in Blake's trusty welcome packet to bring, along with probably a plethora of other things mentioned. And now I was making it *their* problem to make up for my fuckup.

See, this was the problem with having a personality that centered around irony being the butt of *every* joke. Too many people took me seriously.

"Well, good thing I've got one of those fancy spin brushes back at my cabin." I plastered on a smile to, hopefully, make sure I came across as sincere.

The last thing I wanted was for this poor girl to force one of her coworkers to take a trip into town just to buy me a bunch of bathroom essentials because I was coming across as too good to use what would've been provided for me.

I was a rich asshole, but I wasn't one of *those* types.

I liked my luxury commodities as much as the next guy, but I also knew how to handle being without. I'd had a rude awakening in college when I was given the famous figure-it-the-fuck-out-on-your-own speech the second I found myself in my admission advisor's office the second week of classes after complaining about professor biases. I figured it out fast.

Took that alumni legacy wind right out of my sails.

Lydia cleared her throat. "Well, I'm glad you brought what you needed. But don't hesitate to go down to Guest Services if you need anything. There is always someone on duty."

"Even if I have a midnight craving for those bread pudding squares you guys had out last night?"

Her face pinched again. "Yeah... I'm sure we can figure something out for you."

Okay, this was officially the time to shut my trap and let our poor guide do her job without feeling the need to let me keep pestering her. A shame, really, that Blake had to ditch. Now, he was probably going to be getting an earful once we reached base camp about how much of a high maintenance client I was.

Maybe that'd get me a swift knock at my cabin door after dinner for a little chat about guide-attendee etiquette.

Actually, I wouldn't hate that.

Was it bad to intentionally cause trouble just to get Blake's attention?

Or maybe that was going too far. I was letting myself get a little *too* wrapped up in this fantasy, or rather, preconceived idea of the camp's director.

All I knew about that man was he was good with banter, had a soft spot for the LGBTQ youth, and was probably a little young for running a large business like this on his own. Outside of that, he was a complete stranger. Clearly, my attraction to him was getting a little out of hand if I was letting my mind wander *this* much.

Looking back at the group following after us, I eyed the couple I'd chatted with during our break—Luke and Aimee. They were nice, friendly and were definitely giving me the once over as soon as I stood to stretch myself after the walk. Now, I could be reading into things, but I could usually smell a pair of swingers from a mile away.

What better time to test out the ole gaydar if not to distract myself from Blake?

THANKFULLY, there were no burning buildings or outposts waiting for us when we got back to base camp. As disappointing as it was to find out my conspiracy theory was in fact, just that, I was also a little relieved to know I wouldn't be getting shipped out on a bus back to Ellington Heights once the fire department gave the all-clear.

Which still left the question: where the fuck did Blake go?

At this point, I supposed it didn't really matter. For whatever reason, he'd ditched and I'd have to deal with it. Tomorrow, I'd most likely wake up to some other camp counselor taking his place, who would no doubt also be freaked out by my motor mouth, but such was life as the life of the party.

The time to rendezvous with my suspected swinger-couple came around just after dinner service ended and the sun was beginning to set just past the mountains, creating an incredible sight of the oranges and reds of the fading rays, glowing against the lake's rippling surface.

I had to say, Craigleith's lake was downright fucking gorgeous. It put the one by Ellington Heights to shame by miles. With ours caught in the middle of separating two small towns, and a third by extension, the banks of it weren't exactly made for pleasure seekers. There were small beaches here and there scattered north of our towns, but nothing like *this*.

Craigleith's lakefront wasn't marred by the lights of a glimmering town in the distance, or the distant sounds of a speedboat or other watercraft operated by one of the spoiled rich kids who lived in Ellington Heights when daddies and mommies simply wanted the kids out of their hair.

Where the camp sat had a clear shot to Craigleith Mountain with not a single thing interrupting its magnificent view.

Fucking breathtaking. Just like that damn waterfall.

I really needed to bring Silas and Avery out here. I couldn't live with myself if I hogged this hidden gem all to myself.

"Hey, Marlow." Turning to the sound of my name, I spotted Aimee walking toward me, a sway in her hips. "You going to join us at the bonfire later?"

Code for: *you're going to come back to our cabin afterward, right?*

Honestly, I was on the money. However, we

were definitely going to need some ground rules laid out before any kind of swords touched. Namely in the form of no swords and sheaths touching. I was all about celebrating female divinity and the delicate nature of the opposite sex, however my dick wasn't exactly in agreement to that same admiration.

Embarrassing myself with a rapidly deflating boner the second poor Aimee got undressed and wagged her finger at me to come fuck her wasn't exactly my idea of a nightcap. Especially, if her husband was laid out on the bed looking like a fucking snack and a half and my divining rod suddenly sprung back to life.

"Yeah, definitely." I shot her a wink. "I'll see what kind of treats I can sneak out of the mess hall. I've got an in with one of the cooks. I heard they've got a ton of whipped cream back there for those bread pudding squares."

She giggled. "Sounds good. We'll see you soon."

As she sauntered off, she flipped her hair over her shoulder, her hips swaying just as much as they did when she first approached me. An obvious show of what she was offering me. Too bad I wasn't a man of both interests. Aimee was beautiful and clearly ready to get down the second I dropped my drawers.

What a shame.

Checking my watch, I realized I had about a half hour to check in with Silas before nighttime plunging the grounds into darkness. I wasn't a poor navigator by any means, but this was unfamiliar territory and trying to find a couple I barely knew in the dark with other people wandering around would be annoying.

Especially, with a few bonfires being erected and having no clue which one they were going to be at.

I was looking for a quick fix, not some long and drawn out chase. I didn't *chase*—I attracted.

As I turned to head back to my cabin, I stopped dead in my tracks, seeing a familiar face walking toward me.

"Glad to see you're making friends." Blake flashed me a smile.

He had on a light jacket that wasn't zipped. His shirt was no longer half tucked in and fell fully out from under his waistband's trap. The clothes were baggy on him, hiding what I was suspecting was a very healthy six pack under all of that fabric.

My toes curled inside my boots. "Well, well. Look who it is."

He had the decency to wince at least. "Sorry about earlier. Had some things to deal with."

The gold and pink rays from the sunset bathed him in a warm tone. His amber eyes mixed with the red hues, giving them a flame-like appearance that drew me in immediately.

What was it about Blake that enchanted me instantly?

A moth to a bonfire, as it were.

This would've been so much easier if I hadn't just gotten laid two days before I came on this trip and had the excuse of a fried libido. Right now, I was just simply being a fucking horndog.

Straight?

Gay?

Bi?

I was dying to know. The LGBTQ youth group threw me off until I remembered that straight people could *also* care about being good allies. Particularly when it came to kids. They were a soft spot for most people.

Maybe it was because he was sporty. They were always hard to read. Homoerotisim was bred into any male-dominated sport, especially if it came with any sort of manhandling, like wrestling.

Who came up with the idea that a sport like that was peak masculinity?

I'd pretzeled more guys into those positions when fucking them then ever in any competition on a mat.

"Hope it was a rescue mission." And not something stupid like someone else needing his attention more than me.

That would be an even bigger insult to him growing bored of me.

Then again, that could also be for the best. I was supposed to be occupying my time with other participants, after all.

He stopped in front of me, crossing his arms over his chest in a loose manner. He wore a playful smile, the corners of his eyes crinkling.

How bad was it that I wanted to reach out and brush my hand through the tangled mess of his hair and smooth the front fringe out of his eyes?

It looked like he'd been running his fingers through it for the better part of the last hour or so.

"Honestly, I wished someone would've come

to rescue *me* from the mountains of paperwork sitting in my office." He laughed lightly.

He ditched me for that?

All right, now I was actually kind of insulted. There was no way I was that boring. I'd gotten him to laugh. To joke back.

Was that not fun enough to stick around and save the paperwork for tomorrow?

"Lydia told me you were looking to visit Guest Services for some things?"

Oh, Lydia. Gone off and ratted me out to the boss.

The reminder of my actual mission for tonight was welcomed, even if I was now feeling a little salty. A good fuck would get my head on straight and wrangle my ego back in. No matter how offended I felt at the moment.

Paperwork.

He ditched me for fucking paperwork...

"Yeah, actually." I crossed my arms, too. "You got any condoms stocked in there?"

Blake instantly choked. "*What?*"

Even in the poor lighting, I could tell his face was instantly going red.

Too easy. Far, far too easy.

"She mentioned you guys had a little of

everything. Figured I'd ask the concierge before I went poking around to the other guests."

He blinked a few times, quickly swiping a hand over his face to cover up how thrown off he was. It was cute, really, how flustered he'd suddenly become. Maybe I was being a little crass but sue me, I was in my feelings. Plus, watching Blake squirm was... fun.

Amusing, even.

What kind of man was he in bed?

Controlling?

Dominant?

The complete opposite?

I usually saved getting into the minds of people for my clients and rarely let it slip into the bedroom. Most men I brought into my bed got squeamish when it came to giving up control, as it was kind of in our nature to crave it.

Me?

I liked a man who wasn't afraid to leave that shit at the door and let *me* do the work for the both of us.

But those were rare cases and ones that seldom ever lasted more than a few months. An unfortunate side effect of our society that demanded constant performance and never rewarded the good behavior of those willing to let their inner submissive thrive.

Too bad, too. That was my ultimate turn on.

"I can check." Blake's voice was drawn out, unsure. "Can't say I've seen that behind the desk before."

"Really? That's surprising."

When he finally made eye contact with me again, his brows pulled together. "Really? Why's that?"

Turning slowly, I gestured to the couples who were now starting to gather around one of the bonfire sites being set up. Two of Blake's coworkers were stacking the wood in a proper angle while another was off to the side, waiting with a gas can in hand. "I mean... you have a bunch of fit, hot people running around. Kind of ignorant *not* to assume some of them were going to be fucking."

Blake slapped another hand over his face.

"Did I burst your innocent bubble? You had to have known that, right? Surely you weren't *that* ignorant." I'd give him a little bit of slack since he was still in his twenties, but come on. Even this was a little naive.

"I thought you came here by yourself," he

mumbled against his hand. "Everyone here is, like, together with someone.

I grinned. "You never heard of swingers, Blake?"

His eyes went wide for a brief second before he turned away from me and cleared his throat once more. He shifted his weight a few times, his attention dancing around the people coming and going around us while he searched for a way out of this conversation.

Guess now I knew where the limit was. Interesting that it was hitting on the sex bit. Most young guys were totally down for some dirty talk, even if it was all hypothetical.

Did this mean he really was straight and was only interested in keeping the LGBTQ stuff at arm's length?

How odd for someone who spoke so fondly of them earlier.

Oh god, unless he was part of some religious sect that was all about the purity before marriage thing.

"Yeah, I'll, uh—" Right before he turned away from me, he gave me a brief nod, pulling himself together. "I'll check on that... uh, inquiry you had."

I gnawed at the inside of my cheek. "Yeah, cool. Stop by my cabin if you find any. If I'm not there, you know what happened."

He didn't say anything in response, simply fast walked back the way he'd come and soon disappeared around one of the buildings. What a shame. Here I thought Blake could handle the banter, but clearly I'd struck some kind of nerve.

Which wasn't expected at all.

What an odd guy.

Couldn't say I wasn't a little disappointed. But hey, there were always more fish in the sea. Bigger and less bashful, even. More my style than hand holding the babies that had only just started flying out of the nest on their own.

Twenty-eight wasn't exactly young by any means, however, I had almost a decade's worth of experience on top of that. Plus my shameless and unabashed attitude to go along with my massive ego. Hardly anything caught me off guard enough to render me speechless, let alone throw me off my groove.

He'd probably avoid me now. Probably for the best, unfortunately.

Clearly, I couldn't contain myself from stepping over the line with him. Not even a full day into knowing him and I'd already fucked up. See, this was why I went after guys that I had no connection with. It was so much easier than trying to weasel my way into the good graces of those that *actually* tickled my brain.

Not that I was going after Blake in the first place. Camp staff was still off limits.

Sighing, I spun on my heel and headed for the bonfire to find my new couple friends.

Ignoring the disappointment was going to be easier said than done, though I was sure once I was balls deep in Luke while Aimee sat on the bed and got off while watching us fool around, I'd soon forget all about Blake and that pinched expression I wanted to kiss right off his face.

CHAPTER 5

BLAKE

I SHIVERED HARD, pulling my jacket tighter around my body. My shoes crunched against the gravel walkway as I trudged alone in the dark, gaze trained ahead to keep from tripping over my next step.

The campgrounds had plenty of flood lights around the main parts, but back here by the staff cabins, there wasn't much aside from the occasional porch light, if someone remembered to leave it on after retiring for the night. I was one of those culprits, unfortunately.

Before leaving my office, I'd neglected to grab

one of my flashlights. I'd had the ridiculous thought of getting back to my own cabin well before the sun set, which of course had been immediately derailed the second I saw Marlow wandering out of the mess hall. Soon, I was standing in front of him with no idea how the hell my feet had carried me so far before I realized what I was doing, and then the rest was history.

A fucking embarrassing history, at that.

Why the hell I let myself get so damn flustered with him was actually a mystery. It wasn't like he was being overly explicit. In fact, it seemed rather tame compared to what could've probably come out of his mouth given he was still sober and had yet to join the bonfire festivities.

There was no reason for me to suddenly become a blushing bride and run away from what was now, upon reflection, a pretty mild conversation about sex.

It wasn't like I was a virgin. I'd had plenty of people occupy my bed before.

"You never heard of swingers, Blake?"

My stomach twisted. The way he'd asked that drove me insane. Like getting laid was some kind of competition and he was definitely winning at it.

What did I care?

I didn't even know this man. I couldn't even call him a friend, let alone an acquaintance. Letting him get under my skin was stupid, seeing as he wasn't trying to in the first place.

So what the fuck was wrong with me?

The wrappers in my pocket made a soft crinkling noise as I headed up the short hill and down to the client cabins.

Fucking condoms.

Who asks for that?

Someone with obviously no shame and a whole lot of self-confidence.

Sneaking a handful into my pocket while Kaylee was rattling off my ear on the group of four who came in earlier demanding their own personal first aid box was a testament to how good my poker face could be if the stakes were high enough.

How many condoms did the typical threesome use in a night?

Four?

Five?

A whole sleeve?

Honestly, I was shocked when I found the box after some digging. Tucked back behind the supplies of tissues and Band-Aids, still new and completely untouched.

Even more surprising?

They were still good. Which had me mentally tallying up my entire staff roster on who the culprit was that not only put them on the supplies list to order, but hid the box behind a bunch of shit so no one else knew we had any.

Clearly, I needed to be more diligent in looking over our order list before sending it off to the supplier.

Though, maybe Marlow had a point.

Wasn't it kind of irresponsible on my part *not* to have some kind of protection for people to take when needed?

Like he said, adults were going to fuck regardless.

Who was I to hamper them from doing so by holding any sort of contraceptive hostage?

Ugh, I wouldn't even have to worry about this if he never asked. I could've lived in blissful ignorance to what he was getting up to on his second night here.

Two nights in and he'd already found someone to sleep with.

That had to be a record, right?

Established couples didn't count.

I shouldn't have been thinking about any of this, anyway. I should've been holed up in my office outlining next week's event. Not walking to Marlow's cabin well after the sun set.

Coming up onto it, I pulled in a deep breath and climbed the few steps onto his porch, the condoms crinkling once more, mocking me.

I shouldn't even be here, let alone raising my hand to knock on his fucking door. This was the job of my staff, to run and fetch things for our guests—within reason—, not the director's. Since he'd arrived on my property, I'd taken it as a personal mission to handle all things Marlow Knight.

And for what?

I raised a hand, poising it over the door to knock. And froze.

The lights were on inside, though there was no movement that I could hear. The curtains were drawn, so that made it hard to tell if anyone was home. I prayed he was alone and wasn't about to show up half naked, sweaty, and with a blissed out smile on his face when he answered the door.

In fact, it'd be best if he didn't answer at all.

Or I got a fucking clue and turned right around before knocking to begin with.

I'd already made a fool out of myself today, why add to it?

Clearly, Marlow was kidding about the swinging—he had to be. He was all jokes and hardly any bite. Nothing he said should be taken seriously, let alone by me.

Knock, you idiot. The sooner you get this over with, the faster you can go home.

With a surge of gusto, I slammed my fist against his door three times.

Please don't be here. Please don't be here.

The night was quiet enough to hear movement through the door, a pounding of feet heading my way with the thumps growing as loud as my heart rate.

The second the knob twisted, I stepped back.

"—yeah, so then I went to... Oh hey!" Marlow tilted the phone from his ear.

There was a soft and subtle chattering from the other end of his phone, though what the other person was saying, I couldn't really make out. Whatever it was, Marlow snorted and rolled his eyes, then leaned his body weight against the doorframe.

I thumbed a finger over my shoulder. "I can come back if I'm bugging you."

He shook his head, tilting the phone back to his mouth. "I'll call you back later. Got a visitor."

Marlow was dressed still, though not in the same clothes he'd been wearing all day. He had on a pair of gray sweats and a dark colored t-shirt, both of which showed off his athletic build. No signs of sweat or labored breathing, though his hair *was* wet.

Shower, maybe?

"What's up?" he asked.

"That thing you asked me about earlier..."

His eyes lit up. "Oh, yeah. You find any?"

For a moment, my mouth refused to move. My hand hovered over my pocket, just breezing over the subtle bulge that could be mistaken for a wallet, a cell phone, and not the fist full of condoms I'd shoved in there like a kid stealing candy behind his health nut mom's back.

"No," I lied.

What the fuck?

"Bummer." Weirdly, he didn't look all that upset about it.

I forced myself not to look past him and into

his cabin to check if he was actually alone in there. "How was the fire?"

"Eh, got a little toasty, so I headed back early."

Alone?

The word was right on the tip of my tongue, burning. "Gotcha."

Marlow leaned back from the doorway, nodding his head toward the inside. "Want to come in?"

That familiar *'danger!'* warning was screaming at me once again. Not at all working to deter me as one foot was put in front of the other and I was soon crossing the threshold into Marlow's cabin. He swung the door shut behind me, smelling faintly of campfire and whatever expensive shampoo he'd used, while he stepped around me and headed over to his kitchenette.

"You want a drink?"

"Think I'm good on my water intake for the day." I'd forgotten how nice these cabins were.

My granddad had put a lot of time, energy, and *money* into making them top-notch in quality. He'd never been one to cut corners and do things the cheap and easy way. Sourcing the proper material, finding a good contractor and build team, all took plenty of hours that most business owners would turn their noses up at and scoff at for wasting valuable time.

But my granddad believed in things that were worthwhile taking time. As much as needed, so long as at the end of the day, the final result came out better than expected.

I'd always admired that. It was hard to be patient when the world valued a quick turnover. Money was to be made in the fast-paced environment of stocks and corporate profits; case in point, Marlow's entire career.

I couldn't even begin to fathom the kind of money that man made given how nonchalant he'd been about this whole wrong-package ordeal. Barely batting an eye when it came to losing out on a few hundred bucks was eye opening to say the least. I'd taken a peek at his application as soon as I'd gotten back to my office, had gotten one glance at where his residence was, and that had given me all I needed to know.

He was *rich, rich.*

"Actually—" He pulled the fridge door open, producing two uncapped beer bottles. "I snagged these from the cooler down at the fire."

I winced.

Drinking with him seemed like a bad idea on more levels than I could count. However, the temptation was certainly there. A beer wouldn't kill me, could hardly make me any stupider than I already was, running away earlier.

"Come on." He waggled it at me. "Don't you let loose sometimes, Mr. Director? You can't be that much of a stick in the mud when you're not even thirty yet."

Ironic he was calling me that when I was currently holding his condoms hostage like some lunatic and lying about finding them altogether. Or like a jealous ex refusing to let him move on because they were still hung up on the relationship.

Holy fuck.

Was I jealous?

My hand shot out, gesturing for him to toss me the bottle.

Instead of doing so, he laughed and nodded to the couches. "Go sit."

Responsible. Not willing to trash my property on the off chance he threw it too wide or I was shit at hand-eye coordination. He wasn't as reckless as I thought.

Toeing off my shoes, I trudged over to his living room and let my body flop down on one of the couches. My muscles were sore from being bent over my desk all day, trying to map out an appropriate timeline for next week's activities. The problem with having a bunch of teenagers coming onto the property was that they tended to scatter like rats when trying to be wrangled.

There was too much fun, too many things to look at, too much for them to get their hands on, for it to be a quick and easy process to get them all accounted for and assigned to their cabins. Thankfully, they were going to be at the back of the property, away from all of the adults and accidentally witnessing any lascivious activities.

The last thing I needed on my hands was the police showing up for indecent exposure to a minor.

"I'd ask if you had a long day but we did hike a trail together." Marlow hovered the freshly uncapped beer over me, waiting until I had a solid grip around the base before letting it go. "Before you ditched me, of course."

I sighed, sitting up straight. "I'm sorry, again, about that."

"Hey, I get it. I'd rather be in the AC some-times, too."

"I'll remember that when I'm elbow deep in tax forms." The beer was cheap tasting when I took a healthy swig, and weirdly, it reminded me of my undergrad days.

College had been a quick two years to get my Associates Degree before taking over the busi-ness. Simply a way to prove to vendors, investors, staff, *whoever*, that I wasn't going to be running this place on hopes and dreams and had an actual solid business plan on what the fuck I was doing.

"Here's a crazy idea." He shifted down onto the couch across from me, his legs spreading wide and catching my attention just long enough to dart my eyes down to see what he was packing between those muscled thighs of his. "Shred them."

"You're right. Fuck the government."

His grin was diabolical. All dimples and mischief. It had my heart skipping a beat. "Love the sound of that. Anarchy looks good on you."

"I'm surprised you're not trying to sell me on some stock portfolio."

He chuckled. "Nah. I can't do that in good

conscience. I'd actually feel bad if I lost your money."

I slammed back another swig before saying, "You're that bad at your job, huh."

"Wow, really going for the jugular there, Blake."

"Have to make up for earlier. I let you off too easily." My head was beginning to swim, and not from the beer. What I really should've done was get Lydia to quiz him on the way back down to base camp and then report back to me.

Marlow struck me as the type of person to need some kind of constant pushback or else he got bored and started to create his own drama to fill the void. Keeping him contained by proxy would probably save a lot of us from running into some *interesting* situations.

He quirked a brow. "Which time? The waterfall or when I asked you to sneak me some condoms?"

"Do you always like to push people's buttons?"

"Helps me know where the line is. Though, I'm surprised that's a button of yours." He suddenly leaned forward. "Blake, you're not some religious zealot, are you?"

I blinked.

Where did that come from?

"Can't say I've had my fair share of church-going. Why?"

He shrugged, settling back into the couch. "Just curious."

He kicked one leg up over his knee, resting his barely touched beer on top of it. Compared to me, and my half finished bottle, he was looking like a regular Sober Sally. There was a possibility he'd already drank plenty down at the bonfire, though given the lack of slurring in his words, I was going to go with a no on that one.

Not a big drinker, then?

That also seemed surprising. Marlow had the perfect personality type to get anyone hyped up at the bar and feed shots to as many victims that happened to cross into his line of fire as possible. Not to mention, wasn't there a big drinking culture around finance?

I did tell him to detox while he was here. Maybe he was taking it literally.

"I've been wondering... you're from Ellington Heights, aren't you? Why come all the way out here? You've got a lake your way."

He gasped. "Not you exploiting your power and looking at my file."

"Guilty. Arrest me now."

He rolled up onto his feet. "I'm calling the cops."

"Good luck getting a signal." I tilted the rest of my bottle back, draining it.

His eyes twinkled, a bemused smile stretching across his lips.

My mind was growing fuzzy with each passing second.

What was it about Marlow that made me feel so relaxed?

This felt like old times, like we'd been shooting the shit for centuries and this was yet another tally to add to our endless list.

I'd never in my life met someone I clicked with so easily and so quickly. To the point where it was beginning to worry me. I'd had plenty of relationships in the past, platonic and sexual, and none of them had ever made me feel this way.

Not even close, in fact.

I wanted to soak in his presence. To let him keep me here, trapped in this ridiculous back and forth, for as long as humanly possible. The planning for next week could wait. The paperwork continuing to pile up on my desk could wait. Hell, even my weekly phone calls with my siblings could wait.

If it meant staying here for one minute longer.

"To answer your question, I wanted to come here to get in shape," Marlow said.

I raised my brow. "Bit of an odd way to go about that."

He shrugged and then surprised me by settling down onto the couch next to me. His back sunk deep into the cushion, the plush material wrapping around his wide shoulders like an embrace. Strangely, he wasn't looking at me, instead choosing to stare down at his beer bottle while fiddling with it in his hand.

When he finally spoke, he wore a strained smile. "My dad died late last year. Heart attack caused by four blockages. Quite the tragic end."

Shit...

"I'm so sorry."

His expression turned bitter. "Sad thing is, none of us saw it coming. He seemed healthy as a damn horse but clearly that wasn't the case. My mom woke up one morning and he was cold to the touch. What a way to go, I guess."

Jesus. Tragic, indeed.

Nodding, I said, "Makes sense why you'd want to keep up your health regimen. I guess I'm just surprised you'd come all the way out here when you've got a lake back home. No clubs or adventure camps out that way?"

"Listen. I don't know if you know anything about Ellington Heights, but it's full of a bunch of pretentious motherfuckers who'd wither away if they so much as sweat a single drop. They'll buy designer workout gear any day of the week, but ask them to use it outside of going to the grocery store? Forget it."

"Not you though, right?" I teased.

Thankfully, that had him perking up a bit. "All of my gear will come home with me well-worn, trust me. I came from rags. I know how to get my money's worth."

Interesting.

Every sentence that came out of Marlow's mouth was more intriguing than the next, leaving me waiting with baited breath as he geared up for the next one. I'd assumed he came from money and stayed on that path, yet hearing that he *hadn't* was infinitely more fascinating.

I hadn't grown up with money, either. Hell, I

still wasn't. Most of the profit that *Austin Adventures* made went right back into it to pay off labor costs and restock what needed to be replaced. After that, repairs were done and accounted for, and if there was *any* money left over after that, I used it to fund the non-profit.

All in all, I wasn't exactly raking in the dough personally.

I wondered how long it was before Marlow found his way into money.

After he got his job?

A little before that?

My phone went off, scaring the shit out of me. Fishing it out of my *other* pocket, the number for Guest Services flashing across the screen, I held back a sigh. If I was being called this late at night, there was something going down. And not in the good way. "Hey, what's up?"

Kaylee sighed on the other end. "Can you come down here? We've got two couples fighting over the last pack of ramen."

Good grief. "Yeah, I'll swing by in a minute."

Marlow snagged my empty bottle as he rolled to his feet again. "Duty calls?"

"It's never ending, this season."

Though who was I kidding?

This was *every* year in a nutshell.

Normally, I welcomed the busyness that came with the camp being fully open for the summer. It was a nice change of pace compared to the molasses-like winter months that seemed to drag on for years instead of a few weeks.

Yet now, I was wanting to drag my feet in getting back to my duties, wanting to linger for as long as possible until I was getting tracked down and dragged back to the problem waiting to be solved.

What was Marlow doing to me?

"Thanks for stopping by," Marlow said.

"Yeah. Sorry I couldn't get what you were looking for." Getting up from the couch without crinkling *said things* was an Olympic sport. One I was most certainly winning gold in.

"No worries. I'll talk one of my couple friends into sneaking into town and grabbing us a box. There are people who leave the property for lunch and stuff, right?"

My mood instantly dampened, my instincts driving me to saying, "No."

"You can't tell me the food in the mess hall can beat Taco Bell?"

He was clearly ribbing me, but now I was absolutely not feeling it. In fact, all I wanted to do was storm out of here and head back to my cabin to bury my face into a pillow and scream.

Sending one of his future fuck buddies into town for condoms... who the fuck did that?

Responsible adults, Blake.

Obviously, Marlow's whole little setback tonight wasn't stopping him from overseeing his goal in sleeping with this married couple. Enough to already have half a plan devised.

Would it be fucked of me to tell all of my staff not to let anyone off the property tomorrow unless a dire emergency rose?

Oh my god, listen to me. Gatekeeping this man from sex like he was my fucking boyfriend.

What the fuck was wrong with me?

I didn't even know how to date, let alone keep a man like Marlow Knight entertained for longer than a twenty minute window.

He was high energy. Needed constant stimulation or it seemed like he'd implode.

How else was he going to blow off that much energy outside of exercise?

My hand itched to shove it into my pocket and pull out the sleeve I'd taken with me for that exact purpose. Yet, no matter how hard I willed myself to do so, my body wouldn't move—frozen in place while Marlow headed into the kitchenette to wash out both our beer bottles.

It wasn't my place to do this.

Plus, what was stopping him from saying 'fuck it' and hopping into bed with them anyway?

Literally nothing.

"You need a flashlight to get back?" he asked, turning around again. "I got this killer one that has 500,000 lumens."

That snapped me out of my spiral almost instantly. "What the fuck are you doing with the power of the sun in your back pocket?"

"I heard it was good for bears."

"To what, flash bang them?"

He laughed. "You want it or not, Blake?"

My stomach clenched. "All good. I've got my phone's light."

He shrugged. "Suit yourself. Maybe I'll shine it up at the sky. Give you some sort of beacon to follow."

"Do that and we'll have the government showing up with a swat team, ready to apprehend the idiot who took out their satellites."

"Can that actually happen?"

I shrugged, slowly forcing myself to inch toward the door to put my shoes on. "I don't know. Don't they work off lasers?"

"Dunno, I work in finance. Though, I did have one guy on my payroll who worked for the NSA. Maybe I can hit him up."

I rolled my eyes. "Goodnight, Marlow."

"Hey, I'm serious about that beacon offer."

"I don't doubt it." Before he had an actual chance at fishing out that ridiculous flashlight, I quickly hurried out onto the porch, the blast of fresh air hitting me in the face and instantly clearing away any residual fuzziness that had collected in the corners of my brain.

Forcing myself not to turn around and look over my shoulder as I descended down the steps and onto the gravel path again was hard. Harder than I wanted it to be. For that want to be there, broiling just beneath the surface of my subconscious, of Marlow waiting on his porch and watching me go, long enough to make sure I got to where I needed to be, was kind of killing me.

I'd never experienced this deep of a draw to someone before and it was beginning to scare me.

I didn't want to be caught up in the drama of

having some kind of summer crush on someone, let alone letting it distract me *this* badly. I couldn't exactly kick him off the property and rid myself of these blossoming feelings, yet trying to deal with them was apparently only making them worse.

Avoiding him. That's what I needed to do.

At all costs.

No matter what.

CHAPTER 6

Marlow

White water rafting on the official third day of camp was definitely the last thing I expected to walk into upon arriving at our meet up spot for the day.

After roll call, we were all squished into a couple of golf carts and driven down a long path that followed the lake's edge until it branched off into a river heading south. The area was beautiful, lush foliage and trees that lined the riverbank, and the rushing water that kicked up a cool breeze, chasing away the heat already starting to stick to my skin the minute the sun popped up over the horizon.

I never minded the summer sun, as I was a sun worshiper as much as the next guy, but sometimes being around a significantly cooler climate was a nice change of pace.

Once we arrived at the docking area, we were gathered in front of a few rafts already set out on the bank with life jackets draped over the sides. Couples quickly grouped together, each of them snagging a life jacket and helping to put it on while I lingered in the background.

Where was Blake?

"Hey, Marlow?" The man from the first day, Talos, hopped off of one of the golf carts. He held out his hand to shake mine as soon as he was close enough. "I'm going to be partnering with you today."

The second the words were out of his mouth, I was shooting back with, "Where's Blake?"

His brows shot up over his aviators. "He's got a camp to run."

Ah, right. Duty called. Late last night, actually.

Reluctantly, I took his hand and shook it, my mood suddenly plummeting.

There wasn't a reason for me to take it personally after our nice night together. I hated letting him leave even if I had no grounds to stand on when it came to holding him hostage inside of my cabin.

Funny enough, at the time, I could tell he wanted to stay, too. He'd dragged his feet getting to the door, had a hard time saying goodbye, and instead, continued to quip back and forth with me until he forced himself to run out my door and disappear into the dark night.

Was there a chance I was reading into all of that?

Yeah, maybe. But on the other hand, there was a possibility that Blake was *also* picking up on our insane chemistry and fighting it in the name of—what I could only theorize—keeping things professional.

Funny, since that was quickly becoming less and less easy to do the more I got to know him. I'd gotten him to open up a little bit, had cracked that shell apart *just* enough to peek inside, and liked what I saw.

I'd left the bonfire early for a reason that, at the time, I wasn't too sure about. However, the second that knock on my door came around and

I found Blake standing on my porch looking a little frazzled and wide-eyed, I knew the universe was pointing me in the right direction.

Hitting it off with Luke and Aimee seemed like a preamble to what I really wanted.

If I could get Blake to drop down his walls for one night, *just one*, and get him into my bed, I think we'd both walk away happy and satisfied. I'd get him out of my system and be able to move on to the next person and he'd get an unforgettable night.

I'd make damn sure of it.

"You ever white water raft before?" Talos asked, gesturing for me to follow him to one of the rafts where a few spare life jackets were hanging.

"Can't say I have, but I hear it's like riding a bike."

"Something like that. We're going to take you all through a two-hour crash course and then we'll take a few rafts down the smaller swells."

I patted my chest the second I got the life jacket strapped around me. "Count me in. I'm always down to get a little wet."

⁓

SINCE TALOS WAS DOUBLING as my partner *and* one of the guides for this expedition, a lot of my 'training' was done alone or latching on to another couple also learning the ropes.

As I'd suspected, rafting was pretty much self-explanatory in the sense of, you paddled, you kept your weight distributed properly when going through large swells, you listened to your guide, you didn't do anything stupid like try and lean over the side of the raft to scoop up whatever fish or creature decided to float on by.

"All right, everyone! Head to your assigned raft and climb in! Wait for further instruction from your guide!" Talos's voice bellowed over the rushing water behind him.

There were four rafts in total, mine being the last of the bunch with an older couple as my companions, and a couple that looked around my age.

"Marlow, you're going to be in the back with me," Talos said, tossing me a helmet as the others grabbed their own.

"Wow, I'm honored. Does this mean I get to hoist the sails, too?"

He gave me a weird look and then shook his head. "Blake mentioned you were a jokester."

I fought the immediate urge to ask him what else Blake said about me and focused on climbing into the raft as Talos held it in place from floating out into the channel. It wouldn't exactly do me any good to be getting goo-goo eyed in front of his coworkers. Treating this situation delicately meant I needed to keep my trap shut until I got Blake in my bed.

Then maybe I'd go gung ho and figure out what that little minx was saying about me.

As soon as my hands were wrapped firmly around my paddle, Talos asked, "We all ready?"

My stomach twisted in excitement. This was my kind of adrenaline rush. Rollercoasters were boring in comparison and didn't have that same 'near death' tease that an outdoor sport like this had. Sure, we were going down the more tame part of the river with hardly anything too wild, but there was still that element of danger I craved.

Once we were pushed off, Talos hopped into the raft and sat on the bench next to me. He helped guide us to the main channel of water, right behind the other rafts, and kept a modest distance between us all. As the last in line, we were probably going to take this thing slow, and while I'd normally be a little bitter, the older couple in front of me were clearly shaking like leaves the second we hit the first swell.

"All right, everyone! Paddles up!" Talos shouted. "Let's work as a team and have a good time!"

My face hurt from how hard I was grinning.

Sinking my paddle into the water, I drove it back, pulling the water along with me. Feeling the power of a raging current fight back against you was impressive. The commanding presence of a body of water giving no mercy to how it would flow reminded me of my own temperament—giving way to no one and nothing no matter how much they begged or howled.

I used to think it was a negative trait of mine to not bend the knee to anyone, even my own family. However, over time, I began to see it as a blessing. A way to give me the sense of control I needed in order to feel safe.

Growing up in a financially unstable household had done a number on the inner spirit. The constant fear of eviction and food shortage was scary. And when my dad finally hit it big and moved us into a mansion compared to the cramped apartment I'd grown up in for half my life, it seemed too good to be true.

Getting sent off to boarding school, attending an Ivy League, landing myself a seven-figure career—all of it was one single decision away from becoming life ruining.

I could appreciate the gamble that was life, now that I'd had plenty of experience living it. No one was guaranteed a soft and cushy existence, and the more that fact was realized and appreciated, the easier it was to connect the dots to *keep* the lifestyle you got comfortable in.

Much like the raging river. A beast of a force that had no qualms in taking what it wanted. You could be the best swimmer in the world and still be swallowed up by the current.

"River left!" Talos called out. "Rock ahead!"

Driving my paddle down into the water once more, I curved it toward the boat, helping steer us out of the path. For some reason, though, the older couple in front of me began to frantically paddle in opposite directions, creating a counter balance to the motion of what the rest of us were doing.

"River left! Rock!" Talos called out again.

The thing was huge and hard to miss. Even

hard to intentionally drive a raft into it with enough warning ahead of time.

And yet, we were heading right for it.

"Shit," I mumbled, jamming my paddle backward.

My shoulders ached from the force of the water fighting against my paddle. Miraculously, the raft shifted the other way, moving the nose of it away from the rock's direction and scooting us around the other side of it.

Unfortunately, it seemed the river had different plans for us and ended up depositing us toward the rock anyway.

A cruel mistress, indeed.

As soon as our raft slammed into the rock, the woman in front of me screamed.

"All right, calm down!" Talos lifted himself up from the bench to see where the front of our raft was lodged onto the rock. "Paddle backward, everyone! This is an easy one to get out of."

My foot jammed up against the bench in front of me, giving me more leverage to drive my paddle back and scoop more water forward. With the river fighting us from the side, and our raft stuck from the front, this was going to be a bitch to get out of.

"Stick together!" Talos called.

The couple in front of me was clearly panicking, their paddles splashing up more water *into* the raft rather than pushing it out and away from us. I felt bad for them, as they were obviously not at all equipped to be going through an adventure class like this one.

I was surprised they weren't pulled from it and sent back up to camp to tag along with another group doing something way less stressful.

"That's it! One more big tug!" Talos heaved himself backward, slamming into the back of the raft to give us more momentum in dislodging ourselves.

With one last shove, the raft finally scraped away from the rock. We tipped dangerously to the left, leaving us all to grab onto the handles on the sides of the craft quickly.

"Hang on!" Talos stood up again and used his paddle as a rudder against the rock, shoving us out and away from it. Water kicked up, spraying us all right as we hit one of the rapids dead on.

With one last severe dip, the raft was righted and finally we were back in the main channel.

"All right, nice work, everyone!"

"Ellen!" the older man shouted, his face drawn back in a panicked look while his finger pointed out into the water.

My head snapped back, following the line of his finger to someone in a life vest floating down between the rapids. Their arms waved frantically, disappearing beneath the swell and then popping up a harrowing three seconds later, the coughing and sputtering barely heard over the rush of water.

"Ellen!" the man called again, careening toward the side of the raft and tipping the entire party in that direction.

Oh *fuck.*

CHAPTER 7

MARLOW

THE SECOND THE man lunged forward, I snapped my hand out to grab at the back of his life jacket, hauling him away from the side of the raft before he had the bright idea to tip us all over.

The strap I had a hold of pulled taunt while he jerked forward again, a grunt tumbling past his lips while he tossed his paddle down onto the floor next to his wife's unoccupied spot.

Clearly, he was too out of his mind with worry to be thinking straight, but it wouldn't do any of us any good trying to save that poor woman if we were all too busy trying to keep ourselves from getting dragged under one of the rapids while trying to get back into the raft after being flipped.

"Ellen!" he shouted again.

I tightened my hand around the nylon strap while it dug uncomfortably into my skin. For an old guy, he sure knew how to throw his body weight around. As soon as I ripped him back with a sharp jerk, I steered him down toward the floor, practically tucking him between his bench and the one in front of him as gently as I could manage given the small and compacted space.

Talos was already in motion next to me, grabbing the discarded paddle and tossing it into the river to keep it from breaking the man's fall and his back.

"Shit," I heard Talos say, right before a shrill whistle blasted me in the eardrum, rattling my fucking brain in the process.

Two more whistles answered farther down the river from us. Quite useless, seeing as how there was no way any of the other rafter parties were going to be rowing back up this way to help us. Which meant one of two things, we fought the current ourselves to try and get to our fallen comrade or someone was going swimming.

Ellen's figure went down under the water again, popping up a moment later as she sputtered and coughed, her hands desperately clinging to the front panels of her life vest that was coming up near her shoulders from how hard the water was tossing her around. Even if that vest was strapped snug around her body as tight as it could go, it wouldn't matter if she managed to wiggle out of it trying to fight from getting pulled under again.

"Keep focused," Talos barked, his voice sharp. "Remember your training. We're going to cut through the rapids and make our way over there."

I had a feeling by the time we coordinated and got over to her, she'd be floating face down while the current took her to wherever it wanted. We had no time to be fucking around here and letting Talos try and wrangle up the three remaining people able to keep rowing was a waste of that precious time.

So, instead of listening to him bark at me to

grab my paddle and spin us around toward Ellen's direction, I tossed it down onto the floor at my feet.

"Marlow—"

I didn't bother waiting for the inevitable chiding before tossing myself right over the side of the raft and practically rolling down into the next set of rapids. There was a distant *"Fuck!"* that I caught just as I speared my hand through the water, cutting into the force of the spray that kicked up as soon as my body faced west.

Swimming was the only hobby of mine I hadn't yet grown bored of from childhood, making it second nature to fall back into those old and practiced strokes I knew all too well. Call it the fish in me or blame it on the competitive nature of showing off to the academy boys while in boarding school gym class I'd yet to grow out of twenty years later.

The water was much colder than what had been kicked up inside of the raft while we'd been slowly making our way back over to the river's channel, sending my adrenaline spiking through my system and propelling me forward.

Ellen's eyes were wide while she floated aimlessly toward another rapid, her mouth moving while she said something I couldn't quite catch over the swell. Our helmets were a bright yellow, stark against the murky browns of the water, making it easy to keep my eye on her while getting to her.

There was another sharp trill of Talos's whistle, signaling to either the rest of the crew again or using it to belatedly scold me for doing something as stupid as jumping into a raging river with no plan outside of grabbing Ellen and swimming back.

Okay, so maybe this was one of my least smart impulsive choices.

"Hey!" I called out to her as soon as I was close enough to grab at her, "Hold still! I'm going to—"

Her hands seized my arm the moment we made contact, giving her enough leverage to practically crawl up the side of me and use me as a human buoy.

"Help!" she screamed. "Help!"

Naw, fuck.

The worst part about panicked drowning people is they'd always sacrifice you out of pure instinct to get one last meager breath before you both plunged under the water's surface again.

Treading water, I shook her off me. "Jesus, woman. Hold still!"

Before she could reach around to grab at me again, I shoved my hand under the nylon strap wrapped around the back of her life jacket and dragged us both backward, side-stroking toward where I'd last heard Talos blow his whistle from.

The water was high and hard to navigate through with the use of only one of my arms free, and given the added weight of Ellen and us fighting against a very healthy current, my body was feeling the burn.

I was going to wake up jacked as shit tomorrow.

Three more sharp bursts of the whistle sounded out, a little bit to my left and slightly further down from where we were.

Like a guiding fairy light through a dark and decaying forest, I kept us pointed toward the sound. The bright yellow of the raft was hard to miss, much like our helmets, even through the rapids.

Talos had the younger couple working over-time dragging their paddles down and keeping the craft pointed our way while he had his own paddle outstretched in our direction, feverishly waving it.

The last few yards were the worst, with time slowing the moment I reached out to brush my hand along the edge of Talos's paddle, just barely missing it before my hand plunged back into the water. My body ached, the adrenaline already wearing down now that we were so close.

"Grab it, I'll pull you back!" Talos shouted as he waved the paddle again.

His words almost had me rolling my eyes.

Well, yeah. I sure as hell hoped you would.

Because the alternative was getting the cops to come fish our bodies out of the water. I highly doubted Blake was ready to deal with *that* kind of fiasco.

Once I actually managed to get a hold of it, the plastic of the paddle bit into my hand with how hard I gripped it. With a single heave, Talos dragged us back toward the side of the raft. My upper body slammed into it, though not hard enough to hurt.

Or maybe that was still the adrenaline talking.

"All right, Ellen," I heaved her against the craft. "Up you go."

Two sets of hands reached over the side to drag her out of the water, the entire thing tipping dangerously backward with the added force of grabbing her and settling new weight onto the vessel. I kept my hand wrapped tight around one of the rope loops hanging off the side of it while we bobbed, allowing my body to float and recover in the meantime.

If this wasn't a case of someone practically drowning, I would've thought being out here in the water practically freeballing it was lovely.

"Come on." Talos's voice came from above me right as his hands found the front of my life vest and hauled me up. "Blake will kill me if I let you die out here."

My toes curled at the thought of him even giving a shit outside of a business perspective, let alone enough for Talos to say something. There was the possibility of that being exactly what he meant—that letting a client perish on property would be cause for many-a-lawsuit and probably the last thing *Austin Adventures* was looking to garner publicity-wise.

I wasn't by any means a public figure, however, I doubted Avery or Silas would let that shit go peacefully and without raising some kind of hell in order to find out what exactly had gone down at this camp that got my passport stamped with a one way ticket to the meat locker. Avery alone had enough money to hire plenty of lawyers to bury this place into the ground if he so chose to.

My friends could be pains in my ass plenty, but they were also my ride-or-dies through and through. Thick and thin, I knew I could count on them.

I grunted the second Talos dropped me unceremoniously onto the floor of the raft, my body finally flagging as the last of my remaining adrenaline bled out of me. To me, it was crazy how easily my strength had been zapped from my very bones with none of the work I'd spent years maintaining to show for it.

How the hell anyone survived a dip in the rapids was beyond me.

Distant crying caught my attention next, sending me turning my head toward the sound of it.

The older couple was huddled together, their arms wrapped around each other in a sweet way that normally would've had me smiling at the charming sight and almost forgetting about the near-death experience we'd all just shared.

As a silver lining, at least now they'd have an exciting story to tell the grandkids over Christmas dinner.

"River right," Talos called, climbing over top of me and fishing his paddle off of the floor by my head. "Let's park this thing."

CHAPTER 8

Blake

The last thing I expected to come over the radio was a request for emergency medical assistance down at the riverside.

"Couple of guests fell in the water. We're going to need the paramedics down here to check on them. Non-life threatening injuries so far," were Talos's exact words.

I tried to not let my mind run wild while the chattering on the radio continued with rapid-fire questions shooting back and forth from both sides as I heaved myself up from my desk and quickly shoved my shoes back on to sprint out the door.

This wasn't the first time we had a guest or two take a plunge and most certainly wouldn't be the last. We'd trained for plenty of scenarios and seldom took new clients up to the trickier spots on the river without at least some kind of professional training under their belt.

While it was never easy to extract people from the river, the life vests were mandatory for a reason, as were the helmets that kept them from cracking their skulls open on any rocks hidden under the swells of water.

Non-life threatening.

That was a good sign.

Talos reporting it was the real problem my mind was latching on to.

All of it could be chalked up to a coincidence. In fact, there was a strong possibility it wasn't his group at all that had suffered from the predicament and was a simple case of Talos having gotten onto the radio first to report up to base camp about it. Whatever guests had fallen into the water sounded like they were fine and simply a little shaken up from the ordeal.

Most likely this was a case of a younger

couple eager to prove themselves to their peers. Hell, maybe it was Marlow's swinger friends and conveniently would give me the excuse to kick them off the property for violating rule number one when it came to adventure camp: don't be a fucking idiot and get yourself almost killed.

Wishful thinking, sure, but a guy could dream right?

I hitched a ride down with two of my medically trained staff, following after another golf cart that had my other two, and hung on for dear life as our golf cart careened down the steep pathway to get down to the river's edge. The air was much cooler down here than up at base camp, the rapids a soft and distant noise in the background that soothed my weary nerves as we pulled up to the four groups all settled off of an old docking site.

The groups were scattered around the small area, creating a wide berth for us to come through and over to where our river guides were gathered. Two of them were bent over, attending to whomever it was on the ground, while the other two—Talos among them, nodded to the paramedics hustling their way.

As soon as Talos stepped away from the

group, giving our first responders room to work, my entire body froze. An older couple was sitting on the ground, the man's arm wrapped around his wife's shoulders while she had looked visibly shaken and drenched from, presumably, taking a nice dip in the river.

Across from her, looking almost as drenched, was Marlow.

My throat burned as I tried to swallow.

"Hey..." Talos nodded to me, heading my way. "Think we might need to call an ambulance after all."

I forced out a breath. "Someone knock their head?"

"No, but the woman swallowed a lot of water. She threw up some of it when we docked but she's still looking a little sickly."

"And... Marlow?"

God, did I even want to ask?

He looked fine from here, but that was from twenty feet away.

The one day I didn't accompany him on a fucking expedition.

Talos snorted. "You didn't tell me he liked to play hero, too."

My brow popped instantly. "What?"

"Dove in head first after her like it was out of some action movie. He swam all the way out to her and pulled her back one-handed. It would've been pretty impressive to watch if I wasn't busy trying to keep the entire raft from tipping over."

How odd that I could imagine the situation crystal clear without trying.

The determined frown set into Marlow's face while his decision was made to go after his fellow rafter.

The near perfect form of him diving into the water, bobbing up to the surface moments later.

His study build cutting through the water easily as he paddled over to her.

The strain of his powerful shoulders jaw-dropping while he dragged them both back to safety.

I rubbed a hand over my face to clear my head. "How did any of this even happen in the first place?"

"We got beached on a rock. We were having trouble coordinating altogether, especially with the older couple. They seemed pretty freaked out for whatever reason. Caused us to overcorrect and she went overboard."

And then Marlow went in after her.

Honestly, it wasn't at all that far-fetched, given what I knew about him and his boisterous personality. He'd struck me as the hero-type before, yet seeing it put into action was more heartwarming than I expected.

Why I cared if that man was the type to put his money where his mouth was, was beyond me. And yet here I was, trying not to let my rapidly growing smile show while Talos continued to talk.

"I'll call it in so we can have an ambulance waiting for us up there by the time we get them driven back up."

I nodded for one of the golf carts. "Take the couple up. I'll talk to Marlow and see how he's doing."

With that, my second nodded and stepped off to the side to call up to base camp.

Normally, I tried to avoid bringing ambulances down to the grounds at all costs—mainly because it tended to freak the guests out no matter what we said to try and calm everyone down. Worse case scenarios were a frequent topic of gossip whenever something like that happened and no amount of debriefing anyone stopped the rumor mill from churning.

Judging by how shaky the woman still was after she was helped back onto her feet, I'd have to agree with Talos that getting her to a hospital was the best case scenario. Even if it was overkill. In this instance, I'd rather be safe than sorry.

I waited until my staff had the woman and her husband loaded onto the back of the golf cart to head over to where Marlow was still sitting on the ground. His eyes were focused on the couple, a pinched expression pulling at his features.

His hair was still plastered to his head, though the ends of it were starting to curl from where it was drying. It made him look boyish, a stark contrast to the expression he was wearing.

"You doing okay?" I asked.

His head snapped over to me, eyes widening briefly before he flashed me a charming, dimpled smile. "Mr. Director. What a pleasant surprise."

He rolled to his feet easily, a small hop in his step I wasn't expecting but was glad to see nonetheless. Seeing Marlow so chipper after a, what could be argued, *scary* ordeal had my body relaxing instantly. Before this, I'd barely noticed how tense I'd gotten the entire way down from my office to here.

Now, though, the world felt right again.

"Don't tell me you came all the way down here to check on little old me." He grinned.

To save myself the embarrassment from admitting that *yes, I did in fact do that*, I simply shrugged and said, "Part of my job is to make sure everyone survives long enough to leave my campgrounds."

"Yeah, I guess that makes sense. It wouldn't exactly be fun to have a bunch of ghosts haunting this place."

I quirked my brow. "You believe in ghosts?"

"Petrified of them. You're not scared of being haunted?"

I narrowed my eyes. It was hard to tell if he was being serious or not. I had a hard time believing Marlow was scared of *anything*, let alone something imaginary like a *ghost*. Tangible fears were far more unsettling than a bedtime story told to kids to keep them from wandering out of their beds in the middle of the night.

"Can't say I am," I drawled. "But I'll be sure not to invite you to the Halloween weekend we throw every year. Wouldn't want to send you to an early grave by scaring you to death."

He threw his head back and laughed. "Now,

now, don't be hasty. I'm always up for a good party. And slutty costumes."

"Can't forget those," I mused.

Fuck, I was too happy to see he was all right. Far beyond the scope of simply being the director of this place and stressing about a potential lawsuit on the horizon. In all of the years *Austin Adventures* had been open to the public, there was only one time where we'd gotten a knock at our door by a process server and subsequently slapped with a ninety-page document stating we were being sued.

Settling that had been a bitch and a half for my granddad, but since then, we'd been scot-free.

"We should get you checked out either way," I said, my gaze running over his body.

No scratches.

No bruising.

No holes that were bleeding.

Impressive, to say the least. That river wasn't for the weak and even though this group had started farther down where the rapids weren't so severe, it was still a rough ride. That's what made it fun—on normal adventures, at least.

He leaned back slightly, almost like he was

preening. "I'm all good. But hey, if you want to pat me down to check, by all means."

My cheeks flushed with heat.

Jesus, I needed to stop reading into everything that came out of that flirtatious mouth of his. Especially, since I was hoping not even ten minutes ago for a chance to kick his swinger friends off the property.

Get it together.

"Come on." I nodded for him to follow, spinning around on my heel. "Jay, can you make sure everyone's accounted for before you guys head back up to base?"

The last thing we needed was for a straggler to be left behind. Or worse, not accounted for and somehow having wound up in the river without anyone noticing.

"Roger that," the staff member closest to me replied.

I didn't wait for confirmation of Marlow following after me, trusting he'd be a good noodle and do so while I made my way over to where Talos was. He was still talking on the radio to dispatch, confirming that the ambulance was on its way before switching the channel back over to the main one and looking over at me.

"We're all set. They should be down here within fifteen."

I nodded. "Good. I'm going to head back up. I've got Jay doing a headcount. Once you've got everyone back up our way, take them to the mess hall. I'll have the cooks fire up the grills. They deserve an early lunch today after all of this."

Talos glanced behind me and then said, "You taking him with you?"

"It's my special day," Marlow replied, directly behind me.

A shiver raced up my spine unexpectedly from how close he was. "Yeah, I'm going to send him off in the ambulance, too. Think there are still a couple of screws loose in there."

Marlow gasped dramatically the second I tapped my forehead. "My mom had me tested. She said I was fine."

"That's what all parents say when they have a hard time breaking the real news to their kid," I quipped back easily. "Sorry to be the one to tell you."

"No, wait. I have the paperwork to prove it!"

Talos wasn't at all subtle with the befuddled shift of his eyes between us both. "Uh huh... well... I wish you all the best. I guess..."

My poor second. He already had enough to deal with, with just me on a daily basis. Adding Marlow to the mix and doubling down on our eccentric conversations was probably already giving him a migraine.

Without thinking, I reached behind me and grabbed Marlow's wrist, his skin burning my palm the instant I touched him.

Why the fuck did I do that?

Touching him was off-limits with my libido acting like a starved teenager just discovering what a boner meant. Yet, no matter how much I tried to will myself to let him go, I couldn't.

I tightened my grip around his wrist, using it to yank him with me and march toward the remaining golf cart parked haphazardly on the side of the trail. The keys for it were still stuck in the ignition.

Regretfully, I wrenched my hand away from him and flexed my fingers a few times to shake off the feeling of his skin imprinted into mine. Adrenaline was shooting through my veins in rapid bursts, making it hard to concentrate on swinging my body onto the seat and grabbing at the key to start the cart.

"Oh..." Marlow said, catching my attention. To my deep and utter surprise, he began to unclip the life vest from his body and strip himself of it, revealing his rather impressively muscled chest and abs. "You want this?"

Fear at being caught blatantly checking him out slapped me right back into reality. "W-what?"

His smile was cheeky, tinged with a bit of smugness that I didn't at all appreciate in the slightest. "The vest, Blake. You want me to leave it here?"

I swallowed. "Oh. Uh... yeah, clip it to the back seat."

Holy fuck.

Ripping my eyes away from him, I focused on getting the damn cart started and clenched my fingers around the steering wheel, willing myself to behave as he slid himself down onto the bench next to me.

Despite his still damp skin, he was warm next to me, practically radiating heat. I jumped the moment his arm brushed against mine, slamming my foot down onto the gas and jerking the entire cart forward.

"Yeesh," he laughed. "I feel like I'm back on that raft."

I ignored the clenching in my stomach as he shifted next to me and threw an arm around the back of our seat, his hand subtly ghosting close to my arm on the other side of me and just barely not making contact as long as I sat up ramrod straight.

He had to be doing this on purpose. Pushing my buttons to get a reaction out of me just like he'd been doing the past few days. All of this was a game to him, plain and simple. I was conveniently the most fun target he had so far. Until he found himself entangled with someone else to occupy his time until this vacation was over.

I tried not to let that thought taste bitter on my tongue while we headed up the incline in silence. I should've been happy he was all right and made it out of that harrowing situation all in one piece with not a single scratch on him. It was a miracle, really. One I should be celebrating.

Blowing out a breath, I gunned it up the rest of the incline until we were at the top, base camp coming into view just beyond the end of the pathway.

Fingers lightly trailed along my arm. "Don't tell me you ditched me again for paperwork."

My knuckles were white from how hard I was holding onto the steering wheel. "Got that event next week, remember?"

Actually, the small miracle was in fact me being able to form coherent sentences while Marlow's fingers traced halfway up my arm and then back down again at a maddening leisure.

"Want help?"

I forced out a laugh to keep from doing something way more embarrassing, like moaning. How fucking sad I was getting turned on by being *touched*. "You a party planner?"

"Had a few shindigs in my time."

"That business lingo for 'rager'?"

He laughed. "Nah, I know how to tone it down for the right occasion."

Tempting. Too tempting to take him up on the offer, if only to spend more time with him. A bad idea, given how rapidly hard my dick was getting.

From a fucking arm caress.

How goddamn sad was that?

"Think I've got most of it figured out." My

mouth felt full of cotton, along with the inside of my skull.

What would happen if I jammed on the brakes and parked us off the path somewhere and see where else that hand of his would wander off to?

"So, that means you'll be at the bonfire tonight." His tone was firm. A little surprising considering how light it'd been second before.

I chanced a glance over at him right as we were passing through the entrance back into the main part of the grounds. He wore a playful smile, but there was something in his eyes that spoke differently—that same darkness he'd had the night before when he'd practically cornered me into bringing him condoms.

"It... depends," was all I could think to say.

He shook his head slowly. "You'll be at the bonfire."

Was this some sort of hypnosis trick?

If so, I was falling for it hook, line and sinker.

I let my foot off the gas, letting the cart roll until it finally stopped near the drop-off station. The ambulance was just pulling in from the main road right when I parked the cart, the lights flashing but the siren off. The second it cleared the entrance, it parked along the roundabout, two EMTs popping their doors open.

I killed the ignition and quickly scrambled out of the cart. "Come on, let's go get you checked."

So I can get as far away from you as I can.

CHAPTER 9

MARLOW

BLAKE WAS SO DAMN adorable when he was flustered.

As hard as it was to keep myself from crossing more boundaries than I already had, toeing the line and seeing where exactly what it was that made him crack was infinitely more fun. As reserved as he tried to make himself seem, he was damn expressive to a fault. To the point where I doubted he even knew how many faces he was capable of pulling.

The game was fun to play. And much more satisfying now that I knew he was *definitely* attracted to me. If his flustered demeanor didn't clue me in, the boner in his shorts certainly did.

He was lucky we'd made it back to camp by the time I spotted that thing, or else I would've grabbed a hold of the wheel and driven us off the path to somewhere secluded so I could see just how turned on he was pretending he wasn't.

Who knew Blake was a man of simple tastes?

But hey, I could handle that. I loved a partner who got off on anything. Even if that meant blowing in his ear and watching him bust in his shorts.

Now the challenge was getting him to lean into the desire he was clearly feeling, and convincing him to come back to my cabin to explore it.

I had a feeling he was new to all of this, given how out of sorts he was the past two times I'd made it quite obvious about my attraction toward him. I usually wasn't too keen on taking a virgin to bed—or rather in Blake's case, a *gay* virgin—as they tended to get too clingy afterward, however, this was a special case.

Because by the end of it, we'd both be forced to move on. Blake was a busy man, and far too responsible to let himself get tangled up with me for the rest of these six weeks. One night together wouldn't kill either of us, and once he was done and out of my system, I'd be able to breathe again.

Tonight was going to be the night—that's what I'd decided on.

As long as Blake showed up at the bonfire, it was go-time.

To no one's surprise, I was quickly cleared and sent on my way by the EMTs, just in time for the rest of the rafting group to arrive back for an early lunch. Catching up with Luke and Aimee in order to pass the time for the rest of the day until sunset felt like a no-brainer, since keeping myself occupied until I could sneak off with Blake was going to be the ultimate test in patience.

He'd quickly run off the second the EMT had given me the thumbs up that I was good to go, spouting off something about checking in with the rest of the group and leaving me to fend for myself.

I had half a mind to follow him to see if he was telling the truth or bluffing in order to go hide away in his office, stopping myself at the last minute. Overwhelming Blake was the worst thing I could do if I wanted him to trust me. Coming off as overbearing and pushy, especially with a man with no experience in gay relationships, was setting myself up for a harsh rejection I wasn't ready to receive.

Not until I actually had the chance to shoot my shot properly.

He seemed open to the idea, or at least attracted to it. That I could work with. It was all a matter of perspective and seeing things from his point of view, and how confusing all of this newness must be.

And who was I to deny helping him work through it?

Especially, since it seemed like he trusted me a good amount.

The day pushed forward at a sluggish pace, nearly making me tear my hair out the seventh time I looked at the clock and realized it was only three. There was a part of me that kind of wished Blake took me up on my offer to help him plan his youth group event, even if it was to file papers while he figured out whatever logistics still needed to be worked on.

I missed the bump and grind of a laborious day.

Vacationing in the mountains near this incredible lake was amazing, there was no doubt about it. And yet, on some level, that sick and twisted part of my brain *missed* work. Missed the drudgery that came with toiling away at files and portfolios until I felt like I was going cross-eyed.

Avery would be appalled to know how much I missed being in my office only three and a half days into my vacation, while Silas would no doubt agree with me. We were both workaholics by nature and with no boyfriends to occupy us outside of our 9-5's like Avery had the luxury of —or in Silas's case, 11-11's—, there wasn't much else we had going for us.

Sad?

Sure, but a reality nonetheless.

I didn't hate it—far from it, actually. My brain needed to be worked. Like a border collie needed to herd their livestock. It was a driving need that would never be satiated until I got my hands on what gave me that 'fix' in the first place.

I hoped Blake was open to the idea. I wouldn't push him, not if he gave me a hard stop and told me to fuck off.

But goddamn it, I needed him out from

under my skin. I needed to scratch the itch before I tore myself apart trying to get to it.

Was that too much to ask for?

NIGHTFALL CAME FAR TOO SLOWLY.

By the time the bonfires were just starting to go up, I was pacing around the congressional area, my gaze pinned in the direction of Blake's office. Too bad I didn't know the exact building, or I'd be marching over there and dragging him out of that office myself.

"Marlow..." Turning to the sound of my name, I spotted Aimee walking over to me, a smile playing on her lips. "We snagged a few beers if you want to join us."

A *Nah* was on the tip of my tongue, barely held back while I scoped a look back over my shoulder to make sure I hadn't missed Blake trying to sneak by in the five seconds I wasn't hawk-eyeing the entire campground.

"A drink, you say. How generous."

She let out a giggle behind her hand, waving her other toward me. "Come on, Luke saved us a seat."

Us was said in a poignant way. Filled with promises of an evening with her and her husband just on the horizon.

I supposed it was rather shitty of me to keep them on the back burner until I got this Blake thing all sorted out. However, at the same time, I also wasn't exactly ready to sit them both down and have that annoying, and frankly tiring, conversation about how being gay meant I was *only* attracted to men and no matter how much a woman swayed her hips at me, the old pecker wasn't interested.

Not to mention, I wasn't exactly in the mood to ruin whatever night was in store for me with a tough reality check to poor Aimee. I wasn't a stranger to women finding me attractive, the hard part was letting them down gently.

Following after her, I snagged the beer that was held out to me by her husband and settled down on the log furthest away from them that faced out toward the main part of the camp.

Were the staff camps over by ours?

Or were they tucked back somewhere else?

And how far away was Blake's office from them?

"So, Marlow..." Luke took a long swig of his

beer. "Heard you were caught up in some trouble earlier."

"Oh, saving poor Ellen? All in a day's work, my friend."

Aimee giggled. "There's a rumor going around that you pulled her out of the water yourself. Dove right in after she went overboard."

"What can I say, I like to play hero sometimes."

Where the fuck was Blake?

It was well past sunset and the sky was rapidly becoming dark.

"What else do you like to play?"

The hand that suddenly found my thigh wasn't subtle in the slightest, nor was the way long fingernails walked up toward my crotch and settled right near the junction of my hip. Ripping my attention away from the roaming crowd of people coming and going from the mess hall, I glanced down to Aimee's red fingernails hand.

Nothing stirred. Not even an iota of interest.

Poor thing.

Look, if I had a choice, I'd take up the offer. Turning down sex was stupid, especially if a threesome was a strong possibility. I liked the chaos that came with the confusing mess of tangled limbs and frantic touching. It was fun and messy and all the kinds of things I liked about sex.

I hated formality. The mechanics of going through the motions.

What was the point in living if everything felt robotic?

"So, confession time," I said, throwing back a healthy swig of my own. "I'm picking up some *vibes* from you guys."

"Oh?" Aimee leaned forward. "And what kind of *vibes* are those?"

I had to hand it to her, I loved the unapologetic nature she possessed. She clearly was a woman who knew what she wanted and wasn't about to back down in the face of possible rejection or embarrassment.

It was damn admirable. And also a damn shame it wasn't doing anything for me.

"So, I'm into men," I said, flashing a quick smile.

"What a coincidence." Her own smile widened. "So are we."

Nice.

My gaydar was so damn good it was scary sometimes.

"Wow, that *is* a crazy coincidence," I replied.

Her hand squeezed my thigh. "So, why don't you say we sneak back to our cabin and get to know each other a little better?"

Well, it wasn't like I was doing anything else. And clearly, Blake was off hiding wherever, or holed up in his office still, avoiding the entire world. Which gave my chest a little bit of a twinge—a sting to my pride, as it were.

I wasn't trying to overstep the line of whatever it was between us by huge margins, at least not in the way that had him too scared to run into me. He was a busy man, not exactly the type to be running around and hanging out at bonfires while sipping on a beer or two after work.

My paranoia was all likely in my head anyway and was giving me *far* too much fodder to read into.

This entire place was his *job*. Not a hangout spot like it was for me and the rest of the guests staying here.

Just go, what's stopping you?

Slapping my free hand against my thigh, I

pushed myself up onto my feet again. My beer swung at my side, the liquid inside of it sloshing dangerously as I turned toward the mess hall again out of instinct, freezing the second I spotted a figure standing close to me.

My eyes widened.

Blake had his arms crossed over his chest, a loose-fitting zip-up jacket draped over his shoulders, one side having fallen to reveal part of his tanned arm. The reflection of the fire caught in his eyes, creating a mesmerizing glow that seemed to come from within, bursting out of him like the sun, barely being contained inside of his body.

The scowl that was plastered on his beautiful face was so out of place that it took me a minute to register it was being directed at *me*.

Well, that's a first.

Before I could open my mouth, he said, "Came to check on you. How's your head."

I furrowed my brows.

My head?

The last time I checked, I'd been looked at for muscle strains and possible torn ligaments trying to move through the water that was fighting tooth and nail to take me as one of its victims. I wasn't aware that anyone, Talos, Blake, or the EMTs, were worried about a possible head injury.

Unless that was simply a convenience excuse. If so, it was clever and not at all revealing as to the true reason Blake was seeking me out.

"I didn't..." My voice trailed off the second I noticed his attention being directed toward Aimee and Luke, that stormy expression becoming downright turbulent.

Oh.

Oh, this is good.

I liked jealousy.

Twisting at my waist, I set my beer bottle down on the log I'd taken up residence on only a moment before and shot them both a wink before turning back around. Blake was focused back on me, his shoulders bunched up near his ears. That wasn't doing anything to hide his mood.

Adorable.

Seriously.

Why was he still single?

I stepped toward him and threw my arm out to catch him around the shoulders. I cupped the side where his bare arm was and pulled him closer to me, a soft noise escaping him that shot straight down to my dick.

"Why don't we go talk, hmm?"

He sucked in a sharp breath. "Uh..."

I didn't give him time to over think this one. Not when I was so damn close to getting what I wanted—what we *both* clearly wanted. I wasn't about to let this man talk himself out of giving in to his desires that he clearly was used to squashing down until they were nothing but dust floating away in the wind.

"Marlow," he mumbled, stumbling into me as I guided him away from the bonfire.

"You wanted to play doctor and check on me, right?" I didn't even need to look at his face to know his freckled cheeks were growing red at a rapid pace. "Why don't we do that somewhere more *private*, hmm?"

"Goddamn it." I heard him mumble under his breath as I whisked him away.

CHAPTER 10

BLAKE

I WAS SO FUCKING SCREWED.

Allowing Marlow to take me to a secondary location was probably just as bad as allowing a serial killer to do the same. Only in this instance, I wasn't sure if making it out alive was going to leave me better off than if I'd just been taken out by a psychopath.

The thing about Marlow was he wasn't the kind of guy to be dissuaded easily. Not when there was clearly some kind of plan set in motion and I had no way of knowing *what* exactly it entailed.

Other than the main focal point being me.

I didn't like how much I felt flattered by that. Or how desperate I was to see where this went. If I were smart, I would've pushed him away and given him a polite *"no, thank you"* before running like my life depended on it back to my cabin and locking myself behind the door before I bent myself over like a dog in heat.

How fucking embarrassing that I was acting like a lovesick teenager when I barely knew this man.

The problem was that our chemistry was off the fucking charts. I knew it. He knew it. Hell, the whole fucking world probably did.

And that therein was the problem, wasn't it?

Denying anything to Marlow's keen eye was only going to get him to back me into another corner again and see just how far he could push my buttons before I cracked. It wasn't like I made it that hard to do, either. All it took was a little poking and prodding and I was breaking down into fucking putty in his hands, begging for even a simple lick of affection.

Driving in the cart with him earlier had sent me spiraling. Letting myself spend time with him in his cabin even more so.

This growing attraction was only getting worse and trying to deny myself by plunging into work was apparently just staving off the inevitable.

But how the hell was I supposed to go from *Director* of the fucking campgrounds to... whatever it was Marlow wanted from me?

A one-night stand?

"Blake." His voice jolted me out of my thoughts. "You're thinking so loudly."

Fuck me.

"All I'm thinking about is how you reek of bonfire and booze." A lame jab, one that had hardly any bite given how nervous I was the closer we were getting to his cabin.

"Aw, come on. I think it smells manly."

"Did you ever shower from when you took a dip in the river?" Deflection was going to be my best friend today, I could feel it.

He barked out a laugh. "What kind of scumbag do you take me for? I'll have you know I'm *very* well kempt."

"Could've fooled me."

The light from his porch was just up ahead.

Fuck.

Fuck, fuck, fuck.

I didn't even have the foresight to shove a few condoms in my pocket. I'd left them back at my own cabin, shoved into the back corner of my sock drawer, never to be looked at again. Rolling up on the bonfire after Marlow had requested my presence was... impulsive.

And coming up upon him with that *couple* was fucking maddening. To the point where I almost grabbed his beer out of his hand and tossed it at her the second she slipped her nail-polished hand on his thigh.

Actually, I was being ridiculous. In hindsight, I was stupid to give in and see him so soon after the golf cart incident. And so soon after I'd gotten a grip of myself and actually given in and rubbed one out before I'd gone back to work.

Had it helped stave off the burning in my veins?

Well, up until I saw Marlow again, I thought it had. Clearly, that was fucking delusional.

Warm light spilled out from the door's window, colliding with the stark white of the porch light that had my head spinning.

Or maybe that was from Marlow's hand on my arm?

"You eat at all?" He grabbed the knob of the door, unlocked of course, and shoved it inward.

Did I?

I couldn't remember. My brain was failing to connect the synapses and form a coherent thought outside of *Marlow is touching me* repeating over and over in my head.

How in the world did people deal with sexual attraction like this?

I'd had the subtle hints of it every so often since I was sixteen; small whispers that alluded to something bigger and better in the future that never quite seemed to come, no matter who I took to bed. I'd tried the docile partners, the rough partners, the in-between-ers.

Nothing ever satiated that part of me that wanted *something* more.

I always knew there was something wrong with me and had yet to be confronted by it with my stark avoidance of making anything official with anyone. That was the trick to keeping your secrets. If you always kept people at arm's length, they didn't get the privilege of knowing your deep, dark insecurities.

Marlow shoved me through the doorway, a

snicker following along with shutting and locking the door behind us.

I tried to not let the sound of the deadbolt sliding into the jam send my stomach into doing somersaults, and instead, pretended it was my body's way of screaming at me for forgetting to eat both lunch *and* dinner.

The place was still immaculately kept and looked barely lived in. There were two dishes drying on the rack next to the sink, a single coffee cup placed next to that facing upright, and a fork and knife in the cutlery slot. The couch had only a subtle impression of a body rippled into the surface of it, and past that, there was only one door open to a bedroom, the inside of it dark.

Interesting.

I had a feeling Marlow had a thing for control, seeing as he worked in finance. That bled into his dwelling, apparently. Everything was neat and organized with the only things moved that *needed* to be moved and nothing more.

An art to the practicality that I could appreciate.

A wave of pressure came up from behind me, hovering right out of my peripheral. It had me freezing, holding my breath to wait for it to pass.

It didn't. It stayed right there, close behind me.

"You sure are chatty today," Marlow murmured.

"Is that a joke?"

He snickered again. "Nope. Your thoughts are written all over your face, Blake."

Ugh.

"Sorry."

He trailed a hand along my shoulder, moving it across to the other one like a trainer would do with a spooked horse. "Listen, you don't need to over think things. This doesn't have to be scary."

Was I that obvious?

Did I read like a book to him?

Marlow was, on the surface, a playful personality with plenty of wisecracks ready to rip at any moment. And yet, under all of that, his calculating side was ever-present.

How else could he get to be so successful in the financial world?

It wasn't solely on his charm. There was a knack to analyzing and picking apart your opponent that would fly over the head of someone like me, but for me, it was like learning a second language.

Hard at first and then a fucking breeze.

"No need to be sorry." When he stood in front of me, he was close enough to lean into, his hand still hooked around my shoulder in a casual way that felt anything but. "We're just getting to know each other."

"Are we?"

Yeah, right.

He huffed out another laugh. "What do you think this is?"

"You can't honestly think I'm *that* dense, right? I got the jab about being naive yesterday. But come on."

To my surprise, his grip on my shoulder tightened and he used it to drive me backward until my back hit the wall right next to the door. My heart stuttered in my chest, a hard thump that was so loud in my ear I was convinced he'd heard it too by the way his smile grew into something smug.

"Blake."

I swallowed. "Marlow."

He leaned down, his breath tickling my face. "You want me. You don't need to be ashamed of it."

My breath shook as I exhaled slowly. He was

so close and smelled like a fucking pine-infused bonfire.

How was it possible for a man to smell *that* good?

It was unfair. I was no match against a man like him.

His lips were slightly wet from his tongue darting out to swipe at them, pink and a little swollen from sucking on the lip of his beer bottle a few minutes ago when I'd stolen him from his friends.

Or had he stolen me?

"Tell me I'm wrong." His voice dropped down an octave.

My dick ached in my pants.

"You... We're supposed to be—"

"Professional?" he teased.

"*Yes.*" I was too acutely aware of how badly my face was burning. "You're my *client.*"

"Guest. We don't need to go all corporate."

"*Marlow.*"

His hand grazed down to flatten over my pec, keeping me pinned to the wall. "Listen. This doesn't have to be a forever thing. I want you, you want me. What's the harm in giving in?"

Every-fucking-thing for one.

For two... would it be?

A one-time thing sounded too blasé for whatever the fuck this was.

Could we let it go after tonight, hang up the towel, call it a day and be on our way?

Could I?

I wanted to believe it was possible. Like Marlow said, there was no getting around this. I couldn't deny the quite obvious attraction I had for him and it was sort of ruining my focus on anything work-related unless it involved him.

Perhaps there was something to this offer. Get him out of my system and then move on with my life—as it were.

I blew out a breath. "Listen to me. If we... if *I* do this with you, we need to keep this between us. I can't have my entire staff knowing I slept with a guest."

He winked. "You got it. I'm good at keeping it on the down low. Trust."

Yeah, I highly doubted it. But at this point, Marlow wasn't giving me any reason to distrust him. So far, he'd been as best behaved as it seemed possible for him.

A hand cupped my chin, tilting my face to

the side. I bit my tongue hard enough to hurt as he brushed the tip of his nose along my jaw, trailing down to the spot just below my ear. His breath was hot against my skin.

"How's this sound, you leave all your troubles, your worries, your *control* at the door. You let me take all of that. I'll take good care of you. I'll make tonight worth your while."

My knees almost buckled at the promise.

Giving up control—fuck, I wanted that. All I did was delegate and spit out orders all day. I wanted—*needed*—someone to pamper me in the most fucked up way possible. Take me and turn me inside out, molding me into someone new.

Reaching down to the hand still pressed against my chest, I curled my fingers around his wrist and tugged at it, guiding the long digits up until I had them wrapped around my throat.

"You better not break your promise. Or I'll kick you off the property first thing in the morning."

The chuckle I received in return to my threat was a deep and throaty call as to what was to come. "A promise, is a promise. I'm a man of my word. And I *always* deliver on what I say I will."

Desire thrummed through me. "Good. Show me what you've got, Knight. Don't keep me waiting."

CHAPTER 11

BLAKE

THOSE FINGERS FLEXED around my neck just tight enough to draw a soft noise past my lips. I heard a soft chuckle that accompanied it, the sound traveling up to my ear where Marlow's nose brushed briefly against it before pulling back from me.

"I like you making those sounds." As he spoke, he kept his grip firm while leading me away from the wall. "Let's see what other ones you're capable of making."

This was such a bad idea but at this point, I was too far gone to care. My dick throbbed between my legs, making it too hard to focus on anything else but the subtle stabs of pleasure that rocked through me right when Marlow shoved me backward and tossed me back onto the couch.

My ass hit it first, my body bouncing with the motion before settling down onto the plush cushion and I let my legs fall apart to accommodate my tented shorts.

Marlow's gaze was glued to that spot, a hungry smile slowly tilting the corners of his mouth upward. "Tell me something, Austin."

My hands found the sides of the cushion to latch onto as he drew near, preparing myself for whatever was to come next. "What?"

"You ever do anything like this before?"

"Sleep with a guest? No." Obviously.

What kind of director would I be if I made this a regular thing?

He let out a soft laugh, completely contrasting with the hooded look in his eyes. "That's not what I meant."

My mouth fell open. "I'm not a *virgin*."

Is that the vibe I gave off?

How fucking mortifying.

I knew I was bad at this whole flirting thing,

but I figured he could at least tell I wasn't an amateur in the bedroom. I was twenty-eight, for god's sake. That was plenty of years worth of experience to get to know the in's and out's of sexual gratification.

He reached down to cup my jaw, forcing my head back until it was pressed against the back of the couch. He sunk his knee down onto the cushion between my legs, resting all of his weight there and dipping us both while he leaned forward. "With *men*, Blake."

Thick saliva coated my tongue and throat. "Y-Yeah. Why?"

His brow popped up suddenly. "Really? Before this?"

"*Yes*." Okay, that was an even worse assumption that he thought I was *straight* rather than simply being a virgin. "Marlow, I'm not—I *am* gay. I run an LBGTQ youth retreat."

"Didn't know if that was you being a really good ally or not."

If I wasn't currently trying to fight off coming in my shorts from how close he was and how intimate him touching me like this felt, I would've reached out and slammed my first right into his shoulder for good measure because what the *fuck* was that.

He was lucky he was charming.

"You're stalling."

He flashed me a cheeky grin. "You're right."

Suddenly, my world flipped on itself, tilting sideways with a hand catching me in the ribs and forcing me flat onto my back lying horizontally on the couch. My legs were kicked apart by a rogue knee, giving Marlow enough room to settle between them while looming over me once again.

His face was shadowed by the way the light fixtures in this room were laid out. His expression going from playful and amused to one that had my toes curling in my shoes. There was an intensity in his eyes that I'd only ever seen once before the last time I'd been in this cabin and on this very same couch.

He pulled me in without a single word, entrancing me by his presence in a way that was so abnormally foreign, I couldn't help but seek out more. I wanted to know how he ticked, how he was able to break through my years of fog when it came to finding anyone even remotely attractive enough to send me into this near frenzy of want.

"You know what's funny," he murmured, surprising me. "You're the first one to ever do this to me."

His hand snuck under my t-shirt to run along the outline of my abs like he was tracing the details to commit them to memory. My stomach jumped at the contact, contracting involuntarily while I tried not to squirm from the subtle touches.

I was overly sensitive to a fault. Every graze, every brush of those fingertips over my skin were small shots of adrenaline rocketing through my system. While I wanted to reach down between us and kick my shorts down to my ankles and free my poor erection, the angle Marlow had me twisted in gave little room to move.

"I don't know how you do it." He continued to talk, his voice barely above a whisper. "You get me somehow. And that turns me the fuck on."

I wheezed the second he glided his hand up and pinched one of my nipples. The pain licked through the pleasure perfectly, perking my hips up to grind against whatever was close enough to give me some sort of relief.

Marlow's hand caught the side of my hip, slamming me back down into the cushion.

"Thought we agreed on you letting me take care of this."

Any more stalling and I was going to come in my shorts. "Hurry up."

He squeezed my nipple hard enough to hurt. "So demanding."

A whimpering moan slipped out of me involuntarily then, before I could stop it. The worst part about being a closet masochist was that usually it freaked people out enough to steer clear of it entirely, hence why locking it down before I let myself get carried away was usually the only way I actually got laid without scaring off the other party.

There were only the few rare occasions when I got someone to sleep with me who actually wanted to get rough, and unfortunately, they never tended to last long relationship-wise. Too many disguised as 'good men' when in actuality, they were little more than abusers catfishing as 'doms'.

Thankfully, I had a pretty good sense to weed them out early.

He paused for a second, his eyes focused intently on my face. "Blake."

Oh my god.

"Marlow."

He titled his head curiously, assessing me for a long moment before pulling his hand out from under my shirt. My stomach flipped instantly. I knew where this was going—he'd tell me that he changed his mind about this whole thing and would quickly pack me up and send me on my way with some lame excuse that he had to get up early in the morning.

I'd had the same song and dance happen one too many times not to know the signs before they slapped me clear across the cheek the way most rejections did. The worst part was this was actually going to crush me. My attraction toward Marlow was off the fucking charts and having it stomped out before anything could really begin was tragic.

When he leaned back, I held in a sigh and began to sit up as well.

If I left quickly, I could probably save myself the humiliation of him watching me do the walk of shame back to my cabin. The next five weeks were going to be rough avoiding him but I had plenty of work to keep me from seeking him out again.

Suddenly, he grabbed at my hips again and

flipped me over onto my stomach with a dizzying quickness. I had no time to react, or ever question what the fuck he was doing, before one of his hands threaded through the hair at the base of my skull and held me there while his other grabbed at the back of my shorts and pulled my up from the couch in order to prop me up on my knees.

"Are you into this?" he asked

Into what?

The crack against my ass cheek was my answer to that question. It was hard enough to sting, even through the thick polyester fabric. The loud moan I choked out was laced with a curse, the pain from the hit vibrating my entire body and arching my back enough to perk my ass up high in the air.

Oh my *god* that was fucking good.

Marlow chuckled. "Oh. He is. Interesting."

My ass was instantly met with another slap to mirror the first, his hand making contact with my other cheek to make it even on both sides. I moaned again, clutching the side of the couch while I rocked my hips forward against an imaginary body while my balls drew up painfully tight against the base of my cock.

Shit, if he kept doing that, I wasn't going to last long at all.

The fingers in my hair shifted slightly, along with the dip in the cushion behind me. Marlow moved back away from me while keeping me pinned, two fingers hooked at the waistband of my shorts in order to yank them down just enough to expose my ass completely.

The cool air forced a shiver down my spine.

"Damn, I wish I had my phone on me." He grabbed one of my cheeks, kneading his fingers into the muscle. "You've got a perfect handprint here."

"Admiring your work?"

Man, why did I find it so hot he wanted to immortalize this somehow?

I should've been running for the damn hills with the threat of him wanting picture evidence this situation was even happening but instead, I was too wrapped up in the audible pride in his voice.

"You wouldn't mind another, right?" he said right before clapping his hand against my skin once more.

The sound was loud in the quietness of his cabin. I could feel the impression of his hand he left behind, the digits creating a tangible pressure on my skin even as I kept still for him while he moved to do the same thing to the other side.

"Or another..." He chuckled again.

My hips shot forward to buck against thin air, cum shooting out to coat the inside of my shorts where my cock was still tucked inside as my orgasm rolled through me. Coming so soon into this was unexpected, but not at all surprising considering how deeply I'd been trying to bury my want for this man over the past few days and having it fail fucking spectacularly.

My eyes stung.

Holy fuck.

Being this out of my mind for a man was disconcerting. I was the king at keeping people at arm's length and never getting too invested, even sexually, with someone I hardly knew for the simple fact of showing all my cards too early into the hand.

How did Marlow unravel me so easily?

Take me from being someone with strict boundaries and walls that safeguarded myself to one that was coming ten minutes into this?

How was he able to read me so fucking easily that he knew *just* what would get me going?

His fingers dug painfully in my hair, pulling me up from the couch and sitting me back onto my sore ass cheeks. He wrapped an arm around my waist and hauled me against his chest, his hand leaving my hair briefly to travel down my body and shove past the waistband of my shorts.

"*Fuck*," came my choked out reply the second his hand wrapped around my slicked cock.

"Oh, you did come." He stroked down from the tip to the base, coating me entirely in my own fluids.

I had half a mind to apologize and try to explain away with a '*this never happens*' kind of bullshit that would probably do nothing but make me look more guilty. Even if he did believe me, where was the fun in all of this ending so goddamn soon?

My only solace was the fact that I was now currently sitting in his lap and his very obvious arousal was poking at me.

His hand tented my shorts, lazily moving up and down my softening shaft a few more times. "You know, Blake, if I knew you were that sensitive, I would've had you suck me off first."

I dropped my head back onto his shoulder, my legs spreading further. It felt so fucking good to have his hands on me like this. "Okay, then why don't you?"

"I should. Give that mouth something to do other than backtalk me all the time."

"You start half of this shit, might I remind you."

"Hm, I can't seem to recall. My memory is rather fuzzy." His teeth found my earlobe. "Maybe you should remind me."

Such a shameless bastard.

He drew his hand out and wiped it on my covered thigh, bucking his hips up against my ass to get me off of his lap and stand while he pulled himself up onto his feet. He made quick work of my zip-up and t-shirt, gesturing with a head nod to toe off my shoes and leave them by the side of the couch before he grabbed my wrist and tugged me toward the bedroom.

I had no time to look around at what he'd done with the place before I was tossed onto the bed like a ragdoll—a rather impressive thing to do considering I wasn't at all light like one. As I bounced on the mattress, he stripped off his own t-shirt and shoes and dropped his sweats to the floor.

CHAPTER 12

HE HAD no underwear on underneath, leaving me to get a nice long view at what he had packing under those layers of fabric.

Marlow had the kind of body that most gym rats prayed for. Cut abs that had a soft dusting of hair trailing down his stomach and a small patch right between his pecs. His shoulders were wide and dense with muscle, making his form look strong and imposing, even in the bedroom's poor lighting.

His thighs were the kind weight lifters had—

large and bulky and were capable of taking him up mountains with barely any kind of effort.

Between his thighs, his cock hung low, half hard and jutting out at an already impressive size. It twitched once as I stared at it, my own doing the same in response.

"Like what you see?" he teased, though I could tell he was preening under my enraptured attention.

"Thought you were going to keep me from talking?" The compliments on his body were on the tip of my tongue, but wouldn't be so easily won. He'd need to work for them if he wanted them that badly.

He smirked and strode forward, his cock bouncing proudly. "I did promise that, didn't I?"

Pushing myself to sit up fully, I swallowed back the nervousness that had my guts suddenly twisting up. I'd had plenty of cocks in my mouth before, and everywhere else, so why I was suddenly taking on the blushing bride attributes was beyond me.

It wasn't like I didn't know how to handle a man of Marlow's size.

He took the initiative for me, reaching over and grabbing the back of my hair again to guide me forward until my lips were practically kissing his dick. I parted them automatically, letting him feed himself into my mouth.

The musky taste of him had me moaning once more. I missed the heady taste of a man like this. Having been too wrapped up in my programs and this business, I had little time to let myself unwind and enjoy the pleasures of someone else. It'd been a while since the last time I got laid. Too long, in fact.

Marlow let out a shaky breath, his hips rolling slightly to rock himself farther inside my mouth.

I watched his face twist while his attention was focused on where his cock was disappearing past my lips, the flesh growing wet from my tongue lapping at the underside of him with each thrust.

"My bad," he murmured. "For accusing you of being a virgin."

I almost smirked.

He better be.

He soon got lost in fucking himself into my mouth, small grunts being drawn out of him every time I tightened the suction around him. His head fell back, eyes screwing shut while pleasure had him already getting lost in it. To the point where he reared himself back fully and rammed his dick down my throat, choking me.

His eyes snapped open, instantly ripping my head back to release himself from my mouth. "Shit, Blake. Sorry."

Spit dribbled down from my lips to coat my chin, my brows pulling together in confusion.

What the hell was there to be sorry for?

I didn't tell him to stop.

"Are you okay?" His eyes were earnest, filled with worry.

How ridiculous. The man makes me cum by slapping my ass hard enough to leave handprints and he's worried about me choking on his dick.

Where was the line with him?

It was kind of sweet in a fucked up way.

A very *Marlow* way.

Instead of answering him, I shook my hair free from his hand in order to scoot back further onto the bed and flopped down onto it. His curious gaze followed me, growing even more so when I gestured for him to come closer.

He sunk one knee down onto the mattress and then the other, his hand coming down close to my hip where he hovered for a second looking lost on how to proceed.

I huffed out a laugh. "Come here."

"I... Blake."

"Marlow, come here."

The only downside tonight was we weren't going to be able to fuck—which was probably for the best. For one, we had no protection because I'd been a goddamn gatekeep keeping those condoms from him, and two, this was more than enough to hopefully get our bearings back once morning came.

"Where?" he asked as he crawled closer.

"I want you to fuck my mouth. Now, get over here."

His eyes practically popped out of his head. Thankfully, he didn't argue with me on the subject and quickly scrambled to throw a leg over the other side of me, scooting up until he was straddling my chest.

I leaned forward until my lips were around his tip again, greedily sucking him into my mouth and getting that musky taste coating my tongue again.

He swore under his breath. "Who knew you were so fucking needy for dick."

Would it be better or worse to admit it was only his that I'd craved this badly?

It was probably best to keep that to myself and take it to my grave.

He planted his hands just above my head while his knees came down next to my ears. He spread his thighs wide, giving me plenty of room to curl my arms up and grab onto the sides of them, giving myself some kind of leverage in order to bob my head up and down his shaft.

My own dick was waking up from its nap, the tingling of an erection in my near future making itself known. I had no idea if Marlow would last till I was at full attention again, but if he did, I'd love to come together.

"Hey." He quickly grabbed my chin and forced my head back. "Didn't I say to leave all of that at the door?"

I practically melted into the mattress.

I wasn't used to someone taking charge in anything, had needed the relief from it so damn badly, but was disappointed around every corner whenever I sought it out intentionally. Not many were up for that task, or at least at the point that *I* needed. It wasn't just the seldom things like making decisions about the grocery list or what position to get into when fucking.

I needed more than that—I needed serious commitment to taking the choices off my plate and letting me fall back into a submissive role that still allowed me the chance to get off in the end and not simply cater to whoever I was inviting into my bedroom.

"Behave." He traced his thumb along my jaw. "I'm in control, Blake. Remember?"

I dug my nails into his thighs, a whiny and needy moan bubbling up my throat. I wrapped my tongue around his tip, stroking along the underside of his head a few times until the bitter taste of his precum leaked out.

I wanted what he was promising so fucking bad. I'd do anything. *Anything* to experience the fantasy I'd built up in my head.

Could Marlow do that?

Actually fulfill that seemingly impossible desire?

He appeared up for the challenge.

His laugh was soft, though thick with lust. "I have a feeling no one's treated you the way you need to be, Blake."

Fuck, how did he know?

How did he read me *so* easily?

He nodded as if I'd answered him. "Yeah, we're gonna fix that."

His words shot straight down to my dick, causing my balls to squeeze painfully with the need to already come again.

"Open your mouth," he instructed, shifting his weight onto the hand still planted next to my head.

I did so obediently, opening wide for him, and flattened my tongue to catch whatever came leaking out of that tip again. He took his hand off my jaw to grip himself, rubbing his leaking head against my tongue a few times to clean it.

"You like it a little rough, Blake?"

I nodded quickly.

He swore under his breath and then shoved himself back into my mouth without warning. My eyes went wide but I kept my throat relaxed in order to keep from gagging the moment his dick touched the back of it. He gripped my hair by the fringe, using it as a lever to work himself in and out of my mouth.

"Oh fuck," he growled.

Spit mixed with precum drooled from the corners of my lips, streaking across my cheeks and down to the mattress. I held onto his thighs, feeling his muscles flexing under the skin with each rock of his body. There was hardly any time to pull in short and quick breaths in between thrusts, making it nearly impossible to keep my eyes from watering.

My body was buzzing with pleasure, so turned on that if I was as rock hard as earlier, I would've come simply at the wet, sloppy sound of Marlow's dick sliding down and out of my throat.

He dug his hips down against my lips, holding himself there while slowing his thrusts and staying in place. He burrowed his cock down my throat, pulsing as he drew closer to coming.

"Hold it there," he said, keeping us both steady. "Little more…"

I swallowed around him, blinking back the tears that were springing to my eyes.

"Fuck…" His skin was flushed with a light sheen. "Oh, fuck, Blake. Little more…"

Oh, he's close.

Marlow's face was blissed out with his jaw slack and eyes slightly wide while he stared down at me—almost like he couldn't believe what he was seeing. He drew back suddenly, trying to quickly get himself out of my mouth, a garbled curse leaving his lips.

Where the hell did he think he was going?

I bit my nails down into his thighs, startling him from actually going any farther than a few inches and giving me enough leverage with how lax his grip had become in my hair to lean forward and draw him back fully into my mouth.

If he was that worried about coming, he didn't need to be. I'd drink it down like fucking water in the middle of the desert.

"Blake—" He stopped himself, forcing my head back down again and then leaning into it. "God, you fucking want this so bad, don't you."

He rolled his hips again, spreading his thighs farther apart and then shifting his weight onto them in order to steady himself while he used my mouth as a Fleshlight. He kept a close hold on my hair, using it to ground himself while his dick made a mess of me.

I choked on him again the second he slammed against the back of my throat, the sudden tightening around him finally tipping him over the edge. He came with a deep moan, hips jerking with each pulse of his cum bleeding down my throat.

He shuddered, slowly letting go of me. "Okay, I take it all back. Really sorry about the virgin thing."

I laughed around him, keeping my lips taunt and my tongue gliding up and down his shaft.

If he let me suck on this thing all night, I would.

Gladly.

CHAPTER 13

MARLOW

THE SOUND of my phone's shrill ringtone pulled me out of a dead sleep, rocketing me clear out from under the burrow of my covers in order to slap my hand down onto it before it woke Blake up. Whoever the fuck was calling me at the actual ass-crack of dawn was going to get a long text telling them to fuck the hell off.

Only, when I reached over to grab where I'd plugged it in last night before heading down to the bonfire, the side next to me was completely empty.

My body froze at the sight of the depressed

sheets no longer containing the shape of another body, nor the familiar golden brown head of hair blending in with the stark white of the pillow I'd laid him down on after his body had finally given in to its exhaustion.

I shot my hand under the covers to brush along his side, feeling that it was cold to the touch with no lingering body heat anywhere other than the spot I was currently occupying.

Long gone by now.

Slowly, I fisted my hand around the fitted sheet.

He could be off getting us breakfast. He was the caretaker type, after all. He could be down at the mess hall right now trying to talk one of the cooks into firing up the grills early to make him something to smuggle back to me before the rest of the property woke up for the day.

There was no way he skipped out on me literally before the sun rose. That was impossible. We had a fantastic night together—one I was having a very hard time convincing myself I didn't want a repeat of.

My phone continued to ring, cutting through my thoughts and forcing me to fish it off of the night stand next to the bed. Yanking the charging cord out of the port, I put it up to my ear.

"*What?*"

There was a long and exaggerated scoff on the other end. "Wow, really? You don't call me at all yesterday and answer the phone like you've got something better to do?"

I was already feeling the buzz of annoyance crawling over my skin. Normally, I'd take Silas worrying over me as a good thing, a flattering gesture even, since he wasn't one to outwardly show his care and compassion for people outside of snarky comments and showing up to take care of business in times of trouble.

Today, however, my patience was already running thin and it was barely past six in the morning. "You're not my boyfriend. I don't need to check in with you every hour of the day."

"What the fuck crawled up your ass and died?"

My covers snapped against the wall behind me as I tossed them off of me and rolled out of bed and headed out into the living area. There were no signs of Blake's clothes scattered on the floor from where I'd peeled them off of him piece by piece, nor were his shoes by the couch where he'd last left them.

In fact, it didn't look like he'd been here at all last night.

There were only signs of me that lingered in this cabin.

Did he actually ditch me?

He certainly had a track record for it, but this was a little much.

No goodbye or note left behind?

Not even a '*thanks, I had a nice time*'?

He had to be coming back here soon. I had a hard time believing he'd leave me like I was some hookup brought home from the bar that had to be escaped from before the early morning '*what are we's* started rolling in.

But isn't that what you wanted? A one-night stand with no strings attached?

"*Marlow.*"

"What!" I snapped.

"Jesus, I'm talking to you. Don't tell me you hit your head on something and have a concussion."

My stomach churned at his tone—quite different than the usual sarcastic drawl. There was a tinge of worry snuck between the words, showing his actual concern outside of the usual barring jabs he threw at me.

I had to reel it back in. Blake going MIA wasn't Silas's fault and I was a dick for not at least texting him before I dragged Blake to bed and forgot that there was a world that existed outside of these cabin walls for the last twelve hours.

We'd made it a point to contact each other so he knew I was still well and breathing.

What other way did he have to make sure I was still good aside from calling Guest Services and making sure there were no active missing person reports?

I let out a slow breath. "Sorry. Had a rough morning."

"What happened?"

There wasn't any harm in telling him, especially since he had no clue who Blake was or that we'd technically broken some kind of ethical code by messing around last night and would therefore judge me for sleeping with the program's director.

Or worse, accuse Blake of using his influence to crawl into my bed when that couldn't be the furthest thing from the truth.

A part of me was still hesitant, though.

Would keeping all of this close to my chest stop me from jinxing it?

There was a very good and very real possibility I was jumping the gun and overreacting to finding my cabin empty and Blake was coming back from the mess hall, or wherever, right at this very moment and I was going to look like a complete fool for ever worrying.

I wanted to believe that was true, even if to save my own ego the embarrassment from getting walked out on. Something that had never happened to me in my thirty plus years on this planet.

Trudging over to the window that faced out toward the main part of camp, the glass was clouded with a thin layer of fog from how much the temperature had dropped during the night, making it a little hard to see out. "I... brought someone back to my cabin last night and we got to messing around. He wasn't here when I woke up."

There was a short pause on the other end of the phone, and then a, "Huh."

"I *thought* we had a good time. At least, in my mind we did."

Never in a million years did I expect the

adorable, blushing, and who I *thought* was a virgin, director of *Austin Adventures* to be into getting his ass slapped and choked to tears by my dick being shoved down his throat until I came.

Even thinking about it now, I was growing hard again.

Those swollen lips wrapping tight around me, his tongue lapping at the underside of my shaft while I buried the head against the back of his throat hard enough to make him gag. The way his nails had bitten into my thighs to keep me from pulling back to give him room to breathe, and the intense look in his eyes when I told him how close I was getting.

Fuck.

How was I supposed to keep this a one-night stand?

I shot my hand down to my cock to squeeze around it to give me some sort of relief from the throbbing ache that was settling there.

"That's odd. You're usually the dine and dasher," Silas commented.

I grunted in response. "Yeah, I know. Hence the rough morning."

"Are you going to see him around later today?"

"Hard to say."

If I played my cards right, and charmed the right people, I could figure out where Blake's cabin was located. At the very least, I could get someone to direct me toward his office and try to camp out there until he had no choice but to run into me and tell me what the fuck was up.

This was all speculating he didn't come back in the next twenty minutes. I still was clinging onto those last few shreds of hope I was wrong about all of this and I'd soon be telling Silas I had to go because I saw a figure in the distance clutching a to-go container stuffed full of break-fast food.

I forced myself to step back from the window and pace around the living room instead. The longer I looked out through the fogged glass like a dog waiting for its owner to get back from the store, the more depressed I was getting by the second.

"I'll be honest," Silas said after another pause. "I'm surprised you care."

"About being ditched?"

"Yeah, Marlow. Who cares if some guy needed to dip before his partner caught him in someone else's cabin? Aren't you out there with a bunch of couples? Last time I heard, you were trying to hook up with a couple of swingers."

"This guy *is* single."

"Okay, but is that what he's telling you or is that something you know personally because you verified it with your own two eyes?"

I sighed heavily.

There was no way to actually know Blake wasn't with someone, sure, but I found it hard to believe that man had the time to entertain anyone with how much running around he did as the director. And that wasn't at all including getting involved with being my partner for the first few days I'd been here.

Two separate staff members had corroborated as much, anyway.

"That's not that point." I hated how defensive I was getting over this subject.

Silas was right—I had no reason to be this bent out of shape about a man who had made it clear last night we were keeping all of this on the down low. Why in the world I expected to wake up to him cuddled against me like we'd been exclusive for weeks was beyond me, and so far off from how I usually went about my hookups.

Getting ditched made it easier for both of us.

We wouldn't have to do that awkward song and dance as I quietly led him out of my cabin while making sure no one spotted us as I bid him a farewell before going back to pretending like none of it ever happened in the first place.

Yet, the more I paced around the living room, the more agitated I got.

Why didn't he say anything?

Why not wake me up before going and telling me it was a good run but he had to get home?

Did he honestly think I was the type to cling and therefore had to make his grand escape before I roped him into something?

"Then what is?" Silas asked.

I really didn't know. That pang of *something* still lingered in my chest regardless of how hard I was trying to stamp it down. "You know, this is the part of the conversation when you tell me 'there there, everything will work out' and then give me some sort of pep talk about how there's more fish in the sea."

"Are you hearing yourself right now? Since when do you need a pep talk to get over a one-night stand? Marlow, you've been there for five days. How fucking deep did you fall for this guy after sticking your dick in him?"

My face flushed hot instantly. "I *haven't.*"

"Then get a fucking grip. This isn't like you at all."

I wanted to argue so fucking bad—just to get some of this anger off of my chest and tossed to an opponent who I knew could take it.

Silas and I were supposed to be perpetual bachelors for life. We'd made that pact long before we'd both made it big in our respective careers and right around the time we were about to graduate college. Avery hadn't been keen on agreeing to the pact, finding it rather childish when it was far from that.

We were promising not to let something as stupid as dating and relationships get in the way of our friendship. I'd seen too many people get wrapped up in trying to find 'their person' while dropping whatever relationships they had with their friends before that, finding it inconvenient to balance the two in a healthy way and instead made it the other party's problem.

I never wanted to be like that. Lost in my own bubble of happiness that I forgot everyone else around me who helped me get there.

Relationships didn't scare or terrify me, but I knew the damage they could do if left to their self-actualization.

Hence why getting involved with Blake in the first place was supposed to remain off limits. I'd made that decision day one and here I was, not even a week into this program, and I'd already gone back on my own promise.

Damn it.

"Yeah, you're right." I sighed.

"I know I am. The weekend's coming up. You should come back to Ellington for a bit."

"Can't. Got to stay close to the property." It was a grand idea, though.

Before this, Blake probably would've given me the all -clear to sneak off the property and covered for me, giving me the leeway because he still felt bad about my package getting mixed up with the wrong one and wanted to continue to make it right even if I was slightly taking advantage of the situation.

But now... now I really didn't know where we stood.

My entire body ached.

"Okay, then I'll come to you," Silas said.

"Wait, really?"

"Yeah. I'll drag Avery along."

I smiled a little. "Good luck trying to peel him from Brandon's side."

"I have my ways. I'll make it happen."

I had no doubt about that. In fact, if anyone were to guilt Avery into spending time with us again, it was definitely Silas.

Glancing out the window again, and with still no sign of Blake coming back, I heaved a sigh. Sitting around all weekend trying to distract myself while pretending not to look for Blake's face in every crowd that passed by was going to be nearly impossible. I'd wind up getting distracted and doing something stupid, like getting up on one of the adventure courses and plunging to my death because I wasn't paying attention to how to properly strap myself into the harness.

It was going to be hard trying to talk the staff into letting me off the property for the weekend without somehow involving Blake, but that would just have to be my mission for the day— figuring out a way to get out of here with as little people noticing as possible.

The ideal solution would be no one noticing *at all.*

Unfortunately, role call was taken every morning, so that would be impossible.

Unless I got Talos to agree to marking me off for the weekend as long as I kept him in the loop of my location.

Would he tattle to Blake about it?

Probably. But hopefully that wasn't until I was off the property and didn't piss him off enough to not let me back *on* come Monday morning.

"All right, I'll see what I can manage on my end," I said. "No promises, but I'll try to get out of here by dinner time."

"I'll be waiting with a car at the entrance. We can fake a grandparent's death or something."

I let out a dramatic gasp. "Silas, that's asking for trouble from the spirits. They'll haunt you for lying about the dead."

"Okay, if I'm haunted by spirits, it's not from dead grandparents unless you count the ones that die on my table."

"How many grandparents have you killed?!"

"Intentionally or accidentally?" Obviously, he was joking. I wouldn't be friends with a serial killer.

Unless, of course, he was like Dexter and did

it in a vigilante sort of way. *Then* maybe I could excuse a murder or two.

"I'll call you tonight."

"You better," he nipped. "If you forget, I'm calling the cops."

"Yeah, okay, message received." And he liked to call me the dramatic one. "See you later."

"I better."

Ending the call, I felt a weight slowly being lifted off my shoulders. There was still a lingering pain in my chest that probably wasn't going to go away any time soon, but at least I had something to distract me for the next few days.

Even if it was most likely going to end with Silas and I drinking until Avery had to carry us out of there and to whatever local hotel we rented for the next few days.

Monday morning would come sooner than I wanted it to, but at least there was a high chance I wouldn't be running into Blake. His youth program was supposed to start early next week, which he was no doubt going to be stressed out of his mind about up until the day the kids arrived.

That gave me the clear all next week to do whatever I wanted without accidentally having to have that awkward shuffle while he tried his best to avoid eye contact with me as much as possible and I tried to not grab him by the back of the shirt and haul him to the nearest secluded corner to shake the truth out of him.

Neither of us would get what we needed out of a confrontation like that, so things were best left as they were for now until I could actually cool the anger inside of me.

Perhaps by the end of this program, I'd be ready to have a civil conversation with him, but for now, I needed to avoid him at all costs.

Or else I was likely to do something way more stupid than I wanted to. The man deserved to run this camp in peace and without me barking up his tree demanding answers he probably didn't even have.

Avoid. Forget about it. Move on.

That was what needed to happen.

That was what I needed to keep reminding myself.

CHAPTER 14

Blake

Two and a half days.

For two entire days, I'd avoided the main camp like the plague and only took the back routes to get to and from where I needed to go.

Two days of jumping at every person walking by, every call that came over the radio, and every single tall, tanned man with reddish brown hair that I happened to see out of the corner of my eye that soon turned out to be just another stranger.

God, I was losing my fucking mind.

I was stupid to think this thing was never

going to affect me. That I could fool around with Marlow and purge myself from the desperation to have him and work it out of my system like a bad cold, never to be infected again.

I was so wrong. So dead fucking wrong it was painful.

Waking up in his bed, tucked against his side like I was a long time lover was the most unnerving situation I'd ever woken up in and had freaked me out into high-tailing it the fuck out of there the second I could.

I was well aware of how much of a coward I was, particularly when Marlow had done nothing wrong and it was all *me*.

Leaving him without an explanation was probably the only way to go, though, considering all I had in terms of explaining myself was '*I'm fucked up in the head*'.

There was no good reason for me to feel some sort of attachment to him now that we'd fooled around. We were dating and we certainly weren't making anything exclusive. He was a flirtatious playboy at heart and I was a workaholic loner who was only supposed to be focusing on the rest of the camp's season and not letting himself get tangled up in a fucking torrid love affair.

Marlow and I were in two completely different classes of life. Not compatible in the slightest and with no way to actually workout, even if there was actually some semblance of a budding relationship between us.

I was never leaving Wakefield and he was going back to Ellington Heights soon to live among the ritzy upper class he'd grown up with.

And that was that.

Getting upset about it was stupid. It wasn't worth my time.

No matter how often I caught my attention drifting out the windows of my office and down to the camp below looking for a familiar head of hair, or found my hand wandering over to the walkie settled on its cradle on my desk to check in on Marlow's assigned group for the day, I quickly stopped myself from escalating any further.

I had a full day before my youth groups were here and I'd be swamped with making sure they were being kept from the adult section of the property as well as behaving amongst themselves. This was going to be the first time I had so many kids staying on the property and so far, all was going according to plan.

Hopefully, it stayed that way.

My walkie's shrill alert sound had me jumping a mile off my chair.

"Blake, can you come down to registration?" Talos's voice came through the speaker of the communication device.

Wasn't he supposed to be with Marlow's group again today?

Anxiety hit me instantly. There was no way another white water rafting incident was occurring so soon after the first one. Marlow seemed to be a magnet for getting into interesting situations, and so far, he'd made it out alive and without a single scratch.

But soon, that luck would eventually dry up and I really didn't want to be the cause of that.

I may be avoiding him like the damn plague currently, however, that didn't mean I wished him ill will.

"Everything okay?" I asked.

There was an agonizingly long pause on the other end of the walkie that had me up and out of my chair and already shoving my shoes back on my feet.

"Yeah, you got a visitor."

I stared down at the walkie.

Who the hell would be coming all the way out here to visit me?

We were in our busy season, which my siblings knew to steer clear of unless they wanted to get roped into some off-hours volunteer work.

Same with my parents.

That left only one person...

Smiling, I held the walkie up to my mouth again. "Did he just come in?"

"No, he's been chatting with Lindsay for twenty minutes. I just happened to walk by and spot them. Better come quick before he gets talked into heading up to the adventure courses."

In the background of the call, right before Talos's line cut, my granddad's distinct laugh filtered through the speaker, warming my heart instantly.

"I'll be right down."

Tossing the walkie back onto the receiver, I grabbed my keys and headed out into the afternoon sunlight. My granddad didn't make it up here as often as we both liked nowadays but I was always excited to see him, nonetheless.

Along with the rest of the staff on property.

He was a beloved figure among us all, starting *Austin Adventures* from the ground up and building it into the incredible destination spot that it currently was. All I did was maintain it and keep a little extra money flowing in from some of the young students that came through here on field trips—and now my youth group.

Everything else was all him.

I was damn proud to be a part of his bloodline and even more so when he'd passed the torch to me a few years back once he thought I was good and ready. The first two years had been nerve-wracking as fuck, even with him at my side on a part-time basis. By year three, though, I had gotten into the swing of things. And now year five, I was finally feeling comfortable with calling the shots and not consulting with him first about it.

He had full faith in me, which meant I needed to as well.

Taking the back route to the registration office, I quickly arrived with Talos still there chatting with Lindsay and Lydia, both of whom were leaning against the desk under the fan blowing overhead.

My granddad was sitting on the rolling stool

behind the desk, elbow deep in the registration book with a cord phone tucked between his ear and shoulder while his pen quickly flitted over the page in front of him.

The sight had me shaking my head instantly. "You're already putting him to work?"

Lindsay's head whipped around to the sound of my voice. "I swear, he volunteered."

"Took the phone right out of her hand and everything," Lydia corroborated.

I didn't doubt any of it for a second.

That was the one thing my granddad absolutely hated about his retirement. He missed the daily grind and operations of this place. While in its hay day, he loved to claim he hated paper pushing and preferred getting off the property and heading out to explore with our tour groups, in reality, though, he loved it all. The behind the scenes, the on-field work.

All of it.

There wasn't a single thing that man wouldn't volunteer to do given the opportunity.

Turning my attention toward Talos, I said, "Thought you were supposed to be with a group today?"

He shrugged. "Came back early. Temp got a

little hot so we turned back. If any of them want to go out later, there's that firefly path hike we can do but most of them were keen on coming back to swim in the lake."

I wondered what side Marlow was on: be grateful to head back to camp for the day or antsy to take up another course if given the chance.

It was hard to say. He was such an enigma that it made him hard to read. He had so much energy that made him the perfect client to take on any of the tougher courses to burn it off, but at the same time, he'd been content sitting around the bonfires at night, hanging out with the other groups he'd joined earlier that day.

"I see. Anyone giving you any trouble?"

He shook his head. "Nope. All good on my end."

"Mine too," Lydia answered. "Though, Chatterbox was in quite the mood today."

My brow shot up. "Who?"

"Marlow Knight," Talos supplied.

Now I was confused. "I thought he was assigned with your group today?"

I made that plan specifically because it was

going to be tougher on him, and therefore, give him the challenge he was always craving.

Why the hell would Lydia take him when her guides were usually on the lighter side?

Talos shrugged. "He wasn't interested in the hike. Wanted to head out on the jet skis."

"Which was weird," Lydia replied. "Because he didn't even get on one. Just sat on the dock with his feet in the water and watched everyone."

That... *was* odd.

My stomach churned.

I hoped it wasn't because of me. Or what we did Thursday night. The last thing I wanted was for his time here to be less fun because I'd given in and let myself cross that line that never should've been crossed in the first place.

Putting distance between us this weekend was my only solution to try and combat the wave of guilt I felt, along with what I was beginning to suspect were budding feelings I was trying to do everything to *not* let take root.

"Mood... as in?" I ventured.

Lydia shrugged. "Uh, tired I guess? He said he had a headache but he seemed fine other than that. Just wasn't as chipper, I guess you could say."

Oh god.

I rubbed a hand over my face, hiding the sudden panic that was coursing through me.

Seeking him out to talk to him was probably the worst idea I'd ever had. Then again, if he needed to vent or be mad at someone, it most definitely should be me. If I was the source of him no longer enjoying staying here, that was for me to deal with and address and not anyone else.

Putting that on someone else's plate wasn't fair in the slightest.

Right as I dropped my hand to tell Lydia I'd talk to him, my granddad's phone call finally ended. "Ah ha, there's my grandson."

His cheery smile was had to not mirror. "Didn't expect you today. Everything okay?"

He winked and pushed himself up from the stool, his body wobbling slightly as it slowly balanced out again. "Of course. You up to taking a walk with me?"

"Always." Nodding to the rest of my staff, I held out an arm for my granddad and escorted him out into the sunshine.

"Ah, nice day today. As always," he commented. "Why don't we head over to the docks? I'd love to dip my feet in the water."

My heart lurched at the suggestion. Hopefully, by now, Marlow was moved on to some other activity. With Lydia down visiting Lindsay, that was a good sign that her group had dispersed and had absorbed themselves into other ones.

"Yeah, definitely," I said, turning and leading the way.

Please, please, don't be there.

CHAPTER 15

Blake

As luck would have it, the moment my granddad and I cleared the bend and came face-to-face with the beautiful sparkling waters of Mt. Craigleith's lake, so too did we find ourselves coming up on the sunbathing Marlow freaking Knight.

He was stretched out on the dock, laying flat on his back with a pair of dark-tinted sunglasses covering his eyes, his feet still hanging over the edge and submerged under the cool water, just like Lydia had said. His fingers were laced and tucked under his head, cushioning him from the hard wood under him.

But that wasn't the part that was catching my eye the most. It was the fact that he was in nothing but a pair of swimming trunks that were pulled dangerously low on his hips, showing off the beginnings of his pelvis, that I had to rip my gaze away from before I got dangerously turned on.

Of course he was out here looking like a damn catalog model posing from a shoot that was beach-theme inspired. All washboard abs and thick, ropey arms that looked like they could pick up anyone under two hundred and throw them right over his shoulder like they were merely a beach towel slung out of the way in order to carry the precious cooler of beers down to the water's edge.

Bet the veins in his arms would pop if he did that.

Bet he could carry two *coolers.*

His tanned skin was definitely getting dark from when I'd met him a week ago, a full shade at least, and damn, did a little color look good on him. He wasn't pale to begin with but now no one would definitely be accusing him of spending too much time indoors.

"Nice day for sunning yourself," my granddad called out, snapping me out of my lust-filled thoughts while taking in a long sweep of the waters and the guests currently swimming in the roped off area.

"Can't beat it," Marlow replied instantly.

My heart thudded uncomfortably in my chest.

He didn't *sound* upset, so that was at least a positive sign. Perhaps Lydia was reading too much into his behavior. She'd only gotten to know him one other time during the hike back down from the waterfall where she couldn't wait to tell me *all* about Marlow's quirky antics the moment she got back to base camp.

Since then, she'd kept a skeptical eye on him.

That was the man she'd had her first opportunity to know—a vivacious and eccentric personality that was both the life of the party and a master at charming anyone he talked to. A snake charmer that could flatter even the coldest of hearts.

In reality, Marlow was so much more than that.

He had depth to him. More sides than simply the class-clown mask he liked to wear when in social situations. I'd seen it for myself first hand in those passing moments when I'd actually allowed myself to stop with the professionalism and let him in a bit. When I'd actually set aside my worry with crossing boundaries and given in to the itch.

I *liked* that side of him. It was just as compelling as his eccentric self.

If only we'd met five years ago. Maybe then, I would've let myself get caught up in the whirlwind.

It would've absolutely ended in heartbreak, but aren't all first loves like that?

"You enjoying your time here so far?" my granddad asked.

"Besides the hangover? Absolutely."

My brows knitted together.

Hangover?

How in the world did he manage that when we only permitted two alcoholic drinks per guest per night?

Unless he hoarded them all over the weekend from the bonfires... But then again, getting drunk off four beers, *maybe* six, enough that he'd woken up with a hangover this morning, seemed a little... unbelievable.

There was no way he was that much of a lightweight.

"Did you talk someone into getting you something off the property?" I asked.

Marlow shifted on the dock, his hand popping out from under his head to shove the sunglasses down under his eyes to stare at me over the rim of them. "Ah, Mr. Director... so nice of you to leave your cave and join us for a little sunlight. AC getting a little too cold up there?"

The jab, aimed true, right for my chest and hitting home. Dead center.

Talk about a sucker punch.

Ouch.

So he is pissed at me.

Unfortunately, his comment made my granddad practically double over with laughter. "Don't tell me you've been hiding away in the damn office."

Clearly, I wasn't as scot-free as I thought I was. The unmistakable taunting was barely covered up with his usual light tone. A simple tease to any other person that wasn't familiar with the way he spoke or joked around, but to anyone that was a little more seasoned like me, it became quite obvious he wasn't at all kidding in his mockery.

If this was how it was going to be for the next five weeks, I wasn't sure how the hell we were going to both manage. Having such thick tension had already been practically suffocating when it was simply sexual. Slap on a dose of irritation and it turned into a regular recipe for disaster.

Goddamn it.

This was why I was supposed to keep my damn dick in my pants.

"I haven't."

My granddad shook me by my shoulder. "The paperwork can wait, Blake. Enjoy the summer while it's here."

"Yeah, Mr. Director. Enjoy the summer while it lasts," Marlow chimed right in, stoking the fire like the fucking pot-stirrer he was determined to be. "Unless you're avoiding something down here with us common folk."

I shot him a subtle glare.

Knock it off.

He sent back a cheeky smile and then winced. "Ugh."

I tried to narrow down the list in my head one-by-one. Talos was too much of a rule follower to be talked into leaving the property in order to make a booze run for a guest. Lydia was usually in bed before the sun went down, and Lindsay was definitely not the type to be hanging around the guests after her shift was done.

There was the possibility of my other set of crew, my night shift-ers, but would Marlow have approached a staff member he wasn't at least a little bit familiar with?

I supposed it didn't really matter, considering he was good at disarming anyone he came in contact with. It'd take one long and meaningful conversation after the sun went down and the bonfires were blazing against the night sky before he had them fishing their keys out of their pocket and scurrying off to the staff parking lot to run into town for him.

"Who's your hook up?" I asked, crossing my arms over my chest.

I had to know. If he had anyone in his back pocket, I wanted their name and once I had it, they'd immediately be switched to day crew for the next five weeks. No way was I tolerating this bullshit flying under my nose. He wasn't about to be getting a special on-call meal service whenever he pleased just because he sweet-talked someone into feeling special.

He'd signed up to come here for a reason. He wanted a life change and goddamn it, he'd get just that. He'd get the full authentic experience of living at a wilderness and survival adventure camp, I'd make sure of it.

While I was also going to pretend that a spark of jealousy most *definitely* wasn't brewing in my chest at the possibility of Marlow talking someone else up like he had me—cornering them against the mess hall and inviting them back to his cabin for a little getting-to-know-each-other.

My jaw tinged suddenly from grinding my teeth together.

I wasn't supposed to care about being a passing interest. That's what our whole one-time arrangement had been agreed to. He had no loyalty to me, and nor did I have anything for him. I wasn't *supposed to,* anyway. I was only another notch on his bedpost. A consequence of giving in to my stupid desires like I had no control over them in the first place.

That was it.

Why the hell did that sting so badly?

"Can't say, my lips are sealed," he muttered, a hand coming up to massage his temple.

My granddad's eyes were lazering into me. "I see we've gotten quite familiar with the guests."

I almost groaned.

This was not how I wanted any of this to go. We'd come out here to walk the grounds and catch up, not run into Marlow and have my whole cover blown. Him calling me out on everything because of his bitchy mood wasn't what I'd signed up for after agreeing to leave the safety of my office and coming down here to spend time with my granddad.

Marlow was the *last* on my list of people I wanted to run into at this point.

"I don't know if you can tell but I'm kind of his favorite," Marlow said as he shoved his sunglasses over his eyes once again and relaxed back down onto the dock.

"Is that what you think," I challenged.

"Oh, that's what I *know*."

"I'm glad to see my grandson is making friends." My granddad beamed.

That had Marlow lowering his shades once again. "Grandson? Blake, why didn't you say we were in the presence of royalty?"

In a surprising show of resilience, he pushed up from the dock and rolled to his feet. There was a brief wince that I caught right before he smothered it in order to plaster a pleasant smile on his face, offering his hand out to my granddad to shake.

As the two men shook hands, my gaze wandered to Marlow's body again, shamelessly taking in every little line of his muscles and the slight difference in tan shade starting right above the hem of his swim trunks. I bet if I placed my hand right over his pec, he'd be hot to the touch.

Scorching, even.

"Marlow Knight," he said with a flourish. "Your grandson's been keeping me company since I signed up for the wrong package. Turns out, I got in on a couple's retreat and had no idea until I got here. Who knew!"

"The welcome packet, for one," I said.

"Since then...." An arm was thrown around my shoulders, pulling me toward a *very* warm body. "Blake's been filling in as my partner. It's been great, other than him constantly ditching me for paperwork halfway through our adventures."

The worst part about being so close to him

was how easily it was to melt into his side. Like my legs were suddenly turned to Jello and all I wanted to do was let him hold me like this while I soaked up the heat radiating off of him from his sun exposure like a fucking lizard.

Since I was little, I always knew I was gay. Had never tried to hide it or explain it away to anyone, including my granddad, who wasn't at all phased when he caught me making out with one of my classmates while we were at the campgrounds for a class field trip.

All he'd told me as I got older was to keep myself safe and to never give into anything that I wasn't comfortable doing. He'd always been my rock throughout my life. My sage advisor.

Who was hopefully totally oblivious to what Marlow's arm around me was doing to my brain by practically melting it into mush.

Fraternizing with the clientele was a big ole' fat no-no.

Getting caught doing exactly that by my granddad?

I'd rather throw myself into the lake and try to drown before facing *that* lecture.

"Blake." The head shake was all the scolding I needed.

"I wasn't—I'm not." The words were hard to form. Worse with me trying to find what kind of sentence to string them into.

"It's okay." Marlow's long and drawn out sigh snapped me out of my delusional thoughts. "I get it. I'm not fun enough to hang out with. The glitz and glam have all worn off. I'm simply a rusted up toy, no longer used and tossed into the bottom of the toy box."

I nearly rolled my eyes.

I slammed my elbow right into his side, digging in hard enough to force him off of me. "Don't you have a hangover to nurse?"

The second he let go of me, my stomach sank. What a traitorous bastard my body was being at the moment.

"That's what I was doing before you came over here and interrupted my nap."

My granddad was watching us with abject fascination. An amused smile playing on his lips that had an all-too-knowing uptick to it. If he was making assumptions about anything, I sure as hell hoped it was all innocent.

A simple case of me falling into an easy friendship with a bodacious man that clearly had too much fun ribbing me whenever he got the chance to.

So far, I still had plausible deniability. However, if Marlow kept this up—the teasing, the poking, the slightly bitchy attitude—we were going to become *real* fucking obvious soon enough.

I was trying not to be paranoid, however, my granddad also wasn't a stupid man. Far from it, actually.

Not much flew by him without him taking notice, storing it away for later in that file cabinet of a mind he had until the relevant time came around to extract the file and lay all of the evidence out on the table for both parties to see.

There was a reason not many people fought him on how he ran this place back in the day. I'd simply ridden in on his coattails and maintained the status quo.

"My apologies," I said, stepping away from him. "We'll let you get back to it."

Marlow's smile turned tight. "Yeah, of course."

Don't fall into it. Just turn around and walk away.

"It was nice to meet you, Marlow. I hope I'll

be seeing more of you later this evening at the bonfires." My granddad's tone was pleasant, betraying nothing of whatever was swirling around in his mind—theories, questions, evidence pointing toward a particular opinion.

My head snapped back around to him. "You're staying that late?"

He chuckled. "Planning on kicking me off of the property soon?"

My cheeks grew hot from embarrassment. "No. Not at all. Stay as long as you'd like. You know you're welcome to."

Not to mention my entire staff would riot if they found out I booted our former owner off the property. This man had done everything for this place, birthing it into existence from nothing and turning it into something incredible. I'd never be able to face myself in the mirror if I did something as stupidly selfish as sending him on his way in order to avoid accountability.

Whatever lecture was on the horizon for me, I'd have to take in stride. Hopefully, I could cover my own ass and make all of this seem like one giant misunderstanding, depending on what the hell kind of vibes he was picking up on.

"We should get going." I looped my arm back around his. "Ready?"

My granddad threw one last amused smile Marlow's way before letting me tug him away from the docks.

The farther we got away from here, the better.

I needed to put as much distance between me and this man as soon as possible before I did something stupid, like invite him back to my cabin to join us for dinner. The last thing I needed was for him and my granddad to share a dinner table like I was bringing him home to meet the family.

"See you soon!" Marlow called after us.

CHAPTER 16

Marlow

My headache stabbed at me from right behind my eyeballs, threatening what little breakfast I was able to force down my throat before heading down for roll call this morning. I'd been fighting the nausea ever since—my penance for getting blasted all weekend with my friends with no cares as to what Monday's future held.

In a rather dramatic bit of irony, meeting Blake's grandfather felt like divine timing.

Had I known such a bigwig was going to be cruising around the campgrounds with Blake trailing after him, I would've tried to look a little bit more presentable. As it stood, they got the best efforts I could manage for the time being.

Honestly, it was a miracle I didn't throw up right on Blake's shoes the moment he got close enough for me to touch him.

He was stiff in my hold, his body growing rigid the second my arm fell over his shoulder in a way that was mostly insulting to my ego, considering seventy-two hours prior I had him contorting under me as he came.

This new tension between us wasn't sexy at all.

In fact, it was downright exasperating.

Look, I was no stranger to regret. Had my fair share of it in my thirty-four years on this spinning rock in space more times than I could count. College had been filled with those. Each experience a steep learning curve from the last that finally culminated into a nice little portfolio of 'no's and 'hell no's that I still followed to this day.

There was no shame in realizing that the decision you made the night before was best left untouched in the future and to not fall into the trap of it being repeated again once the dust finally settled.

But for Blake to clearly be that remorseful over what we'd gotten up to hurt my feelings more than finding him gone from my bed Friday morning.

Had he woken up with that sick feeling in his gut that told him to run? Or did that come much later, after he'd finally gotten back to the safety of his own cabin and the events from the night before had finally hit him?

I wanted to know, yet at the same time, the answer was definitely going to force me to drown my sorrows in booze like I had all weekend with Silas and Avery. Tossing back drink after drink until I was numb from the rejection and could no longer remember why I was so damn beaten up about it in the first place.

I barely remembered my weekend outside of getting dragged back to the campgrounds and carefully snuck back into my cabin by a very foolishly wasted pair of friends who ended up crashing on the couch and in the other guest bedroom until I'd had to kick them both out before the sun chased away the morning dew.

The worst part about all of this was how *good* being with Blake felt before it all went to shit. I'd *never* gotten off like that in my life, and now, to find out the other party wanted nothing to do with me, it stung like a fucking wasp to the eyeball.

Where did I go wrong? Did I go too hard on him? Scare him away?

Maybe he thought he wanted it rough like that but in hindsight, realized he'd let himself go too far into some unknown territory he had yet to explore within himself or with a partner in bed.

I wasn't sure.

Whatever was going on, and whatever feelings were stirred up the moment I'd had Blake standing in front of me again, was forcing me to reevaluate everything.

I was thankful—no, *grateful*—that both Silas and Avery had shown up for me, whisking me away in a black Mercedes like I was Cinderella going to the ball. I'd pulled the sick card with the medical staff, playing up my symptoms from the white water rafting incident as a residual sickness that seemed to come over me a day later.

They were all too inclined to believe me, promising not to bug me outside of the occasional check-in's I'd wormed my way into doing by handing over my phone number the minute it was asked of me.

Sneaking off the grounds was easy enough once the sun set, and soon, I was feeling like a kid sneaking out past curfew.

Blake's ability to sniff me out was impressive. Enough that it had me considering ratting out his coworkers as a reward for him connecting the dots so easily. I wouldn't, of course, but the temptation was certainly there if only to get Blake to talk to me again, even if it resulted in a scolding.

I longed for any sort of attention from him. A sad side effect from having him on my mind the entire weekend and having no good outlet to waste my energy on outside of drinking myself stupid.

Avery and Silas had listening to my drunk rambles I don't know how many times, each one circling back to the main focal point of: what the fuck happened?

With no real theories from either of them, or myself, my brain refused to move on to something else. Too stuck in trying to rewrite history until it finally made sense.

It never would. Not unless I got Blake to

actually talk to me and I doubted that was happening anytime soon.

He had his youth program to run come tomorrow morning and now with his grandfather hanging around the campgrounds, I would be to be lucky to see passing glimpses of him for the next week or so.

My stomach squeezed pitifully.

"Ugh." Settling my head down onto the table, I let my eyes fall closed while my headache throbbed dully.

I wasn't up to lying out in the sun after Blake and his grandfather had stopped by, the situation causing me to feel too raw and way too exposed for my liking. I doubted they'd be swinging back around after whatever they were out doing, but regardless, it had me hightailing it back to the mess hall where I could wallow in one of the forgotten corners.

There was no motivation in me to do anything today. Not go hiking, jet skiing, try my hand at the challenge courses further up into the wooded area. Nothing.

Forcing myself out of bed this morning had been a chore and a half, and now that I was among people, I was feeling even less social than I was before I'd thrown on an outfit to come down here.

What was stopping me from sneaking away and going back to my cabin for the rest of the day to sleep off my hangover and avoid anyone else from bugging me?

There wasn't much time left before the sun started to set and nighttime activities were in full swing. Plus, I wasn't partnered with anyone today, so I had free rein to do whatever I wanted, which should include doing *nothing,* too.

Given my foul mood, avoiding people was probably a blessing in disguise. No one wanted to be around a total bummer.

I didn't get the need for the staff here to make sure I was getting my money's worth with this package. Sure, maybe this was all stemming from the fact that I was absolutely not in the mood to do *anything* at the moment, but still, it wasn't like I was going to be demanding a refund because every second of my day wasn't jam-packed with activities.

How often did that happen?

Imagining poor Lindsay down at Guest Services getting screamed at for something that stupid by some rich-ass snobs had my blood boiling. I hated entitlement more than anything.

Having not grown up with a silver spoon in my mouth, and now having the ability to bestow that onto whatever offspring I happened to *maybe* have in the future, I could confidently say that people like that needed to get a fucking grip.

Much like me with this whole Blake thing.

Silas's words rang in my head loudly.

Get over it.

Easier said than done.

Though, he had a point.

Why the fuck was I getting *so* hung up about this?

It couldn't just be an ego thing. I'd had my fair share of being knocked down a peg or two in my time and this was nothing in comparison to that.

Seeing Blake again had re-ignited the flame of betrayal. Like the wound had slowly been staring to heal and then was unceremoniously ripped right back open, leaving me bleeding all over the damn place yet again.

Get. Over. It.

Something cold shocked the back of my neck, heavy and slightly wet. Instantly, I brought my hand up to slap at it, coming into contact with something solid in the process, along with whatever it was that had been placed there.

"Relax," a familiar voice said from above me.

My entire body froze in disbelief.

He moved it—an ice pack I was starting to realize—up toward my hairline, keeping it there with a firm hold. Relief rippled through me at the compress. My chin met with the table again, my attention pinned on the figure moving just out of my peripheral and then slowly shifting into it when he hopped up onto the table to sit on it next to me.

"Who gave you the booze?"

I rolled my eyes. Wasn't even going to allow me to enjoy a second of this without some kind of interrogation. "Is that what you came back over here to bug me about?"

"Yeah. I want to know who I have to fire." Blake's tone was hard to read. If he was serious about that, then I *definitely* wasn't going to be ratting anyone out no matter how many times he poked and prodded at me to do so.

The medical staff were good people and actually seemed like they gave a shit when I'd walked in there playing up my cat-with-a-limp-paw scheme and pretended like I needed the weekend to recuperate without anyone coming around to bug me as I slept off my cold.

"Technically..." I tilted my head to the side, letting my cheek rest against the table instead. "A bartender gave me the booze."

I heard him mutter 'bartender?' under his breath while rearranging the ice pack, following the curve of my neck in order to rest it right at the junction right below my ear. I nearly groaned at the pressure, both pain and relief reverberating inside of my poor skull at the same time.

Fuck, the last time I had a hangover this bad was when I went out to celebrate my first million-dollar trade.

To this day, I still couldn't stomach tequila.

"You snuck off the property?" He sounded bewildered. Which was so cute.

It wasn't like he was running a fucking jail. Anyone could come and go if they really wanted to. The only reason I'd gone through such great lengths not to be found out was because I didn't want any of the staff to have to call Blake up for approval. I was still salty about Friday. Getting him to give me the thumbs up or down was the last thing I wanted.

"Why?" he asked.

"Why not?" I challenged.

My skin buzzed being so close to him after being in withdrawal all weekend. I really wasn't prepared to see him so soon after our run-in earlier and for him to seek me out himself... didn't that mean something?

Get over it.

"No one called me. So, I'm guessing you didn't tell anyone because you thought I'd say no or something."

Partially true.

Blake wasn't a warden. He wasn't the type to hold anyone hostage on account of some power trip or ego boost he got from lording over a bunch of adventuring adults. If anything, he probably would've sent someone with me to make sure I got to and from camp okay and didn't get lost on my journey coming back.

He was the caretaker type, after all.

So why didn't I involve him?

The reason was simply this: I wasn't ready to face him or hear his voice so soon after being rejected.

There, that was the full and god's honest truth.

The jailbreak had been my little form of rebellion. Even if it was stupid in the end and meant nothing.

"Maybe you would've." The words came spilling out of my mouth before I could stop them.

I didn't actually believe that. Not in the slightest. My pettiness wasn't letting me say the things I wanted to and was filling in the blanks for me with nonsense.

He only sighed in response.

My heart felt heavy when he pulled away, leaving me feeling ever more raw and exposed than on the docks.

What was wrong with me?

This man was trying to be nice and figure out what my problem was and here I came barreling in with insults and snippy words.

No wonder he was so quick to leave with his grandfather earlier.

Speaking of which. "Where's your pops?"

I lifted my head up from the table, cupping the back of my neck to keep the ice pack suctioned there while I turned toward him. He had one foot kicked up on the seat in front of him, the other dangling down by me. He wore a frown that twisted my inside up—an expression that looked way too foreign on his face for it to be a common thing.

I was used to Blake's cheerful expressions. Even his neutral faces had a lightness to them.

This one was downright upset.

"He got pulled away for a bit. I didn't have the heart to tell him no when he loves this place so much. I figured in the meantime, I could send over something to help with your head. Unfortunately, everyone else seemed to be tied up with something, so you got to deal with me delivering it."

'*Got to deal with*'. Like that was an actual bad thing when in reality it was the best case scenario. My hand itched to reach over and grab his thigh. Squeeze it until I had him squirming.

Then again, he'd probably shove me away at this point.

"I'm surprised he retired if he loved being here so much."

Blake shrugged. "He didn't want to. But he's getting older and isn't able to keep up with the demands of this place anymore. It was better to let it go when he still had some health left in him versus having to pry it out of his cold dead hands."

"Quite the imagery," I joked.

He shrugged again. "It's the truth."

Ugh.

What the fuck was I supposed to do with that?

We were literally two feet apart, physically. Emotionally, there might as well have been a giant chasm opened up, swallowing us both in the process.

I wanted the old Blake back. The one that poked and jabbed at me just as much as I did him. Messing around with him couldn't have messed things up *this* badly with him. I refused to accept that answer.

Not when it was so, *so* good.

His eyes darted away from mine, catching sight of one of the cooks leaving the back in order to start setting up the buffet for dinner. At that, he slid off of the table.

"Hope your head feels better."

Fuck, I couldn't handle this.

I grabbed his arm right before he could skirt past me and head out of the mess hall. He froze the second I touched him, his eyes going wide and then snapping over to meet mine. That frown was quickly replaced by surprise.

"Blake... listen."

He rubbed his free hand over his face, brushing at it roughly. "I gotta go, Marlow."

No.

How many cool-guy points would I lose if I refused to let go of him and instead forced him to sit back down and talk to me? 10? 20? 50?

Prying my fingers apart in order to let him go was a new type of agony I'd never experienced before. It felt like ripping my chest open and grabbing at my own beating heart to suffocate with my bare hands.

He stared at me for a long moment, his lips parting as if to say something but quickly clamping shut a second later. With one final headshake, he slipped away from me and headed out of the mess hall, leaving me to wallow once more.

THE THING ABOUT SELF-PITYING, at least for me, was that eventually, it turned into righteous anger.

All of this was unfamiliar territory. One I'd never waded through, let alone figured out how the fuck I was going to get out of this funk now that I was knee-deep in the shit storm of it all. With no one to blame by myself for fucking this up royally with my own emotions, I was beginning to see why Avery had been so fucking bent out of shape about Brandon.

Here were some simple truths I was starting to discover on this own journey of mine.

One: getting ditched was actually starting to grate on my nerves, to the point where I was close to throwing a tantrum the next time my time was cut short with the one person I'd been promised to be sharing it with.

Two: getting iced out by Blake was at the top of my list for *worst things ever* and was steadily getting worse the longer I sat here staring at this damn bonfire while pretending to give a shit about whatever the couple next to me was rambling on about in between sharing a single bottle of beer.

Three: no matter how many times I tried to talk about this to Silas, he wasn't going to get it. No amount of explaining, re-explaining and then explaining myself again was going to get through that thick skull of his. I was convinced he was incapable of feeling most human emotions outside of pure petty spite, but that was me. Avery was *pretty* sure he felt love and deep affection, at least for us, so we had that going for us.

But other than that?

He was like a damn robot with the wrong default settings installed.

Four: I was fucking over my own self.

How I'd gone from coming here with the sole purpose of bettering my health to combat the very real fear I'd drop dead just like my pops and somehow turned that into a *'why doesn't he like me?'* situation was never going to cease from blowing my mind. And pissing me off.

Mainly because I could no longer pretend I *didn't* care.

I did.

A whole lot.

"What do you think, Marlow?" the man next to me asked. Mark, I think his name was?

"About what?"

His wife laughed. "About what we were just discussing. I think the ropes course was way tricker than the rock wall. There was nothing to grab onto and it was all core strength. Which one did you do already?"

Yeah, fuck this.

Pushing myself up from my stump, I nodded to their bottle, waving my own completely full one in the air. "Another round?"

They both glanced at each other. "Oh, uh—"

Before they could tell me no, I stepped around them and headed for the small group of staff huddled at the edge of the fires. Their voices were quiet as they talked amongst themselves, a rumble of laughter rippling through them right as I approached.

"Hey..." I threw on my best endearing smile. "Was looking for the director's office. Would any of you be kind enough to point me in that direction?"

As my eyes adjusted from staring at the fire, I noticed Talos was among the group. I had a hard time seeing his expression from the flickering of the flames behind us making the shadows on all of their faces dance and move in weird patterns. All of them were quiet for a moment, defaulting to Blake's second almost instantly.

He was the first to speak. "What's the matter?"

"Have to return something."

"What's the item?"

This weirdly felt like I was talking to a self-service kiosk trying to return an online order.

I sunk my beer into the dirt next to my foot, unlooping one of the pockets of my cargo pants to fish out the ice pack that had long since melted and grown mildly toasty from the fire. I'd been holding onto it like some fucking up keepsake memento, if only to immortalize Blake caring for me for those ten minutes.

Holding it up to show him, I said, "He gave this to me earlier. Just wanted to give it back."

The second he reached out to take it from me, I snatched it back. His hand paused, mirroring the confusion of the rest of the group.

"I can give that back to him," he said.

I plastered on another smile. "Yeah, but then how am I going to use this to butter him up into getting the cooks to give me another cup of bread pudding?"

The rest of the group, besides Talos, laughed. In the dim lighting, I watched as his eyes narrowed slowly, his fingers twitching while he slowly lowered his arm back down to his side. The suspicion was evident but with nothing to pin it on, he had no reason to call me out for it.

Not at this stage, anyway.

I was good at playing the innocent and bumbling fool that everyone thought was only slightly smarter than a box of rocks. That was my home field advantage and one I used quite often when going into a rather tough meeting with a competitor.

The perks of having a loud and obnoxious personality is how easy it was to sell that image. How simple it was to get people lowering their guard around me in order to collect as much information as I could before flipping it around and using it for my clients.

It seemed as though Talos was slowly starting to peek through the mask I wore. His skepticism gave him a sort of buffer against my charms, causing him to go from curious to suspicious nearly instantly.

Good for him, honestly. Not being easily swindled was a skill not many possessed.

Not naturally, at least.

Among this group of people I'd already won over, he was in a losing battle. The majority were already on my side, seeing my offer as a harmless gesture to thank the camp's director with a bit of flare added to it for a little flavor. They weren't seeing what was underneath—my paralyzing need to see Blake again before tomorrow stole him away from me indefinitely.

One last time. That's all the hit I needed to hold me over.

Talos finally sighed. "The path leading from the mess hall, there's one around the back that goes to the offices. Head that way. He's up on the top level. You'll see the door. The light's probably still on."

I threw him a wink. "Thanks. I'll snag you an extra cup, too, for your troubles."

His expression flattened again. "I'll pass. Thanks, though."

At least Blake had someone solid like him by his side. A man able to see through the bullshit was a valuable asset to have. Especially as the second in charge.

Nodding to the rest of the group and bowing flamboyantly in order to draw one last laugh from them all, I quickly turned and jogged toward the mess hall, leaving my beer behind. I wasn't going to need it, anyway. I wanted to be stone cold sober when I talked to Blake.

A part of me wanted to apologize to him, though for what I wasn't exactly sure.

Pushing him past his limits? Getting too intimate too quickly by tucking him in bed with me? Not kicking him out the moment we both had our breathing back to normal?

Whatever it was, if it got me the old Blake back, I'd fucking do it.

Even if I didn't mean any of it.

Following Talos's directions, I jogged until a large house came into view. It was two stories with an outside staircase leading up to the second level. A lone lightbulb was lit up on the second floor, right above the door with a few bugs bouncing off of it. The night was quiet with no signs of life other than that.

I flexed my hand around the ice pack and sucked in a breath.

I took the stairs two at a time, getting up to the landing in record time. The window facing out toward the camp was covered by a thick curtain, leaving no light spilling through from the other side, and no way to tell if anyone was actually in there.

The *tapping* of the moths bouncing their small bodies against the light met with my heartbeat, a steady rhythm that felt loud enough to hear through the blood rushing in my ear. There was a strong possibility if Blake was in there, he wasn't alone.

Lifting my fist, I pounded it against the door a few times.

His grandfather had expressed wanting to stick around the camp for a while. Staying overnight wasn't a huge stretch.

The door swung open quickly, a gust of wind slapping me in the face from the force.

Brown eyes blinked at me once, twice, and then widened. "Marlow?"

I had every intention to shove the ice pack into his hands and rattle off some quick apology before turning around and heading back down the stairs and leaving him be for the rest of the night. I really did, I swear.

But the second I caught sight of that slightly bewildered expression, coupled with the soft curiosity lingering in that dark gaze of his, I found myself leaning forward until my shoulder hit the side of the door's molding.

The moths dancing above our heads, the irony of them constantly trying to fly into the orb of light with no second thoughts outside of their desire to get as close to it as humanly possible, wasn't lost on me in the slightest.

In fact, the parallels were almost staggering.

Me, a moth.

Blake, the damn flame.

I was powerless to stop myself from any of this. My body moving on its own accord with the desire of my heart at the helm of it all. This was beyond a simple passing sexual interest and was hitting into actual infatuation that I cared very little at the moment to stop.

Why bother?

Why hurt myself anymore than I'd already done so by pretending like I *didn't* care?

Clearly, being in denial wasn't working anymore and was most likely going to send me into an early grave if I continued to drink about it.

Blake's lips parted again.

"Tell me to leave," I said, cutting in before he could.

He blinked one more. "What?"

"You gotta tell me to leave." He was so close, I could reach out and cup his face if I wanted to. Pull him into so I could bury my nose in his hair and breathe whatever shampoo he used like a fucking dog.

"I—why?"

I stayed right where I was, pressing my full body weight into the doorframe and letting the slight pinch of the corner of it dig into me to break through the cloudy haze already trying to muddle up my thoughts.

Here was a moment in time that I had a crossroads right in front of me.

Turn and walk away and leave Blake be, or do what I really wanted to do and shove him back against the door so I could kiss him stupid.

Both options would change things.

Which consequence was I willing to face in the aftermath?

"Blake," my voice was already growing gravely. "If you let me cross over this doorway and into that office, I'm going to lock it behind me and lay you out on that desk you probably have piled high with papers right now."

His throat bobbed.

"And I'm not leaving until I make a mess of you." That was a fucking promise.

He let out a shaky exhale.

"Tell me to leave," I said once more.

His hand flexed around the edge of the door. I was frozen still, waiting for him to make his choice. Either way, I'd behave and do as he asked. If he told me to go, I'd respect it and hurry back to my cabin to lick my wounds. There would be no holding it over him. He'd made his choice and that was that.

If not...

If he let me in—

When he let go of it, he slowly stepped deeper into his office. My heart thudded hard in my chest, the silent invitation almost too hard to believe it was being offered. His tongue darted out to swipe at his lips, the front of his shorts steadily growing tighter the longer I stood here.

"Say it," I whispered.

He pulled in one single breath, and then said, "Come in, Marlow."

CHAPTER 17

BLAKE

MY BODY TINGLED. Every single nerve ending attuned to the man standing in front of me, leaning against my office door. His gaze roamed over me from head to toe, sending a flush of heat rushing through me.

In the back of my mind, hesitation on letting him in here, into what I largely considered the gateway into what the inside of my head looked like at all times, was almost loud enough to stop all of this altogether.

Letting someone into a space I spent the majority of time in felt so intimate. More than if

I'd simply invited him back to my cabin. Here, I had personal trinkets gifted from campers long since moved on, important documents related to the business, and photos of my family tacked to the walls to remind me that no matter how suffocating these four walls got, I had them waiting for me on the other side.

Oddly, Marlow wasn't focused on any of that. His eyes were pinned to me and only me, even as he slowly pushed himself away from the wall and stepped over the threshold.

I stayed rooted to my spot, letting this towering beast of a man fill up the small space with both his body and his presence. He shut the door behind him and then tossed something toward my desk, the sound of it hitting with a *thunk*ing sound that nearly drew my attention away for a split second.

He cupped his hands around my face almost at the same time, pulling me right back into the moment where all I could focus on was him.

He descended until his lips were pressed to mine, a feverish hunger taking over my body instantly the moment we were finally connected once again. A moan ripped from my throat as I clawed at his shirt, my desperation to force him to make good on his promise far outweighing whatever lingering embarrassment I had for the state of my tiny little office.

He lapped against my lips with his tongue, tilting his mouth until it was flush against mine. I let him in, let him taste every damn inch of me while my knees were beginning to go weak from how fucking turned on I was.

Trying to get this man out of my system was a fool's game, one that I was sorely losing and not at all caring about doing so. I'd tried to bargain with myself over the weekend about getting through this next week, promising to take those rare vacation days and get out of here to find something to entertain myself with that wasn't at all attached to Marlow Knight.

What was inherently stupid was how convinced I was that I could beat whatever sorcery he'd woven around us both to attach us so tightly together. Binding us and making it nearly impossible to walk away, even if it was the right thing to do.

Falling into this man's trap again was stupid on all levels. And yet, I didn't care at all.

I was happy. *Finally* happy after my miserable weekend of pretending like I was fine all along.

Marlow turned me and then pushed me back with his hips until my ass met the lip of my desk. One second he had his hands cupping my face, and the next, he was sliding them down my body to grab at my hips and pick me up.

I kept our mouths fused together as he set me down on top of the desk, bending me back until I was lying flat amongst the papers I'd been in the middle of working through when I'd gotten that knock on my door so late into the evening.

I instinctively parted my legs for him, welcoming his large body to fit right where I needed him to. A slow rock of his hips had me groaning again, the friction of my cock pinned against the inside of my shorts as painful as it was fucking mouthwatering.

Belatedly, I remembered the condoms I still had back at my cabin and kicked myself all over again for not storing them here instead. In hindsight, this was karma getting back at me for trying to gatekeep Marlow's sex life, because now it was affecting mine, too.

Marlow's lips popped off mine, the wet sucking sound making my dick twitch. He trailed his mouth along my cheek, working his way to my neck, while one of his hands wandered under my shirt to find my nipple.

"Oh *fuck*." The second he had it pinched between his two fingers, he pulled on it.

My body twisted under his, one leg coming up to hook around his hip and force him down to practically mold himself against me, giving me enough leverage to grind against the hard line in his pants.

The soft moan in my ear shot straight down to my dick.

"I want to fuck you so bad," he murmured.

I wanted it, too. I wanted to feel that hard rod in his pants jamming against my hole until he pushed his way inside and split me in two. I wanted it to hurt so fucking good until tears were streaming down my cheeks and I was begging him to keep going.

He could give it to me good. I knew he could.

"Condoms," I choked out, barely coherent anymore.

"I know." He pecked the spot right below my ear. "We'll improvise."

I was fine with whatever. Honestly, at this

stage, I was so raw with need that I'd probably let him fuck me raw. A decision I'd absolutely regret later once I sobered up and actually thought about how many fucking STDs we could unknowingly pass back and forth to each other because we were being fucking dumbasses.

But right now, my dick was calling the shots. It was screaming at me to fuck around and find out. I was tired of being responsible and always having to think ten steps ahead. I didn't want to have to plan for shit. I wanted to live in the moment, *be* in the thick of it with no worries about the consequences later on down the line.

I'd lived my entire life afraid of the future and what butterfly effect I'd unknowingly cause to fuck myself over, eventually. I was a chronic planner and an even more chronic worrier. I had plans for plans and plans for those plans, too.

Nothing would ever get past me. Not so long as I had a strict idea of what needed to get done.

But here, in this moment, I wasn't afraid to let go, to give up my rambling thoughts and let myself sink into oblivion. Marlow could take that for me—take it *from* me and allow me to just... *be*.

He swiped his tongue over my skin, leaving a

cool trail of spit behind before straightening up and towering over me once again. His breathing was a little labored, his tanned skin flushed slightly pink. He was honest to god the sexiest man I'd ever seen, let alone allowed myself to let touch me.

He worked the belt around my waist off, tugging it through the loops and then tossing it onto the desk next to me. I shivered at the implication of him leaving it there and not simply tossing it onto the floor like he was getting ready to do with my shorts.

I'd only been tied up a few times and each experience was... lackluster, to say the least.

In concept, being at the complete mercy of the other party was enticing as fuck, yet in practice, gave little room for error when choosing said partner. Namely, those who got lost in the heat of things and started trying to default on their responsibilities, aka pleasuring and seeking pleasure themselves, back onto the other party who had little to no mobility to do *anything* other than lay there.

So... those had been short-lived stints.

Marlow wasn't easily flustered—case and point, diving into the rapids to rescue an older woman and barely batting an eye before, during, and afterward.

He took things in stride, dealt with the punches and kept on rolling.

That was the kind of dominant you wanted controlling the bedroom activities. Not one who thought they knew what they were doing and then got too overwhelmed when they realized they were in over their head with a partner who wasn't just going to lay there and take whatever was given to them.

I'd admit to being hard to please, at times, but I also wasn't asking for a left kidney in return.

Commit to what you promised or get out.

Simple as that.

"Blake."

My eyes shot up to meet his.

"Stop thinking."

Ugh, fuck. Caught in high-def.

The amused smirk that played across his lips suddenly untangled the knot that had formed in my belly from over-thinking yet again. I let myself ease back into the moment, unhooking my leg from his hip so he could fully tug off my shorts and underwear and toss them onto the floor away from us.

He splayed his hands over my hips, framing my aching dick between them. "I'll never get tired of looking at you."

My back arched instinctively at the compliment. Now look who was preening at the praise and attention.

"I could say the same for you."

He chuckled. "Look, I won't lie, we look good together."

We really fucking did.

He grabbed the belt, sending my heart racing instantly. He grabbed one of my wrists and brought it up to pin above my head, shoving a stack of docs out of the way with his elbow while he asked, "You ever do something like this before?"

"Uh, once or twice."

Amusement danced in his eyes. "Blake, you keep surprising me here."

"Let's just say I've had a healthy sex life."

"And still single?" he muttered.

What did that *mean?*

Before I could ask, he pinched the belt

between his teeth and then grabbed my other wrist, drawing it up to meet its match, and then shifted hands to hold them both together in his one. Taking the belt from his mouth, he brought it up to tie around my wrists and part of my arms, tugging it tight enough to keep me from wiggling free but not enough to cut off circulation.

Clearly practiced in this area.

A stab of jealousy rocketed through me.

"You know what I've been thinking about?" he asked.

"Tell me," I said to distract myself from obsessing over the imaginary list of people he probably had on his roster who were most likely dying for him to get home.

"I want to mark you."

My mouth fell open. "W-What?"

"See, a funny thing I've noticed about you is that you get this look in your eye sometimes." As he spoke, he moved his hands down from my chest, slowly working his way back down to my pelvis. "It's this weird flash of anger that I couldn't really figure out what I was saying to cause it."

I could barely focus on the words coming out of his mouth over how he was pushing up the hem of my shirt until my entire torso was exposed.

"But then it happened again when we were back at my cabin and just now, too. And each time it was after I mentioned something about my sex life." He pinched both of my nipples between his fingers.

I groaned immediately.

"Tell me, Blake, are you normally this jealous?"

I wanted to smack my head against the fucking desk.

How?

How?

"No," I moaned miserably.

Fuck, how did he know—how did he *figure that out?*

Fucking financial analysts. Fucking business tycoons who were all about reading the room and picking out the weakest link. I hated how hot it was, how turned on I got from him reading me like a damn book.

No one could. *No one did.*

No one but Marlow fucking Knight.

He laughed, delighted. "Just for me, huh. I'm honored."

"Oh, fuck off—" A gasp ripping from my throat cut me off as he dealt a slap to the side of my hip. "*Ohhhh.*"

"I really need to figure out what to do with that mouth of yours."

"Fill it," I begged.

Another sharp slap, this one coupled with a gruff. "Oh, I plan to."

CHAPTER 18

M ARLOW

S TREWN out on his desk like this, his legs kicked up and hiked partially back to give me a perfect shot of what I had to work with between his legs —his cock already glistening at the tip, balls drawn up tight to his shaft, and a pucker that clenched each time I pinched his nipples between my fingers—I was having trouble not ripping my own cargos down and gripping both of us in my hand while I rutted against him.

His fingers twitched above his head while he watched me, phantom movements left over from the desire to reach out to touch and being restrained from doing so in the process. His chest quivered like a baby bird's, pulling in short shocks of oxygen while I continued to play with what I was quickly realizing was his very sensitive body.

Every ghost of my fingers over his skin, or subtle caress along his inner thighs to circle back up to where his cock was resting against his belly, was making him squirm and twist on the desk, writhing with the need for me to *keep going*.

How long had it been since someone had him like this?

Laid out like a fucking all-you-can-eat buffet just ready to be swallowed up whole?

Funny, he was the one that was getting jealous when it should've been me after he'd whipped out that little nugget of knowledge earlier.

I'd admit, he surprised me with the getting tied-up bit. Clearly, I'd been underestimating my dear director and had pegged him as more of a square than he actually was. That was my bad. I'd misjudged him in a way I hated others doing to me. I'd taken a few characteristics he'd shown me on that first day we met and let my imagination fill in the rest of the blanks before stamping it as 'FINAL'.

Types like him, the kind who were wound a little tighter than normal, were the best to unravel. They always turned out fucking beautiful by the time you were done having your way with them and that satisfaction in getting them there was half the fucking fun of it.

I was curious to see how much of a freak he really was hiding under all those layers of professionalism he liked to dress himself up in.

What kind of nasty shit got him coming all over himself while gasping for more?

Clearly, the corporal punishment was doing wonders so far.

Having Blake spread out like this, with his stacks of important documents piled high next to his twitching body, just ready to be ruined by him getting off, got my own dick twitching in my pants.

The dichotomy between what we were doing right now and what he'd been up to less than ten minutes ago—being an actual responsible adult running a million dollar business—was staggering. The kind of irony that struck you days later after a full decompression.

While I wasn't exactly going to apologize for having a hand in Blake slacking off on his duties, I'd take full responsibility for giving him a much-needed break he clearly needed.

I could sit back and look at him all day. Watch that flush slowly crawling across his chest, pinkening his skin, and see what other parts of him it'd soon manifest on.

He was such a fucking vision.

My hands itched to grab and squeeze every part of him. Leave my fingerprints bruised into his skin so that each time he stretched or reached for something, he felt the apparition of my hands still on him.

I worked my bottom lip between my teeth until it felt raw, using it to control the energy burning through my veins before I got carried away. I wanted this to be a nice and slow kind of ride, not like the ones where it was a thirty second ultra high and over and gone too soon.

Who knew what fresh bullshit tomorrow would bring and what regrets would come with it. Right at this moment, in the here and now, I wanted Blake to focus on what was right in front of him. To stop thinking so damn loudly that it drowned out everything else, including my hands on him.

Every shift of his eyes darting away from me, every downturn of those pouty lips the second I didn't have him fully engaged, gave me a snapshot into what the chaos going on inside his head at all times was like. The noise that was never going to let up if he didn't allow me to get in there and turn the fucking sound system off.

He needed someone to force him into letting it all go, to table the responsibilities and the pressure for the time being, and let himself simply exist in the moment.

The world would keep on spinning regardless of how many papers he pushed, so why not make the most of it and enjoy the time outside of the mess for a while?

Another moan slipped out of Blake's mouth, his lashes fluttering over his dark eyes, the second I trailed the back of my finger up the length of him. He was a nice size, perfect for gripping in my hand while I railed him. Too bad we were going to have to pivot in a different direction from that tonight.

I'd been looking forward to feeling his tight heat wrapped around me, seeing how firmly he squeezed me right before he came. It would happen one way or another before these next five weeks were up and I was being shipped off on a bus back to Ellington Heights.

Before coming here, Silas had taunted me about not bringing my own stash, ragging on me for thinking I was above my own hormones. It wasn't like spending six weeks out in the woods was going to be a deterrent for my very enthusiastic libido, according to him.

At the time, I'd waved it off and told him to mind his own business.

What did he care if I got laid on my self-imposed sabbatical?

Now I was severely regretting my choices.

Like usual, Silas was right and I was the bastard too stubborn to admit it.

"Fuck. You—" Blake's chest heaved. "You're such a tease."

A few beads of precum slowly drooled onto his stomach, a trail of pearly wetness creating a nice sheen against his flushed skin. I drew a shape around it, following the smattering of freckles he had peppering the spot.

Not just the bridge of his nose, then. Wonder where else you've got these.

"Where should I leave it, Blake?"

By now, it was quite obvious how much he liked all of this. I was a fool to think my first impression of him when I had him back in my cabin was all wrong. I'd gaslit myself into thinking I crossed the line when, in reality, I was only just scratching the surface of what he truly wanted.

How he liked to be treated in bed.

"I'm thinking it'll go right here." I gave him no warning before I moved down to his inner thigh and gathered the soft skin between my fingers and squeezed it tight into a pinch.

He nearly leapt off the desk with a choked gasp, his back arching far enough to contort him into an entirely different position. The stack of papers closest to him tipped to the side danger- ously, swaying with the movement just enough to push it right over the edge. The pile exploded into a heap of a mess, individual pages launched across the small space between the desk and wall.

Oops.

Turning my attention back, I held his skin between my fingers until it turned a flaming red, mimicking exactly what I was going to do with that spot with my mouth in a second.

Blake rocked himself forward in response, his cock desperate for attention I wasn't giving him just yet. Soon, though, we'd get there.

Letting him go, I split his thighs apart further, practically pressing them both down flush against the desk. His pink hole was taunting me, daring me to swipe a finger over it to test how tight he was. "Maybe I should leave a mark right where everyone can see it."

"You'd like that, wouldn't you?" His thighs were trembling in my hands while he goaded me. "You'd love it if someone pointed it out and asked me about it and I had to make up some excuse to throw them off the trail."

Yeah, I fucking would.

That shit would have me preening like a damn cockatoo. Loudly and obnoxiously.

Normally, I wasn't the type to care for marking up my bedmates. It wasn't that I found the practice distasteful, I simply didn't care enough to show the world who the person warming my bed was.

They weren't mine to keep, so why go through the hassle of pretending like they were?

This thing with Blake was different, though. The little flashes of anger, the barely hidden envy for something he didn't have, *that* was what got me. I *liked* seeing it. I liked seeing him getting all riled up when no one was holding a candle to him to begin with.

It meant he felt something outside of a temporary curiosity I once believed he had. I wasn't naive or delusional enough to think there would be something more to this by the end of these five weeks, or that we were preordained for something more. Nonetheless, wherever this was going, I'd had my boarding pass already stamped for the destination ready to go.

"You know me so well." Stepping back from where I was pressed against the desk, giving myself enough room to lower my mouth down to ghost against his thigh. His balls clenched when I blew on them. "Maybe a little *too* well."

I supposed that should've been a scary thought—for someone I just met to already start seeing the deeper parts of me and connecting the dots it took most people years to do. Blake was always some kind of special case, though. A paradox I needed to stop trying to question.

I suctioned my mouth around the spot I'd pinched, sinking my teeth down into the soft, meaty flesh. The musk of him was intoxicating, the slightly salty taste of his skin mouthwatering. I ran my tongue over it, tracing the edges of my teeth where they would soon be leaving a lasting impression.

I caught his thigh in my hand before he could clap it against the side of my head and pin me against him. I sucked on his skin, rolling the spot between my teeth a few times until I got it nice and tender, enough for it to bruise, at least, and stay that way for a few days.

Every time he bent over or squatted, every time he pulled on a pair of pants or shorts that brushed over the spot, every time he climbed up a set of stairs or walked from his office to the mess hall, I wanted it to be tender enough to remind him of me with every step, every movement.

Call it an ego thing or the sliver of narcissism I was bound to have in me from my chosen career path.

Pulling back to survey my work, his thigh was a sharp shade of red, the outer edges of it turning slightly purple. "Perfect."

He swallowed audibly, his face flushed. "Marlow..."

Such a pathetic way to say my name.

I loved it.

Letting him go just for a second, I stripped my shirt off and made quick work of my pants next. My dick bobbed the moment it was free, the head of it red and angry looking from how rough I had it grinding against the inside of my cargos.

Taking it in my fist, I stroked along the shaft a few times, giving myself a little bit of relief in the meantime. It wasn't much, not in the way I wanted, but it would do for now.

Blake's eyes were locked onto my hand, his lips wet from where he'd just swiped his tongue over them. A part of me was desperate to get that mouth around me again, to feel his throat tighten until I spilled down his throat and fed him the dinner he most likely skipped in order to hole himself up here longer.

Another time.

I'd figure out a way to steal him away from his youth groups this week. I had to. Going an entire week without him wasn't going to fly. Not this time. Not now when I finally had confirmation we were in the same damn boat of instability when it came to the energy radiating between us.

This street wasn't as one-sided as I thought it was and I'd be damned to let it return that way.

"Say that again." My cock brushed up against his thigh when I moved closer to him again, smearing the leftover saliva still coating his mark on my tip. "I want you to keep saying it."

"*Marlow.*"

Oh, he was indulging me tonight.

What a good and obedient thing he was.

In return, I gave him a nice hard slap on the underside of his thigh, earning a wail in response. "Marlow!"

Fuck, that was turning me on so bad.

Who knew my own name out of those plush lips would rev me up like that?

Actually, Blake could probably recite the fucking alphabet and it would get me going. He was lucky at this point, I wasn't giving into my baser instincts to jack off over him and use my cum as a mark instead.

I lowered my mouth again down onto his other thigh, mirroring the mark on the other side and giving him a matching one there. His squirming made the process sloppy, his thigh slick from my mouth when I finally pulled away to judge my work. His skin shined slightly in the lighting, a thin sheen causing his skin to glisten.

An idea sparking, I drew his legs together. "Like I said, we're going to improvise."

He let out a harsh breath. "Ohhh... Marlow..."

Wrapping an arm around his shins, I kept them pressed against my shoulder, one hand trapping his ankles together to keep him from moving around too much. Using my other, I let a trail of spit fall from my lips and hit my dick, using it to cover my shaft. Inching closer to him once again, I dragged my tip along the seam of Blake's thighs, rearing back my hips to thrust against that line.

This would have to do for now. As much as I wanted to sink into that tight heat of his that was teasing me so badly right now, we'd have to save it for another time.

Pressing against the seam of his thighs once more, I reared back again and shoved my way through the tight folds. Blake's gasp was all I needed to hear to send my balls tightening up and a few beads of precum to leak out of me, coating his inner thighs and wetting them more.

"Next time," I said. He was slick enough now

that I could glide in between his thighs easily. Those thick, ropey muscles were a nice pressure against me as I fucked them, enough where I could envision I was someplace else instead. "Next time we see each other, I'm going to have a whole box of condoms waiting. I'll get someone to do a drugstore run for me. I'm not letting you leave until we use at least a sleeve."

I was so tired of us dancing around this fucking subject. It was actually torturing me at this point.

Maybe using an entire sleeve was a bit of wishful thinking on my part, but at the rate we were going at and what I still needed to explore of him, we'd be lucky if we only needed *one* box.

Turning my head to brush my lips against his ankle, I grazed my teeth along the bone, following it until it gave way to muscle. I bit down until I felt his foot spasm in my grasp.

"Have some," he choked out.

My hips stuttered and then clapped against the backs of his thighs hard.

What the hell did he say?

He already had some?

What the fuck, I thought he was single?

My teeth let go of him. "What does that mean?"

Blake's head was resting back against the desk, his eyes closed and a blissed out expression relaxing his features. His fingers were still flexing in their makeshift restraint, though he was being good and keeping them above his head where they belonged. His stomach clenched with each thrust of my dick between his thighs, his skin growing slick with sweat.

He was so fucking perfect it was painful.

"Blake," I prompted again.

Actually, if it turned out he'd been propositioned by someone, I was going to have a fucking meltdown. Or worse? If he'd told them yes and then simply hadn't gotten around to bringing them over yet.

I wasn't going to compete. I'd lay that other fucker out on the ground before they ever touched Blake.

"You," he said cryptically.

I brushed my other hand down the side of his leg, following the curve of his hip, and then swatted him back into reality. "Me what?"

He groaned in response. "*You* wanted them."

Now, I was really confused. Since when the hell did I—

"Are you talking about when I asked you to go find me condoms to sleep with that swinger couple?"

He let out a disgusted noise.

Oh.

Oh, man.

Did he keep them from me on purpose?

"Blake. Did you lie to me? When did you find them?"

"Stop," he whined.

Oh, he so did.

What a shit.

I threw my head back to laugh, rearing my hips back just enough before slamming them forward into him and burying my cock between his thighs. This is exactly how I'd fuck the jealousy out of him. I'd stretch that hole of his until he knew exactly who the hell I was taking to my bed.

The clapping sound our bodies sent a shiver racing up my spine.

"You are the most jealous man I've ever met. What, you thought not giving them to me would stop me?"

He turned his head to try and bury his face into the crook of his arm. The odd angle from how his upper limbs were tied together wasn't giving him a very successful hiding spot, leaving the right half of his face completely exposed.

From this angle, I could see most of his expression—a pulled back pucker of his lips that told me he was indeed not having fun talking about this subject.

I swatted the curve of his ass again. "Answer me."

"Fuck off," he muttered.

"Where are they?"

There was another pause. I swiped my hand against his hip, giving it a hard love tap. "My cabin," he said, instantly.

Good. Excellent. No bribing his staff necessary. "How many?"

"Ugh."

"Blake." I nipped at his ankle again. "How many?"

"*Enough.*"

"A whole box, one might say?" I ventured.

He simply grunted in response.

Oh, this was even better.

That sold it. I was absolutely stealing him

away this week from his teenage ducklings. I wasn't taking any excuses from him and allowing him to try and play the good director by avoiding me in order to pretend he was still keeping up the professional boundaries. There was no point in denying the chemistry we had. Not when we were dying to follow it through all the way.

Why torture ourselves when we'd eventually stumble our way into bed anyway?

Turning back to his legs, I sunk my teeth down deep into his skin, clenching my jaw until I was locked into him, holding him in place in order to really drill between his thighs. I needed to cover him in a grotesque way. To the point where there were *no* questions on who I was entertaining and who was simply a fleeting flirtation.

"Oh, fuck!" His back arched again, nearly lifting his entire upper body off of the desk. "Marlow... please!"

He asks so nicely.

My legs burned from the endurance, pounding myself between his thighs while they clenched around me with each thrust. Fuck, if he felt this good from the outside, imagine how incredible he was going to be once I finally had him sitting on my dick.

The image of him bouncing in my lap, driving me deeper into that pulsating hole while he leaned against me and was sweating from the exertion, his eyes glassy with how turned on he was. Fuck, it immediately sent me right over the edge.

My balls gave a firm squeeze, staining his skin with my cum and smearing it front to back with each residual pump of my hips to draw out my orgasm. It was too good. Too fucking good for this to be another one-time thing.

I let out a long groan.

Fuck.

Releasing his ankles carefully, I lowered his legs back down onto the desk, draping them over the side of it while he went limp. The slick remnants of my cum coated his thighs and parts of his stomach where it'd shot out as I was still fucking him. Seeing him like this, covered in me, was an even better gift to leave him with than the hickeys I'd sucked into his skin.

His breath was coming out of him in harsh pants, his cock still swollen and resting against his belly. Cupping my hand and dragging it along his thigh, I covered my palm and fingers with my own cum, bringing it up to wrap around his cock and move my hand in long, languid swipes.

With barely five passes of my palm over his tip, Blake jerked in my hold, his hips spasming as his own orgasm rolled through him and he spilled all over the both of us. My hand dripped from our spend, tempting me to pop each and every one of my fingers into my mouth to taste.

Blake let out a shuddering exhale, slowly blinking his eyes open as his body grew limp once more. "Wow."

My mouth twisted up into a smirk.

I trailed my dirty hand up from his belly, to his chest, tracing winding patterns until I reached his neck. The second I had my hand wrapped around his throat, his eyes rolled into the back of his head, a shudder rippling through him.

"Blake."

He let out a soft grunt in response.

"You're coming back to my cabin tonight."

If he wanted to accuse me of kidnapping him, then so be it. I wasn't going to take no for an answer this time around.

Aftercare wasn't simply about cleaning up

the mess you made of each other afterward. It was so much more than that, and I'd be damned if I let Blake go back to his place, alone, in order to potentially avoid any wandering eyes and risk facing a comedown from something like this by himself.

There was a reason scenes ended with a specific ritual afterward.

I waited until he slowly blinked his eyes open again, repeating what I said to him until recognition bloomed in his gaze.

Finally, he nodded. "Okay."

My entire body relaxed instantly.

Good.

BLAKE

Cocooned inside of an inferno was the best way I could describe what waking up next to Marlow was like.

For all the times I'd brushed up against him in passing or by accident, and the very few times he'd actually put his hands on me for longer than a moment, he'd emitted a warmth that seemed to chase away whatever chill seemed to settle in my bones where I never thought there was any to begin with.

I'd grown up under a hot sun for most of my life. Spent every summer since I was seven at

Austin Adventures baking each year in the intense UV rays until I'd eventually formed a permanent tan to keep my poor skin from burning away layers of itself like I did every year before that.

I could never get enough, no matter how much I tried to pretend being in my office all day wasn't giving me massive FOMO toward everyone getting outside and enjoying the nice weather.

That was how I grew up, after all, on the lake while the summer skies above me were crystal clear and the sun was a blazing orb in the sky. That was probably how I was going to die, too, honestly, dry-roasting on the damn dock like a fucking lizard.

Sleeping next to Marlow was unreal. He was as hot as a space heater pressed right up against your body, branding you through your clothes with the cage design and leaving the nice lasting memory of a third degree burn in its wake that always seemed to twinge every time a cold front was coming in.

And yet, I didn't want to move away from him at all. I was too cozy lying next to this volcano-turned-man while waiting for my skin to melt off. It was a pleasant kind of slow death in a macabre sort of way.

Wiggling closer to the source got me pressed right up against his back, bare and uncovered, unlike me who had the sheet still wrapped tightly around my entire body to keep whatever lingering heat I stole from him all to myself.

I wasn't even that cold, honestly.

His breathing was slow and steady, a calming rhythm that was already lulling me back down into a dreamless sleep. Coming back from my office last night was hazy, partially because I was so fucking high on my own hormones, I barely remembered stumbling through the dark after Marlow as he led us through the backend way to get to his cabin. After a shower and a change of clothes he'd thrown my way, he'd pulled me into bed without even entertaining the idea of me taking the guest room. Preemptively, not taking my 'no' for an answer.

At the time, I hadn't had the energy to fight him. Still didn't, really. So, I'd given in and let him tuck me in, wish me sweet dreams, and then, before I could wait for him to climb into bed on his own side, I was out like a damn light.

Yesterday was intense. Not for the actual sex

things we'd done—I'd had far more crazy encounters than that in my life—but for the simple fact of how *locked in* we both were to each other during the entire thing. Every move he made, every touch he placed on my body that had me quivering like a newborn calf, I was hooked up to a damn amp to receive it.

Everything felt like it was in high-def.

That was something I'd never experienced before, even after having my fair share of sexual encounters already under my belt.

How could I go back to things after this? After Marlow was long gone and back in his own hometown while I stayed here in Wakefield, trying to figure out how the fuck I was going to find a man *half* as tuned in to my needs as this man next to me was.

The worst part about all of this, though, by far, was that I should've left a long time ago. Before the sun came up to peek in through Marlow's bedroom blinds. Now, I was going to have to figure out a way to leave his cabin without anyone spotting me, along with my walk of shame back to my own place to grab an actual change of clothes.

Fuck, and the youth groups are coming today.

I had until noon to set everything up, double check my plans, cross reference my staff's jobs to make sure everyone knew what the fuck they were doing before we had dozens of teenagers piling off buses, and run through the roster *one* more time to solidify enough food was going to be coming over to the event's pavilions.

Judging by the way the sun was coming in through the window, only partially blocked out by the curtains drawn over the glass panes, it was close to eight.

Ugh, I really didn't want to get out of bed.

I was too comfortable.

By now, there was a healthy chance my granddad was already up and running through my list of to-dos before I even made my way down to the mess hall to grab a cup of coffee. He was known to be an early riser with no signs of retirement slowing him down in the slightest, which tended to give him a leg up on all of us mid-morning people.

Before we'd parted ways last night, he had already been planning on acting as my second-hand during the first set of events today, along with offering to help for the rest of the week if I needed him to. The gesture was sweet and, of course, one I wanted to take him up on, but only in order to spend time together and not force him back into the chaotic role he'd given up five years earlier.

Retirement was his chance to go out and travel like he and my grandma always talked about before she passed. Not get stuck half-running a business he'd handed over to me and trusted me to manage all on my own.

I was confident this youth group was going to go well. It had to, considering how much time and energy I'd put into perfecting it. I wasn't looking for everything to go off without a hitch, much the opposite, in fact. There would be hiccups along the way, but that was to be expected. Rolling with the punches and figuring it out as the days progressed was what mattered in the end.

So then, why the hell was I still feeling so damn nervous?

The bed dipped forward as Marlow shifted in his sleep, my body almost rolling with him as he moved. Sticking out a hand to keep myself from face planting into the mattress, I used it to lean and roll onto my side of the bed. For a moment, Marlow's overwhelming warmth wasn't engulfing me and for the first time since waking up this morning, a gut punch hit me.

But as soon as it'd come, it was quickly chased away by a figure looming over me, half covered in the bed's comforter, messy hair poking out from where it was gently resting on the crown of his head. There was no time for me to react before he was leaning back down, his arms digging under me and circling my waist while his upper half laid down on top of me.

I struggled under the added weight, suddenly flustered at the unexpected intimate position.

"Uh..." was all I managed to get out before Marlow was burrowing his face into the crook of my neck.

"I can *hear* you thinking..." His lips tickled my neck as he spoke, sending a shiver rolling down my spine.

My face felt like it was on fire. He had to still be half asleep. "*How?*"

"Because your thoughts are loud as fuck. I can literally hear the stress sirens going off."

Okay, that was uncalled for.

I was only stressed because my body refused to roll out of bed and kick itself into high gear. While running on a finite amount of time before all hell broke loose, there was very little dilly-dallying I was allotted before I royally fucked myself over.

Not to mention, my granddad feeling oblig-ated to pick up the slack. Which was absolutely something I *didn't* want him doing.

"*Blake.*" There was a sharp pinch at my side, snapping me out of my thoughts instantly.

"What?"

"Jesus." He nipped at my skin next. "Stop it. It's not even ten yet."

"That's the problem. The kids arrive at noon."

"Plenty of time."

That's what he thought. Time tended to fly by on busy days. Even more so when there was an actual set schedule set in place.

My stomach clenched the moment I felt Marlow's lips moving along my neck. Soft presses that were making my toes curl with each one. One of his hands unhooked from around my waist to come up and thread through my hair.

He gripped the strands gently, using them to tilt my head back to give him better access.

Oh...

My hips were still sore from last night, a lasting reminder of what we'd done in my office and the mess I had to go back and clean once I finally forced myself out of this damn bed. Yet, despite all of that, they still managed to kick up against his body in return, coming alive under his touch like some fucking soothsayer calling to me.

I'd never been used in quite the way Marlow's creatively had allowed for. Often when I found myself in sexual situations similar to what happened last night, they either ended one of two ways: unsatisfied or downright *weird*. Neither of which were pleasant and ultimately had me swearing off hopping into bed with someone for a long while.

Until Marlow came around and completely bulldozed his way through all of those carefully laid plans.

At this point, I really shouldn't be surprised anymore. After all, he was a man that was all about the unexpected.

Who could predict someone like him when before that, there were set rules to everything?

"Fuck," I muttered when he sank his teeth into my skin.

Making good on his promise from last night, no doubt. I'd definitely have to wear one of my sports jackets today to keep my granddad from questioning the random love bite suddenly appearing on my skin with no boyfriend in the picture. I was going to end up sweating my balls off but that was the far better alternative than getting interrogated about a secret situationship I was currently engaging in.

Marlow shifted over me, keeping his mouth attached to my neck. He hooked a leg over mine to grind his pelvis against me, the thin material of his sweats doing hardly anything to hide how hard his cock was underneath them.

Oh, that felt good.

Getting off two days in a row?

I wasn't going to complain.

When he finally released my neck, he ran his tongue over the marking a few times. The spot felt raw and tender, mirroring the ones on my thighs that sparked every time his hips collided with mine in that slow roll of his.

Now this was perfect, a little bit of pain mixed with the pleasure.

Why was that so hard for people to grasp?

Too many times I'd been in an all-or-nothing situation that never left me coming back wanting more.

"I should keep you here," he whispered. "Tie you to my bed until you actually let go like I want you to."

What was a clear sign that something was definitely wrong with me was how little I cared about anything else other than those words—the *promise* in his voice. Skipping out on the first day of an event I'd been planning for months would go down in the history of dumbest decisions I'd ever made.

And yet...

"Hm?" He nuzzled his nose against my ear. "What do you say?"

Oh, god. He was making me choose.

What the hell.

"Marlow..."

He dove back for my neck, swiping his tongue along the love bite again and then latching on once more right below it. I squirmed under him, feeling completely powerless under his heavy weight pinning me to the bed.

He bucked against me, his hard length

teasing mine through my boxers. With each pass of his hips, I tried to follow after, to get a little bit more of that delicious friction to bring me to the promised oasis of pleasure I'd been transported to the night before.

I wanted more.

I *needed* more.

This was what domination was all about. A give and take that was controlled by one party with mutual trust exchanged between both with the understanding that at the end of the day, we both got what we wanted.

My eyes popped open—when had I closed them?—the second Marlow's mouth popped off my neck and he pushed back from me. Dazed from the sudden shift and still trying to chase my high, I wasn't at all expecting it when he scooped me up and dumped me onto my stomach.

His hand splayed between my shoulder blades to fist my t-shirt in a tight hold, keeping me down while kicking my legs apart and getting me to spread them until my hips screamed in pain.

"How about this," he said, lowering himself down until his cock rested against the curve of my ass. "Tonight, after your event is over, you come back here with that box of condoms you hid from me."

I shivered. "It'll be late."

He chuckled, his mouth finding my ear again. "Don't worry, Blake. I'll be waiting up."

CHAPTER 20

M ARLOW

H EADING DOWN for roll call with a pep in my step and feeling like a million fucking bucks with my plans for after the bonfires solidified and squared away, I was ready to blast through the day's activities and get to the part I was really looking forward to: Blake coming over tonight.

I still couldn't believe he actually found a box of condoms and hid them from me, all in an attempt to prevent me from getting laid.

Honestly, what a brat.

I knew I sniffed out envy when he'd caught me with Aimee and Luke. My only problem was not realizing how deep it went, how long he'd been secretly holding onto his possession of me and practically barking at whoever came wandering by wanting to take a gander at what I had to offer.

Blake was the most interesting man I'd ever met.

For someone so hell-bent on keeping me at arm's length, he'd taken some painstaking measures to keep me from growing attached or interested in anyone else here. It was like he was fulfilling a self-imposed prophecy at this point, one I was all too happy to keep feeding into.

Why stop when we were both getting what we desperately wanted?

I was looking forward to finally putting his box of condoms to good use tonight.

He lied right to my face about them, too. No wonder he'd looked so guilty.

The memory had me laughing.

"You're in a good mood today."

Whipping around, I spotted Talos hanging out by the marquee signs, his arms crossed over his chest while his eyes were covered up by dark sunglasses. I fitted him with my best smile and wandered over to where he was standing.

If he'd swung by to check on Blake after I'd headed over to drop off the ice pack, we were totally busted. I doubted that office had sound-proof walls, let alone something that would buffer any kind of noise coming from inside. My dear Director definitely wasn't the quiet type, so I could only imagine what the hell anyone heard while wandering by last night.

Hopefully, they figured it was someone's nearby TV on full blast. Or a young couple getting it on in the woods close to where the offi-cers were and weren't so discreet as to run off to their cabin before getting frisky.

There were plenty of excuses I could come up with to deflect the heat off of Blake and save his poor reputation among his coworkers. The only real problem, it seemed, was Talos being completely immune to bullshit.

It was hard to tell from the way he was staring at me behind those dark sunglasses what exactly he knew. In retrospect, he could've not made the journey up to Blake's office at all and stayed down with the rest of the guides super-vising the fires and called it a night once the last person packed up and headed in for the evening. Or, he could've come around long after we'd picked up and hurried back to my cabin to hunker down, giving him no reason to suspect either Blake or I had had more than a passing conversation exchanged along with the ice pack.

Either way, both situations kept us in the clear.

While the first option was most likely the real timeline of events, that meant Talos no doubt noticed I never returned last night after dropping off the ice pack. On the one hand, he could've chalked it up as me retiring early for the evening. Or two... well.

That stamped a big old GUILTY mark across my forehead.

"What's on the agenda for today, teach?"

All he gave me was a single quirked eyebrow before unfolding the clipboard from under his arm and flipping a few pages. "You're signed up for the overnight hike."

"Pardon?"

He flipped one more page. "You signed up for it Friday. We're taking you all up to Craigleith's peak and camping up there. It's about a day's walk there and a day's walk back. We'll be gone from base camp for about three days."

Trying to keep my jaw from dropping at the

news was a Herculean effort. Especially, when it occurred to me how Friday I'd been a complete yes-man to whatever the fuck the guides were throwing at me in order to get them to let me duck out early to start my weekend with Avery and Silas.

Fuck me.

"Anyway, I can postpone that to next week?"

Talos slowly lifted his head up from the clipboard. "Afraid not."

"What about yanking my participation altogether?"

He stared at me for a long moment. "Seeing as how we all spent the entire weekend painstakingly assigning your entire group to specific sets of hiking partners and matching the athleticism as closely as we could with each of you so neither of you in your group will fall behind, I'm going to have to say no."

Holy shit, this had to be a joke.

Right?

Was this Talos's way of fucking with me because he was suspicious I had the hots for his boss and was trying whatever tactics he could to steer me away from him?

There was no way I was being forced on this

fucking camping trip, especially when all of the other activities were a completely voluntary venture.

"So, what happens if I say I wasn't prepared to go on a journey like that today?" If this man could, for once, give in to my charm, that would be great.

He sighed—oh boy—and then tucked the clipboard underneath his arm again. "Look, I can't force you to do anything you don't want to do. You're an adult and are capable of making your own decisions. I'm not here to parent you. But what I will say, is that if you pull out, you're fucking over your hiking partner. Like I said, we spent all weekend making these teams and if one party backs out, we don't have a backup that can just slip in seamlessly to take their place. That's why on Friday we had you sign all that paperwork to *double check* that you were good with making a commitment like this."

He was laying on the guilt real thick. I had to admit, it was totally working. If not for the fact that he was making me sound and *feel* like a total asshole for signing a bunch of waivers and forms without paying an ounce of attention, it was definitely him piling on that I'd be disappointing my hiking partner, too, who was probably incredibly excited about going on this trip.

I was probably the only dumbass that signed themselves up for an intense excursion like this without reading the fine print. Friday was such a blur with how strung out my emotions were from Blake leaving, I hardly remembered anything before I climbed into Avery's car and jetted off to the closest dive bar.

Shit, how the hell was I going to let Blake know?

My stomach knotted at the thought of him waiting outside of my cabin, knocking in that quietly polite way of his, wondering why the hell I wasn't opening up the goddamn door and sweeping him off his feet.

The last thing I wanted was for him to think I ditched him when that couldn't be further from the truth. He was likely to jump to conclusions, figuring I went off and got distracted with my swinger friends and ended up at their cabin instead.

That would then start our whole vicious cycle from last week over again where we had to gain each other's trust back when we just fucking got it.

I blew out a long breath.

Three days.

Out in the woods, hiking up a mountain to reach the peak.

Three days without coming back to base camp and seeing Blake.

Three fucking days before I was going to be able to touch him again.

Fuck my life.

"So, who's this mysterious partner of mine..."

If he picked up on the defeat in my tone, he completely ignored it. "Her name is Elaine. She's got a lot of energy, like you, so you two should get along fine."

"Wonderful. Sounds like a total blast."

Talos wasn't at all amused by my plummeting mood.

If my hangover on Monday wasn't my karma for being a total idiot last week, this certainly took the cake. By a large margin.

"When do we set off?" I asked.

If it wasn't for another hour or two, that still gave me time to pack and leave a note for Blake up in his office. I doubted he was going to head up there at any point today while his youth group was here, but outside of tapping a note to my own door—which I was absolutely going to be doing—there wasn't much else I could do without being completely obvious.

Asking Talos for directions to Blake's cabin was definitely going to blow my cover. And if it wasn't from him, any other guide I asked would be giving me the side-eye. No matter how peaceful and innocent I could make my intentions seem, no one in their right mind was going to give a guest the directions to the Director's cabin.

That was asking for a lawsuit.

"You've got two hours. I suggest you head back to your cabin and pack what was on the list. You'll need it all."

"So... about that list."

He actually rolled his eyes before slipping a piece of paper off of the clipboard and handing it over to me. "Marlow, I'm going to say this once. Please, be on your best behavior."

Yeah, okay, whatever. Easy to ask that of me when I was internally debating running into the nearest wall to see if I could pop my shoulder out of its socket before we set off for our *three day* journey.

"You got it," I said, throwing him a thumbs up.

His face remained unamused. "I'll see you in two hours."

I plastered a grin on my face before turning around and heading off back to my cabin. What a fucking wet blanket thrown onto my good mood. I was really confident nothing was going to ruin it today, and just had to go and tempt fate like that with my overconfidence.

I hoped Blake wasn't going to be mad. If there was a way I could write him an extensive note apologizing and sticking it to my door without the worry of other people coming around to read it before he got a hold of it, I absolutely would.

All I could do now was pen out a quick note that was vague enough for anyone not to read too much into it if it got into the wrong hands, but had enough small details scattered throughout that Blake would pick up on what the hell I was talking about.

Hopefully, this was a way for me to mitigate whatever fallout was threatening to fall over us again.

The last thing I wanted was to be at odds

with him again when I quite literally just got him back.

Rubbing my face, I let out another sigh.

What a damn mess.

"HEY! It's so nice to meet you!" A woman, tall with a runner's body, stuck out her hand toward me. "I'm Elaine, by the way."

She had her long, blonde hair tied back in a ponytail that swayed as she spoke. Her eyes were a bright hazel that lingered on my bare shoulders before quickly popping back up to meet mine again. She had a sliver of metal across the top set of her teeth, prominently on display as she grinned.

I grabbed her hand, giving it a two-shake. "Marlow. Nice to meet you. Hope I can keep up. It's my first time."

She waved a hand at me. "Oh, no worries! We can go at any pace. I'm really good with anything. I brought a bunch of trail snacks, too, if you get hungry. Oh, and extra water. Were you able to fill yours up at the mess hall before you left? They have giant canteens they're handing out to anyone going on the trip today. I can hold your stuff here if you want to go grab one. Or maybe we can ask one of the staff to bring you one? I don't think they'd mind. I mean, everyone has to stay hydrated, right?"

I blinked twice.

Wow. All right. Talos wasn't exaggerating at all.

Jesus, was that how I sounded to everyone I opened my big yap to?

Poor Blake.

"Lucky for both of us, I've got an in with guest services." I swung my bag off of my shoulder and let it drop down onto the ground. When I squatted, I pulled the zipper apart and brought out *two* canteens. "Pretty cool, right?"

Her mouth dropped. "Oh, that's *excellent.* We definitely won't be going thirsty today! That's going to be great because there are peanuts in the trail mix and they're the salty kind which definitely make you real thirsty after a while. So many people don't realize that when they bring trail mix as a snack and then they go through half a bottle of water, and it's like... where did it all go!"

Talos was a sick bastard.

There was no doubt in my mind assigning me Elaine was giving me a taste of my own medicine. Trying to dress it up with 'taking painstaking measures to pair up matching athletics' my ass.

"How we doing over here?" Turning to look over my shoulder, the devil himself was wandering over at a leisure pace, clipboard in hand and a pen at the ready.

"Oh, we're great!" Elaine replied. "I don't know about Marlow's stamina but I can definitely match paces. I hate when groups get too staggered because what if someone twists an ankle? Or what if there is a mountain lion waiting for a straggler to get too far from their group? You know there is plenty of wildlife out here that are opportunistic predators. I have a whole guide book that shows each one and their hunting habits."

Talos swung his attention down to where I was still squatting, a slow smirk curling at his lips.

This was definitely karma.

"You know what, Elaine?" After shoving the canteens back into my bag and zipping it up, I rose up to my feet again. "I'd *love* to see that guide book. In fact, we should totally dog-ear the ones that are known to be in this area so we can warn the rest of the group. There's no reason only *we* should be privy to such important info like that."

Her eyes immediately widened. "Oh... you're so right." She quickly turned to Talos. "Do I have time to quickly run up to my cabin? I swear it'll only be, like, a second."

Right as his mouth started to form around the word 'no', I butted in. "I mean, it would make us all feel safer. The key to a healthy mindset is through learning. Plus, what an entertaining book to go through while we hike?"

"Oh, yeah, it's a real good one. And! There is a whole chapter dedicated to wild flora you can eat!" Elaine said.

I shot Talos a grin. "A *whole* chapter."

A laugh bubbled up in my chest that I had to bite back when his jaw ticked, clearly resisting the urge to tell me to go fuck myself. "As long as you're back here in five minutes."

"Done!" she said, and quickly spun around to sprint back to her cabin.

The second she was out of earshot, Talos flashed me a look over the rim of his sunglasses.

"Remember what I told you less than two hours ago?"

"Was it the 'behave' thing? Sorry, my memory's a little fuzzy. Lots of packing, you know? That list was extensive."

He muttered something under his breath and then said, "I'm going to be keeping a close eye on you. Don't do anything ridiculous. Please."

"Wouldn't dream of it."

As he walked away to bother the next pair on his list, my shoulders relaxed. Going toe-to-toe with Talos, while fun in the moment, wasn't exactly the kind of attention I wanted on me at the moment. I was going to be focused on keeping my thoughts *away* from my obsessive worrying and that was going to take a lot of dedication. Enough where it would definitely rouse suspicion if someone who knew me a little better than the average stranger would pick up on.

Getting cornered by him to ask me what my problem was wouldn't be good. I needed to *not* spiral during the next three days, and if Talos was too busy riding my back about my weird attitude problem, I would be in trouble.

Blowing out a breath, I slipped my hand

around the strap of my bag and lifted it onto my shoulder again.

Three days. That's all I had to get through.

And then I'd get back to Blake again.

All I had to do was pray he found my note and didn't hate me after he read it.

CHAPTER 21

MARLOW

SETTING off for the summit of Craigleith's peak, I had my fair share of back-and-forth conversations with Elaine while we hiked.

Despite my initial impression of her—and the very obvious mirror that had been kindly shoved into my face—we'd grown to have quite the repertoire between us. She was a nice woman, and while talkative, incredibly knowledgeable in survival.

Having been to *Austin Adventures* twice before this, she'd come well-versed, pointing out spots to avoid along the trail while we walked, giving me tips on how to ascend up the steeper inclines when we finally reached them, and keeping up the reminders to stay well hydrated.

She kept my brain focused on the here and now, refusing to let me get too deep into my thoughts before she was pulling me out with another fun fact or regaling me with her stories about the two other times she'd been here, which was a crazy feat if you asked me.

Austin Adventures was a welcoming place but definitely wasn't for the faint of heart. The waivers that were signed before any sort of payment was taken were the real deal and definitely a component the older couple I'd helped rescue that day on the river failed to consider.

So, to me that meant Elaine was nothing short of a badass.

Plus she shared her snacks with me.

What better partner could I have asked for?

Talos's sabotage had turned into a blessing in disguise. One I was sorry to have judged at first glance but now was entirely onboard with making up, even if Elaine was none the wiser to my inner turmoil.

Making it to the top of the summit, right at sunset, was fucking spectacular.

Reds and oranges collided with the darkening blue of the sky. Peaks of pink were fading in between the stark colors of the dying light, golden rays touching the treetops of the evergreens that littered the side of the mountain and the valley below it.

A breathtaking view and nothing like we had back in Ellington Heights.

I got why Blake stayed up here. Why he refused to go anywhere past Wakefield. Growing up with this kind of scenery, like it was something out of a painting masterfully done by the most skilled of hands, was enough to almost convince me to call up my job and quit right here on the spot.

"Here..." I felt a nudge against my ribs, forcing me to rip my eyes away from the incredible sight as a disposable camera was offered my way by Elaine. "I know they're old school but the pictures that come off of these things are *unreal.*"

"You're the fucking best," I said, carefully taking it from her.

She laughed and quickly moved along the

other side of me to another vantage point, bringing her disposable up to snap a few shots before moving down farther. Other hikers were around us, some sitting, some taking pictures, too, with their digitals or phones, and others were helping Talos and Ivan, another one of our guides, set up our camp for the night.

Following in Elaine's footsteps, the sound of the shutter in the disposable going off sprang up memories from my childhood, back when we were still living on supplemental income and trying to make it by before my dad hit big.

Times like this, I missed my old man. He would've loved to come out here and experience something like this. His heart failing him for too soon was still a sore spot to me. Being thirty-four and well into my adult years was sometimes a hard thing to cope with during those times I just wanted my dad by my side like I was still a kid.

I used to take my time with him for granted and now that I no longer had it, it ate me up inside.

Blake was lucky to have a man like his grandfather still around. I envied him a little bit for it.

I wasn't sure what his family situation was and didn't care to speculate outside of general curiosity with why *he* was given the director spot and his parent wasn't. He'd certainly earned the damn title, but it was still an interesting topic to wonder about.

Maybe I'd ask him once I saw him again. I'd love to get to know him more outside of how he liked to be touched. He was such an interesting man that I was sure extended far beyond what I knew of him already.

A throat clearing right behind me had me swinging around. Talos stood close to me, his sunglasses pushed up into his hairline while he hit me with a sour frown. Right as I was about to ask him what his deal was, he lifted something in his hand.

"For you."

My eyes shot down to the radio he was offering me, confusing me immediately. "Uh..."

"Take it past the tree line. I don't want anyone else coming over to ask me if they can use it."

What the hell?

Slowly slipping it from his grasp, I glanced down at the screen, realizing it was turned to channel six.

My eyes widened.

Quickly brushing past him, I headed for a dense part of the tree line that descended down toward the main trail we used to get up here. It was a little steep, causing my hiking boots to catch on some of the pebbles crumbling away from the face of the rockhead. I caught myself on a nearby tree, stopping right before face planting into the dirt.

Nearly out of breath, I pressed the walkie's button. "Hello?"

"Marlow?" Came Blake's familiar voice.

I swallowed thickly. "Hey. Did you get my note?"

"Yes. Sorry. I got distracted and completely forgot to check the schedule or else I would've reminded you."

The tension in my chest melted away entirely, leaving me feeling like my entire body was turning to Jello. I leaned back against the tree just in time for my legs to give out and slowly sink myself down against the foot of it. The bark bit through my t-shirt, scraping me to hell. Barely any pain was coming through the sheer relief flooding through my system.

He wasn't mad... apologizing to me for my own fuck up, even.

He was too good for me.

"No, I'm sorry. I was the dumbass who signed up for it without realizing what I was doing."

There was a pause on the other end. "Wait, really?" His laugh was cut off too prematurely, quickly followed by, "How in the world did you manage that?"

Rolling the radio's antenna along the bridge of my nose, tracing it up to where my temples were, I contemplated telling the truth. While we were on a private line, it wasn't at all secure or secret.

If Talos was smart, like he'd proven to be in the past, he would've taken Ivan's radio from him and hopped right on this channel to monitor why the fuck the director of the entire property was personally calling up to talk to me.

If *I* were in his shoes, I'd do the same.

It wasn't being nosey, it was being concerned. None of which I blamed Blake's second for. He was a good man with a healthy amount of worry for his boss. Obviously, if I was taking up enough of Blake's time, to the point where I was getting personal calls from him, that was something to feel uneasy over.

Pressing the radio's button, I said, "Well, Friday was kind of... a tough day for me."

There was another long pause of silence on the other end. "I'm sorry."

Smiling, I pressed the button again. "No worries. Just means you owe me three bread pudding cups."

He laughed again into the receiver. "Is that your tax?"

"Yup." Among other things, but I wasn't about to get into that over a semi-private radio channel. "Anyway, how did the first day go?"

"Amazing. The kids did great. You should've seen them."

"Wish I could've. Maybe next time."

"They'll still be here by the time you get back."

Was that an invite?

I flexed my hand around the walkie. Blake wasn't granting anyone permission over to that side of the property. For good reason, of course.

And yet... was that strict rule being lifted for me?

Because he wanted to spend more time with me?

During all of this back-and-forth with him, I

was trying not to get my hopes up about anything. Mainly because mitigating the distress of leaving him and this place behind was already going to be hard enough. Adding more fondness to tether me here was turning this into a recipe for self-flagellation.

"I was actually toying with the idea of coming up there tomorrow."

I reeled back my hand to stare down at the radio. There was no way I heard that right. "Seriously?"

"Yeah. My granddad offered to run the show tomorrow so I can actually get a full night's sleep. He's been picking on the circles under my eyes all day. But... I was thinking about doing something else instead."

I grinned. "Sleep's for losers anyway."

He laughed again. "I take it you won't mind if I crash your party."

"You're going to *love* Elaine."

"Oh. Elaine Matthers? Did Talos set you up with her?"

"Oh yeah, we're getting along like a fire in summer."

"Why am I not surprised..."

How hard would it be to sneak off with Blake once he got up here?

I could probably catch him before he made his grand appearance, sneak off while Talos had his back turned and his attention somewhere else in order to meet Blake somewhere down on the trail.

I'd probably be in deep shit once it was realized I was missing, but honestly, how much did I care when it got me to have a little bit of alone time with Blake for a bit?

All I wanted to do was grab him and kiss him. That soft, sappy shit you saw in romcoms when the two leads finally came together again after being forced to spend an extended amount of time apart. We'd barely been separated for eighteen hours and I already practically wanted to crawl out of my own skin with need.

"Come up here," I said into the radio.

"Okay. I'll start out as soon as the sun comes up. You guys will be there all day so I should see you just after lunch."

"Sounds perfect. I'll save you some trail mix." God, I couldn't wait.

"Want anything from base camp?"

Just you, I almost said before stopping myself.

"Nah. Just promise not to twist your ankle before you get up here."

"You got it. I'll see you soon."

Springing up from my spot on the ground, I pinched the dial to flip it back to the main channel before heading up to the summit again. There were people scattered everywhere, most tents already pitched and a few with their own makeshift hangouts facing out toward the view.

Talos was off to the side with Ivan, a healthy bonfire having been stoked in my absence, that was far enough away from everyone's sleeping quarters, but close enough that the roasted smell of meat was wafting over the entire site.

His eyes immediately narrowed on me once I headed for him.

I waved the radio in my hand. "Here you go."

He took it from me, glancing down at the changed station before saying, "All good?"

I grinned, not being able to help it from splitting my face in half. "Yup."

He stared at me for another long moment, Ivan behind him propping up another log inside of the fire. "You sure?"

It was so obvious he wanted to ask me what the hell that was all about, why his boss was calling to talk to me privately, and why I'd come back with a skip in my step. All very valid curiosities that I wasn't going to give a damn about entertaining.

I threw out a thumbs up instead. "Yup. You want help? I hear I've got a mean way to charcoal."

"We're good, thanks. Might want to go check up on your hiking buddy."

"Okay," I sang, backing away slowly. "If you change your mind, you know where to find me."

Elaine was sitting on an elevated rock that was tall enough to let her long legs swing in the wind, a peaceful smile on her face while she watched the fading like disappear beyond the horizon.

"Hey, you."

Her head snapped to me. "Hey! Did you get some good photos?"

"Oh yeah. I can't wait to get these bad boys developed." Pulling out the disposable from my pocket, I sat down next to her rock and leaned back, getting her in the shot before snapping a picture. "Gotta get some keepsakes for my scrapbook."

"Oh, yeah! That's so right." She grabbed hers from her lap, turning it to me. "Say cheese!"

I threw up a peace sign, grinning wide enough to make my cheeks hurt. "Cheese!"

Her flash went off, and then she lowered it. "Excellent. Say, Marlow, we should totally exchange numbers when we get back to base camp. In case you want a copy of any of my photos for your scrapbook."

"I'll do you one better." Shoving my hand into my pocket, I fished out my phone and turned it on. "Give me your number and I'll text you. That way in case I die on the way back, you'll have a space to send things to me in the afterlife."

Her brow shot up. "Do ghosts have access to their texts in the afterlife?"

"Guess we'll find out."

I HARDLY SLEPT AT ALL, too excited for lunchtime to roll around and for Blake to join us up on the summit.

There wasn't exactly much I wanted to show him up here that he hadn't already seen a million times. Nevertheless, that wasn't going to stop me from putting on my best tour guide persona and doing it anyway.

Thinking about being able to bask in his attention was substituting what little energy I'd gotten from my restless sleep. We weren't going to be doing much hiking today outside of traveling down to some of the lower shelves on the mountain face for better vantage points, so I wasn't in danger of my low energy levels affecting me too badly.

Plus, bothering Talos about the time every nine minutes was the only other thing keeping me going at the moment. "Hey, what's the time again?"

His shoulders rolled back slowly, a gesture I was becoming intimately familiar with as his way of trying to mitigate whatever agitation was currently trying to make its way to the surface over his very carefully crafted facade of indifference.

Funny how it was so easy to rile him. "Like I said the *last* time you asked, it's not even eleven yet."

"Right, right. But how close *are* we to eleven? Actually, how close are we to say... one o'clock?"

He slowly looked up from his notebook full of detailed records he'd been keeping the entire way up here. Line by line in very fine and straight-aligned print were notes about all of us and how we were doing—most likely to report back to Blake once we got back.

I had half a mind to tell him not to bother since the man of the hour would be here—hopefully—soon. Then again, I was trying not to assume Talos had overheard our conversation on the radio and was choosing to believe he was just as ignorant as the rest of our little party.

"At least three hours."

I fought myself with deflating over the information.

Damn it, still so far away.

And that was with the caveat that Blake was traveling as fast as he thought he could. *Or* that he was even making his way up here at all.

The chances of him having been caught up with someone down at base camp were staggering—too much for me to really make any sort of bets either way. I had hope he would've radioed up to me to let me know by now if that were the case, however, it wasn't like he owed me an explanation in general.

He wasn't my boyfriend. He didn't have to answer to me.

I chewed my bottom lip.

"Is there some reason you keep asking me about the time and why noon is so important to you?" he asked.

"Nah, just wondering. Heard one o'clock is the best time to get a good tan up here."

He fitted me with a look of disbelief. "Right. Well, we'll be heading down to the second point in five minutes. Make sure whatever you're bringing with you is packed."

Fuck, how was Blake supposed to know where we went when he got here and no one was around?

"How long are we going to be down there? Are there going to be people staying up here?"

He popped a brow. "Why?"

I gestured to our tents. "Hello, what if someone comes up to steal all our shit?"

"You think someone would spend six hours hiking up here on the off chance a big group has their stuff up here?"

"*Yes*, Talos. Did you not hear Elaine's lecture about the dangers of *bears*?"

He sighed. "Ivan is staying up here. He also has bear spray *and* a horn."

I made a show of wiping my brow, relief flooding through me again. "Phew! *That's* a relief."

Talos waved a hand at me. "Go pack your things. Make sure it's light. The trek down there is a little precarious."

"Roger that." Maybe it was a good thing to not be here when Blake arrived.

As much as I wanted to be the first to greet him, allowing him to get his story straight in the presence of only a few people versus all of us, plus Talos, was the better idea. He was already going to be put on the spot by his second, regardless, and at least if he was up here for a bit to help Ivan with camp, it would seem more like *lending his hand* and not something else, which Talos was no doubt doing to be suspecting the moment they came face-to-face.

I'd sneak him away once nightfall hit. No one would be looking for us then.

Elaine was already packing a small bag when I made my way over to her. She had a blanket spread out under her, cushioning her slightly from the rough terrain of the mountain's face. There was a canteen by one of her knees, along with a half eaten bag of trail mix.

"Hey!" She waved. "Got all your stuff ready?"

"Yup. Still feeling good about our trip?"

"Oh, I'm over the moon. The last time we went down there, we got to see an eagle's nest. Now, you may be thinking, Elaine, I thought eagles usually nest near a water source because they're fishermen. And to that I would say, I know! I did, too! But I guess there is a small river that runs close to here that connects to the falls on the other side of the mountain that they use! How cool is that?"

Damn, actually that was pretty cool. "You'll have to point it out to me once we're down there. I have a friend that'll go bananas if I send him a photo of an actual eagle."

"Definitely. I promise I will. I'm going to be bringing my binoculars, so we can totally use them to scope out some of the trees where I last remember the nest being."

"Perfect."

"All right, everyone!" Talos's voice rang out

across the area. "Everyone heading down to the second vantage point, head this way. All those who are staying, check in with Ivan, please!"

"That's us," I said, offering a hand for her to take.

She slipped hers in mind, folding herself up from the blanket. "Thanks. Oh, I'm so excited!"

Her attitude was definitely infectious. Letting myself be pulled into it was enough to satiate the worry crawling up my throat at missing Blake. Maybe this hike would help me burn off some of this excess energy. Coming in hot the second I met him wasn't exactly sexy.

After a headcount, Talos waved for all of us to follow, giving clear and concise instructions as we descended down to the narrow stonemade footpath along the side of the mountain face. Only wide enough to travel down one-by-one, I held tight to the thin railing jutting out from the mountain's side while we went, keeping my attention locked onto the man in front of me while following him.

More than once, I felt Elaine grip the back of my shirt to slow me down, patting me lightly when I obeyed and kept at least two steps between me and the man in front of me. The problem with being tall I typically ran into more often than not, was overtaking people by accident. Long strides tended to outdo even the most athletic ones more times than not.

When we finally reached the second vantage point, a rock shelf that was far smaller than the one up top and about a mile down from it, we collected together against the mountain's face, keeping away from the edge until all of us were finally down the steps.

Our group was only about twelve people, which gave us all enough room to move around freely on the shelf.

The air felt a little denser down here, strangely enough. I pulled in a deep lungful, the scent of pines and dirt filling my nose. That rough kind of outdoorsy smell not many people tended to appreciate but was my absolutely favorite.

"Wow," Elaine breathed out, her arm brushing against mine. She had her binoculars looped around her neck and was slowly bringing them up to her eyes. "Oh yeah, I definitely see an eagle's nest."

She inched her way over to the side of the

dropoff, carefully keeping her steps small. While I wasn't at all worried she was going get distracted with her binoculars and plunge over the edge from a bad foot placement, I still kept close to her while she moved, on the off chance something happened.

Like parts of the rock shelf crumbling or—

Something moving out of the corner of my eye caught my attention. Glancing over to my left, I spotted more movement, going completely still the moment I realized it was a fucking *snake* slowly climbing up the rock wall.

"Hey, uh, Elaine," I muttered. "Remember what you were saying about those snakes that were super snake-looking with the reddish brown pattern that you said were up here?"

"Oh, yeah. Copperheads."

Here was a little known fact about me: snakes terrified me.

It was a stupid fear left over from childhood after a bad run in with a garden snake my grandma kept fed in her herb bushes that one day crawled up my leg and into the cuff of my shorts and left quite a nasty bite behind before I could scream loud enough for my dad to come rip it off of me.

Since then, I'd steered *very* clear away from the things.

"Yeah, so. What happens if they start crawling toward you?" I asked, noticing the own rising octave to my voice.

Unfortunately, Elaine was far too busy with finding us the eagle nest to pick up on my impending terror. "Staying still is what I'd suggest. Not many copperheads up this way, though. The most we'd run into up here are Western Terrestrial Garter snakes."

Okay, whatever the fuck *that* was. The longer the name, the more venomous in my opinion.

Who named a snake with more than two words?

"Elaine..."

She gasped. "There it is! And I think they have babies in the nest!"

"Yeah, okay, great. Maybe we should move, though."

Holy fuck, it was coming closer.

The snake's head reared toward me as I shifted my weight, its tongue darting out. It was long and fat, clearly well fed up here on whatever it was hunting. It's beady eyes focused on me, tongue darting out one more time before it slithered forward and *right to us.*

"Oh, fuck!" I shoved her back toward the rest of the group.

She stumbled and caught her footing on a small divot under her foot, her heel stopping her from moving back any farther while her body shot back. Recorrecting myself in order to keep her from falling right back onto her head and cracking it open on the rock, I snagged her arm and quickly tugged her forward, righting her suddenly.

"What the—"

"Snake," I hissed, pointing.

"Marlow." She laughed. "It's okay, it's just a garter—"

She didn't get to finish her sentence as the world around me suddenly began to shift, falling away and growing smaller while my body pitched backward. Belatedly, I realized I'd stepped far too close to the edge of the rock shelf when I'd righted her posture, the pieces under my feet crumbling and giving way before either Elaine or I could quickly move away from it.

Time slowed.

Her eyes widened as she registered what was

happening, her hand snapping out far too late to try and catch me back, my body just out of reach.

In the back of my mind, I knew I was already dead. This was simply the build up to that untimely demise I was always staring down the barrel at but had no way of predicting when and where the final nail in my coffin would finally rest.

What a terrible fucking way to go.

"*Marlow*!" I heard Elaine scream.

That was the last thing I heard right before I plunged and hit the ground below.

CHAPTER 22

MARLOW

VOICES FADED in and out along with my consciousness—hard to understand through the sharp pounding in my ears, making everything seem like I was underwater.

Light danced on the inside of my eyelids, strange shapes twisting into odd figures that almost looked inhumane the more I tried to focus on them. I parted my lashes just long enough for the shapes of the trees to come into view overhead, a cool breeze rustling the leaves to allow for sunlight to peek through in speckled moments.

And then once more, it all faded away. Gone again to return me to that inky blackness.

There wasn't much in my life I regretted up to this point.

Having always lived under the belief of going out in a blaze of glory being the better choice compared to wasting away behind the safety net of sense and stability, I had very little in the ways of true remorse for what I'd accomplished these past thirty-five years.

Choosing to embrace every thrill that came my way and push the limits on what life had to offer no matter the cost, I chased the rush and the risks and hardly ever looked back on the consequences that followed close on my coattails.

It was the illusions of a life well-lived that I'd once believed were proof I'd somehow beaten the odds, unlike my dad whose carefully cautious lifestyle had put him into an early grave.

A real carpe diem that had soon fallen short the moment the rocks beneath my feet had crumbled away and I'd plunged to my demise.

At least there was no pain now or a slow, agonizing pull into death to endure.

I supposed that should've made me happy. To have died in a quick accident rather than a long, drawn out one. A snap of a finger and the blink of an eye, my life snuffed out far too soon, just like my father's was.

Poetic. Ironic. And a little bit macabre.

Was that the way the Knight men were meant to leave this world?

Here one minute and gone the next?

Did my mom ever suspect I'd follow in her husband's footsteps so soon after?

God, my poor mom...

She was going to lose it when Silas called her to tell her the news. Both of her family members dead within two years of each other.

How was she going to cope?

She was a mess at my dad's funeral. Soaked from the rain drenching the funeral procession while she cried against his coffin before I finally had to peel her off of it so the groundskeepers could lower it into the ground.

Burying me was going to kill her. She wasn't supposed to outlive us both.

I never even told her I'd come up to Wakefield to spend the summer at a wilderness adventure camp, figuring what was the point in worrying her when I'd be back soon enough and with plenty of stories to entertain her over dinner.

Regret seized me hard.

To think the last time I'd stepped outside my house and into that cool, morning air had been just that. Getting drunk at the dive bar with Avery and Silas while they listened patiently to my romantic woes was the last time I'd ever see them. Talking on the radio to Blake to convince him to come up to Craigleith's peak, only to find me already long gone.

What would he think?

What news had accosted him the moment he'd finally made that final ascension up to where our campsite was?

Sheer panic?

Confused worry?

Neither he, nor his staff, were at fault for my stupid moment of panic that ultimately ended with me going over the edge of that rock shelf. There was nothing anyone could've done differently. Not Elaine, or Talos, or any of the other fifteen who were there simply trying to enjoy the view.

I hoped my death wasn't the end for his business. Having something like that on their record, even if it was a simple and tragic accident, wouldn't matter to the masses of people who would see it reported in the newspaper and demand for the place to be shut down for negligence.

All because of a fucking snake.

Something brushed against my cheek causing my skin to tingle.

"I'm so sorry," someone whispered from somewhere.

Yeah, me too.

I hoped Blake didn't hate me. I hoped my mother could forgive me.

"They just called. Helicopter is being dispatched in five," someone else said, farther away.

Another gentle stroke along my cheek. The voice was closest to me. "How long until they get here?"

Wait, helicopter?

"Hard to say. I've got a flare I'm going to shoot off when they get close enough so they can find us down here. I've got their dispatch on standby."

"Thank you."

Wasn't I dead?

Why the hell were they calling a helicopter if all they needed to do was belay my dead body up the ravine or wherever the fuck I ended up?

Sure, it was going to cause a little bit of an emotional scar to those there witnessing everything, but that was far better than wasting resources trying to do things 'respectfully'.

Who cared about that when I was gone?

"Ivan's going to start taking everyone back down. Lydia finally made it up."

"Good." A soft sigh. "Good."

Why did all of this feel so very real and not some far off dream?

My heart thudded hard in my chest.

This was no out of body experience. I was trapped somewhere, not floating above it all like a ghost drifting in the wind attached to the place its corpse passed at. Like the kind of spirits mediums saw on the side of the highway after a major car accident.

My consciousness was grounded with no sense of anything other than this black void surrounding me.

How was that possible?

If I was still alive, wouldn't I be in pain?

No way I landed all right and ended up with only a slight concussion.

Or—

Holy fuck, was I paralyzed?

My eyes shot open immediately, my sense of being having slammed back into my body with a kickstart that had my body twitching against the cold, solid ground. It was dark all around where I was, faint outlines of the trees and other brush I'd landed in hard to make out, even with whatever lantern lights were set up and trying to illuminate this little piece of land.

Pain ricocheted inside of my body the moment I became aware of this not being some kind of fucked up ferry to the afterlife, so intense it stole the air from my lungs. Minutes before this, I'd been in some kind of void inside of my own mind, free from whatever mortal shackles bound me to my own flesh and bone that I'd somehow shattered the moment I'd forced my eyes open.

A groan rumbled past my lips.

Holy fucking shit—

Now, I felt it all. Every single scrape, bruise, break, and slice inflicted onto my body as I'd dropped and rolled against the sharp rocks below the base of the rock shelf. Whatever I'd landed on and eventually slammed up against to prevent my body from rolling all the way down to the base of the valley had cracked me apart in several things, making it nearly impossible to pull in a full lungful worth of air without causing my eyes to water.

"Marlow?" The voice near me sounded choked up with emotion, hard to make out through how clogged my ears still felt as blood rushed through my skull.

I groaned again.

"Oh my god." A shadow passed over me, blocking out the light from the lantern closest to me. "Tell me where it hurts."

Fucking everywhere.

Was it normal to feel like your body was simultaneously on fire and frozen to the core?

Or was that just a special gift given to me?

"Hey, hey." A hand stroked my cheek. "You're okay. We've got search and rescue on the way to airlift you. They should be here soon. Try not to move your head too much. We need to keep your neck stabilized."

I swallowed thickly.

Was my neck broken?

Wasn't that code for, *don't move or else you'll paralyze yourself more?*

"Are my toes wiggling?" I asked.

There was a pause. "What?"

"Are. My toes. Wiggling."

The shadow disappeared from view, the light from behind him blinding me suddenly and forcing me to squeeze my eyes shut to save my poor retinas from the assault. A hand ghosted over my ankle on the left side, tapping down to the bridge of my shoeless foot. I forced my toes to strain for it, meeting the curved palm as pain shot up my leg in an excruciating way.

Wow, *fuck* that was rough.

But I could feel it. That meant my brain was still firing off those goddamn neurons up and down my spinal cord.

"Yes?" he said. "But don't move your leg too much, okay? It... we have it in a splint—"

I let out a massive sigh of relief and then laughed, a nearly hysterical sounding one.

I lived.

I fucking fell down the side of a goddamn cliff and *lived.*

Oh, Silas was going to owe me more than an IOU. He was going to give me that pretty little savings account he had stashed with enough money to buy a small country and he was going to let me play around with it while I threw most of it at the stock market.

"Marlow?"

The only thing that would make any of this better was if Blake was here.

My heart ached. I missed him so goddamn much. The pain was making me delirious, tricking me into believing if I reached out, I'd be able to touch him. Wherever he was, I hoped it was far away from here. This wasn't exactly the alluring image I wanted him to have stuck in his brain after I'd promised an unforgettable night nearly forty-eight hours prior.

"Hey. Can you do something for me?" I asked.

The shadow came back into view. "Anything."

"Can you tell Blake I'm sorry. He's the director of the place. Tall, tan, light brownish hair that looks kinda dark blonde in the sunlight. Cute little freckles under his eyes. Brown eyes that turn golden during a sunset. You know who I'm talking about?"

There was another long, drawn out pause. "Why in the world would *you* be sorry?"

I let out a long, mourn-filled sigh. "I think my friends are going to sue this place. I swear I'm going to try and talk them out of it, you can tell him that, but one is a billionaire with too much time and money on his hands and the other is a hardass who believes in 'an eye for an eye'."

Was I making any sense?

It was hard to tell with how weird my vision was swimming and the warped shapes that moved while I tried to focus on the dark blob of a man leaning over me.

How long had we been down here for?

It was almost around noon when I fell and now it was pitch dark out.

How many days were long gone?

There were no sounds of a helicopter approaching, blades beating against the silence of the night. Outside of the man next to me and his soft breathing, I couldn't pick up on anything else.

Normally, that would be the promise of a peaceful night if not for the absolutely heinous amount of pain I was in.

I was wrapped up in some kind of cocoon,

the silver tinfoil-thing covering me was bouncing light off from the lanterns in an annoying way. It was tight-locking all of my limbs to my sides, along with something having been tucked under my chin and sides of my head to prevent me from moving it—a towel, maybe?—which felt constrictive and not at all comfortable.

My body hurt but I wanted *out*.

Someone farther away from us snorted softly. "He falls forty feet and still wakes up a motor mouth."

"Is that far?" I asked.

"Far enough." Fingers grazed along my forehead and up through my hairline, the feeling soothing, cutting against the sharp stabs of pain spidering through my body. "Too far."

"Can you please apologize to Blake for me?" I asked.

"You don't need to apologize to me, Marlow. Stop it."

My eyes widened as reality hit me. "*Blake.*"

He was so hard to see but I recognized that soft laugh immediately.

Why did it sound so choked up?

"Yeah..."

"You made it."

"I did." He trailed a finger along the bridge of my brow and down under my eye, circling gently until my lashes fluttered against his skin. "You didn't warn me you'd be surprising me with jumping off the side of a cliff."

"Technically, I was jumping *away* from a snake. The edge of the cliff just happened to be there. Poor planning on my part, I'll admit. Man, I'd kill for my heating pad right about now. Everything fucking hurts so bad."

His touch was retracted almost instantly, my gut tightening in response. His face was hard to make out with how the lantern was shining behind him, only really highlighting the outline of his body. He hunched over to curl his hands up close to his face, sucking in a sharp inhale that sounded caught between a cough and a soft cry.

Why was he upset?

Was it something I said?

The outline of him was all I had to go off of. The shaking in his shoulders was visible while he fought back whatever was trying to burst out of him.

"Blake... I'm not going to let them sue you. I swear."

He breathed out another laugh. This time

around, it sounded less amused and held on to much more sorrow than I'd ever heard from him before. "I'm not worried about that, Marlow..."

The pounding in my head made it so damn hard to hear his softly spoken words.

I twisted my hands at my sides, the sore digits hard to flex from the healed-over cuts and scrapes of being dragged along the rough terrain on my way down. "Can you hold my hand?"

I needed to feel connected to him somehow. Chase whatever it was making him upset away for good and get my dry-humored Blake back. This overly careful, subdued version of him was freaking me out more than my broken body was.

He straightened slowly, clearing his throat. "I can't, I'm sorry. We have you wrapped up in a space blanket so you don't freeze out here."

That explained the tinfoil. "What about you?"

"I'm okay."

"No you're not," I argued. "You're shaking. Get under here."

"I'm fine, Marlow."

"Please?"

He seemed to hesitate, fighting with himself to give in to my pleas and pull away this straitjacket so I could finally breathe again. All I wanted was to feel him curled up next to me like we'd been in my cabin two mornings ago—safe from the world and tucked in where only the two of us existed.

I barely registered the distant beating of a drum coming up over the horizon, a humming sound that just narrowly cut through my clogged ears.

"I'm so sorry," was all he replied with. "I should've been here. You wouldn't have…"

I hated how hopeless he sounded. Distress and anguish were two things I never wanted to associate him with and up until now, I never had to.

What was he even talking about?

In no world could either of us have predicted a damn snake appearing out of nowhere from between a rock formation and deciding I was its next meal. Being here would've prevented nothing, and if I was being honest, it may have resulted in him going over the damn edge with me.

Twenty feet from us, something flared to light and quickly shot up into the air. When it popped, the entire sky exploded in a red, smokey haze, lingering long enough for me to turn to get a good look at the man sitting next to me.

He was looking up at the sky, his tear-stained face bathed in a morbidly red glow.

"Blake..." *Come here.*

I wanted to kiss those tears away. They weren't right.

His gaze shot down to me, lips parting for a moment. The call from a nearby radio was a loud and shrill noise that cut through the quiet of the night. Three trills chimed off on it before being prematurely cut off from Talos speaking into it.

"Flare's up," he said. "ETA?"

"Two minutes out," was the static-y reply.

"They're going to transport you back to Ellington Heights," Blake told me, brushing his hand along my cheek once more. Time was moving too quickly now and I was severely running out of seconds to grasp at. To stay here longer with him. "They'll take good care of you. You're going to be okay."

"You're coming with me."

He forced a smile, his eyes brimming with unshed tears again. What a horrible expression on such a lovely face. "You're going to be okay, Marlow."

He can't leave me. He can't go back to his life and forget all about me.

The drums on the horizon were drawing closer—the unmistakable countdown to my life changing once more for what I would argue was the worst.

After this, I was never going to see him again. Banned from the property would be an understatement, along with whatever else I'd be forced to deal with once I was cleared from Wakefield's air space and out of the Austin family's hair.

And if not from Blake, there would definitely be imposed sanction from Silas and Avery.

I couldn't let that happen. Not when there was still so much of him I needed to know.

"Blake."

"Shhh." A single tear fell down his cheek.

My anxiety choked me, crushing my voice into something small and childlike. "Come with me."

Another flare shot off right as the trees around us hummed with a heavy force of wind whipping and beating against the thin branches. Dust kicked up from the ground, along with whatever fallen brush was littering the well-covered area.

Blake leaned over me to shield me from debris, his eyes forced closed while he curled his hands around the side of my face protectively.

"They're sending down a stretcher!" Talos yelled over the noise.

I fought the blanket's captivity, every single part of me screaming.

If this was the last moment I was ever going to get with Blake, I'd be damned if I wasn't going to touch him one more time. To hold his hand like I wanted to before I was strapped to a damn gurney and catapulted through the air to where Silas was no doubt waiting in the ER for me at Ellington Medical.

My entire arm shook as I forced it up and out from under the blanket, the strain agitating whatever was wrong with my shoulder as I moved it. Even under the flare's lighting, I could tell how swollen and heavily bruised it was— maybe it was even broken from trying to slow my fall.

None of that mattered the moment I grasped my disfigured hand around Blake's wrist and held on tight. His eyes shot open the next second, surprise reflecting in them while he locked onto me.

There was so much I wanted to say, so many things I wanted to thank him for, yet none of them were coming to mind. My body was so damn tired, my energy reserves fading faster than I could force them to keep up with me.

Stay with me...

While falling back into that dark pit of nothingness, where pain and my consciousness evaporated, the last thing I felt was Blake's lips brushing against mine before everything else faded away completely.

CHAPTER 23

BLAKE

THE STERILITY of a hospital was one of the only things in this world that truly got my skin crawling.

There was something about the smell of antibacterial wash clinging to the air, coupled with the soft and distant beeping of machines going off from down the hallway, that turned my typically calm and collected self into a twitched mess of anxiety.

Being crammed in this chair for the last few hours was pure torture. It had nothing to do with how pinched my back was feeling from how tightly I had my legs drawn up to my chest, nor the way I'd been hunched over for the better part of three hours while watching nurses and doctors come and go from the double doors leading into the emergency unit.

None of them stopped to update me on Marlow's condition, which meant one of two things: either he was still in surgery, or something else had gone horribly wrong and they were gearing up to come break the news.

Both of which made my stomach twist.

I was fortunate to arrive alongside Marlow when he was transported to Ellington Medical, the search and rescue team not taking any chances with leaving Talos and I out in the wilderness seventy feet below the plateau of the mountain's peak where we'd eventually found his beaten and broken body.

Seeing that image, belaying down to him while he lay motionless and stuck between a bunch of shrubs that had stopped his fall, was something I was never going to forget. It was going to haunt my worst nightmares for the rest of my life, no matter what the outcome of all of this turned out to be.

Around an hour into sitting in this waiting

room, three people arrived at the nurse's desk asking for Marlow. A woman who looked just like him, and two men, both around the same age as him. Taunt distraught was written in all of their faces, an emotion I felt gripping me tight from deep within me the moment I'd gotten my feet back on solid ground in the ambulance bay.

Talos had left shortly after arriving at Ellington Heights, per my request, even after he fought to stay with me to keep me company. As much as I would've loved the companionship, I needed someone that wasn't my poor granddad back at *Austin Adventures* running everything in my absence.

I could only assume the people sitting on the opposite side of the waiting room from me were Marlow's family, also eagerly awaiting for a status update on his condition.

I'd kept to myself the entire time we were all here, not wanting to interject in whatever quiet solidarity was resonating between all of them while they spoke in hushed whispers and gentle shoulder rubs of support to tell them I was the one mostly responsible for this horrible accident happening in the first place.

What was there to say, anyway?

My confession wouldn't make any of this better.

When the doors to the ER parted, a man in surgery scrubs, a cap over his hair, and clear plastic glasses perched on his nose walked over to Marlow's family. My eyes were locked onto him as he squatted down in front of Marlow's mother, her hands shooting out to grip the surgeon by the shoulders while she spoke to him in a hushed whisper.

The back of the doctor's head nodded and then she burst into tears, thanking him loudly before throwing her arms around him.

Without meaning to, I melted back into my seat.

That was a good sign.

They all exchanged familiar pleasantries with one another, one of the men getting up to bring the surgeon into a one-armed hug while slapping him on the back a few times. After parting, they were gestured to walk through the double doors, a room number I couldn't quite catch being given to them just as they all quickly shuffled beyond the nurse's desk.

Slowly straightening up, I let my legs drop to

the ground while pins and needles raced up from my toes. I supposed that was my cue to—

I froze the moment the surgeon pivoted and headed my way.

He was probably a little shorter than Marlow but not by much, and with slightly wider shoulders. His scrubs fit snug over his muscular build, creasing slightly under his arms when he brought them toward his face. His arms were covered in tattoos, leaving no signs of visibly un-inked skin.

He snapped off his gloves one by one, a silent show of authority that didn't go unnoticed by me.

"Blake, right?" His ice blue eyes were narrowed dangerously behind his protective glasses, the cloth mask covering the lower half of his face giving me nothing to work with outside of the very dull tone he was using.

I swallowed. "How is he?"

"He'll survive."

That was... good.

Great, even. Survival was what we wanted.

Thrived?

That was even better. A bold goal one might say.

The man, his surgeon, clenched the used gloves in one hand and then tucked his arms over his chest. His shoulders rolled once, cracking loud enough for me to catch. "He just woke up a little bit ago."

I nodded. "That's good."

If Marlow was already awake, that was a good sign for his recovery. It meant his surgery wasn't hard enough on his body to require some sort of medically induced coma or an extended dose of meds to knock him out for the time being.

I wasn't going to jump ahead and assume he would be out of here within the next day or two, that would be incredibly naive even if I wanted to remain hopeful, but there was a promise of a good prognosis at the end of this.

One where Marlow walked away from this terrible incident banged up but a plenty alive.

"Strangest thing, though." There was no humor in this man's tone, nor did the coldness in his eyes seem to dull despite the beginning of what should've been a very lighthearted sentence. "The first thing he did when he opened his eyes was ask about you."

My eyes flitted to the badge clipped to the hem of his shirt.

Dr. S. Montgomery.

I glanced back. "He did?"

"Told me to go look for the hot guy in the lobby with a great tan, freckles and honey-colored eyes that you could 'melt in'." He held up one hand to use air quotes.

Inwardly I winced.

Oh, Marlow... what the fuck.

"Which is so weird considering the last time I saw him, he was pretty beaten up about some guy with that same description." Dr. Montgomery tucked his arm back over his chest, popping out a hip while he shifted his weight to one side. "What a weird coincidence, considering the EMTs who brought him in said you were the camp's director... Isn't it?"

Both of my hands flexed around the chair's arm involuntarily.

Clearly, this was some sort of shakedown meant to scare me away. Or at least scold me into feeling worse than I already did. I had a feeling this man was one of Marlow's friends he'd spoken about back on the mountain, the *eye for an eye* one if I had to take a wild guess.

Did I blame him for being pissed?

Absolutely not. I was lucky this guy wasn't asking me to head out to the parking lot with him to settle the score the way he probably wanted to instead of being forced to remain professional.

Whatever Dr. Montgomery was hoping to accomplish by hammering down on my negligence, it was nothing compared to the unwavering storm inside of me, already beating me over and over again with my turbulent regret.

"I'm—" Pulling in a deep breath was doing nothing for my nerves. "You can tell him I left."

He stared me down, his form unmoving like a statue's. Those intense blue eyes glared through the lenses covering them, sharp and piercing with how extreme the silent judgment was.

It seemed as though in that moment, the entire waiting room grew deathly silent. No distance machines chimed with patient codes, no clacking of the nurses on their computer filling out reports, not even the sound of my own labored breathing being forced into my lungs could mitigate whatever soul sucking energy this man was smothering me in.

"Is that your final choice?" he said. The bait was dangling, edging me to take it and disappoint what little opinion he still had left of me.

The truth was that all I really wanted to do

was march down to Marlow's room and throw the door open to see for myself that he was alive and breathing, that he was well enough to be sitting up and talking like not a damn day had passed from our last conversation over the radio as he'd urged me to come join him on his hike.

I wanted the last words he'd said to me before he'd passed out again to become reality and not something I was forced to ignore because I was trying not to cross a line we'd already sprinted over ten times by now.

'Stay with me.'

I shook my head, giving in to my own soft feelings. I couldn't leave. I wasn't strong enough to even if it was for his own good. "No... I want to see him."

Dr. Montgomery rolled his shoulders back once again, breaking out of the all-consuming bubble he'd trapped us in. "All right. I'll let him know. Though, I suggest you visit him after his mother. Getting between her and her baby can be... quite troublesome at times."

And just like that, the world returned to normal.

"Uh... okay."

He gave me one last look before dropping

his arms and pivoting to head back for the double doors. "Once they leave, come to room 207."

He wasted not a single second longer before pushing the doors back and disappearing on the other side of them.

Involuntarily, my body sagged into my chair once more, completely wiped out from whatever the fuck *that* was.

Jesus, that man was intimidating.

How the hell did Marlow make friends with the strangest and most unlikely people?

AROUND TWO A.M. Marlow's family finally filtered out from the ER, looking as exhausted as I felt. I watched them drag their feet through the waiting room, the taller of the two men with his arm around Marlow's mother while she rested her head on his shoulder.

It felt wrong to go in after them, even if I'd been adamant about storming down there only an hour ago.

Was it more appropriate to let Marlow get some much-needed rest after his family visiting?

Or actually follow through with what I'd told his doctor I wanted?

I had a feeling that no matter what I chose, I'd probably end up being in the wrong somehow. And if that was the case, I might as well follow what my heart wanted.

Getting up from my chair, I nodded to the nurses behind the desk before slowly pushing through the doors heading down to the ER. The noise of a bustling hospital greeted me almost immediately, causing more tension to stiffen my body.

As I made my way down the short hallway, it opened up into a large wing with medical staff coming and going from beds lined up against the walls and facing outward. Patients were either lying down on them or sitting up, all with varying stages of trauma or sickness being tended to.

There weren't any room numbers I could see listed on the wall over the backs of the beds. On the left side of the wing, I spotted another nurses station and headed for it.

"I'm looking for room 207."

The nurse's fingers flew over the keyboard. "Name?"

"Uh, Marlow... Knight?"

She typed more, her head shaking. "Honey, he's up in the recovery wing. Not down here. You need to go to the elevators and go to floor two. He's in one of the private rooms up there."

I held back a sigh.

Why did I have a feeling his doctor did that shit on purpose?

Clearly, I wasn't out of the woods yet of whatever kind of hazing he was still interested in inflicting on me. "Thank you."

Pushing away from the desk, I found the elevator and took it to the second floor, thankfully, much quieter than the one below it. I felt the tension ease out of me with each step down the hall, a plaque on the wall pointing to which side I'd find Marlow's room on.

Laughter trickled into the hallway when I approached it, familiar and warm. His door was already open, the curtain above him pulled back while he relaxed into his bed. Machines were hooked up to him on either side, their silent graphs pulsing with his vitals that looked strong and relatively healthy.

Marlow's right leg was wrapped in thick ace bandages up to his hip, a splint underneath it to keep it in place for the time being. He had his opposite side's arm in a sling, also wrapped up in ace bandages. His gown was parted at his chest, only loosely tied at his hip that made it drape dangerously low. More bandages covered him there as well but weren't as intense looking as his leg and arm.

On the right side of his bed, reclining in one of the visitor chairs, was Dr. Montgomery. "Oh, look. He actually did show up."

Marlow's neck snapped as he turned his head toward the door, his eyes going wide.

Without a word, he lifted his good hand toward me, making a grabbing motion with it.

It was hard to push away from the doorway, my guilt fighting to strangle me with every step I took into the room of the man I allowed to get hurt under my watch. I wasn't interested in hearing whatever excuse or explanation anyone was willing to give me to diminish this horrific feeling inside of me.

It didn't matter if all of this was an accident.

Marlow got hurt and that was more than enough for me to blame myself over it.

His lifeless body flashed inside of my mind, causing me to stop dead in my tracks.

I thought he was dead. I thought I was belaying down to recover his dead body.

Marlow frowned. "Come here."

My eyes began to sting.

My hands were still raw from how hard I'd ripped into those pricker bushes to free him, Talos shouting at me when he noticed Marlow pulling in deep, labored breaths. How careful we'd had to be when laying him down because we had no way to tell how badly he'd hit his head or if he'd snapped his neck and was now paralyzed.

"Blake. Come here." He made another grabbing motion.

Blinking hard out of the memories, I drew my hand up to brush against his fingers.

Alive. He was alive. I needed to keep reminding myself.

He tugged me forward in a surprising show of strength, practically collapsing me on top of him as I stumbled and fell onto the side of his bed.

"*Careful,*" Dr. Montgomery snapped. "The wires aren't there for show."

"Yeah, yeah." Marlow dismissed playfully, his hand coming up to cup my jaw immediately.

"Don't listen to him, he's just grouchy he got called in on his day off."

He slid his thumb across my cheek in the same way I'd done for him in the mountains. A small smile played on his lips, not at all tinged with whatever pain had been coursing through his body while we waited for the helicopter to arrive.

Relief shot through me, hard enough to spring more tears to my eyes.

Marlow's soft grunt was followed by him quickly swiping his thumb under my eyes, catching whatever he saw brewing there.

"You would be, too, if you heard the police scanners going off with an emergency airlift from Wakefield." Dr. Montgomery's tone flipped back into being bland, no longer tinged with the residual anger he'd yelled at me with only moments ago.

Marlow glanced over at him. "Stop listening to the police scanners on your day off."

"I think a *'thank you, Silas'* is more appropriate in this situation seeing as I sewed you back up nice and neat after all of your guts were spilling out of you."

"They were not!"

"Tell that to the search and rescue team who had to pack your wounds before you got to me."

That made me wince.

It had taken so long for us to get into contact with search and rescue, to the point where I'd all but given up before Talos had finally gotten a damn answer from our SOS. We had no chances of moving Marlow up the side of the ravine carefully, and with no way of knowing the extent of his injuries, I wasn't willing to move him an inch from where we'd found him.

So many hours had been wasted on us trying to get help; precious moments Marlow needed that were the difference between life and death.

We'd gotten so damn lucky with the way he'd fallen, most of the brush clinging to the side of the mountain having slowed his descent before he actually hit hard ground.

Marlow pulled me against his chest, burying his face into my hair. "Don't listen to him, he's being fucking annoying. I'm okay."

I wasn't sure whether he was doing all of this to make me feel better or himself. At this point, I had no shame left in me to be embarrassed about the blatant displays of PDA in front of his friend, especially when my ear pressed up against his chest and I heard that healthy beating of his heart hammering back at me.

Dr. Montgomery, *Silas,* snorted. "Whatever. We'll see how Avery feels in the morning. He was too tired to argue with you earlier before he left."

Fingers threaded through the hair at the nape of my neck, pulling just enough to soothe me.

"He's not suing."

"We'll see."

Honestly, it would surprise me if we *weren't* sued.

I wouldn't fight it. I'd give Marlow whatever his friends were asking for, save for shutting down the entire property. *That* I'd have to fight, if only to try and protect my granddad's legacy he'd worked so damn hard to build.

I squeezed my eyes shut. I'd never forgive myself if out of the thirty plus years *Austin Adventures* had been in business, I got it shut down in five.

Though at the same time, wouldn't that be my karma?

Letting Marlow get hurt so badly he nearly died?

Maybe this was all the universe's way of punishing me for being careless. For allowing myself a sliver of happiness and reckless abandon and getting myself tangled up in a man I had no business even entertaining, let alone holding a conversation with long enough to actually develop feelings for.

Marlow was in a different league of his own and wasn't meant to be down in the dirt with the rest of us. He was a bird that was supposed to be sailing free on whatever breeze drifted on by, carrying him to whatever heedless destination he happened upon.

I was tied down to a single entity. Living and dying under my family's legacy.

"Blake..." Marlow's voice softened. "It's okay. I'm okay."

His gentle laugh only served to make my eyes leak more, wetting the bandages covering his chest.

"Sorry," I mumbled.

"Don't be. What did you say to me? 'You have nothing to be sorry for'. Same goes for you."

I shook my head.

"Yes," he replied, tugging at my hair.

How could he still want to be around me after all of this?

Why was this man so damn forgiving?

No one else would be acting half as happy to see me if they were in his shoes. In fact, they'd probably send their family after me to try and beat me up in the hallway for risking their family member's life like that.

Marlow was such a damn enigma. One I doubted I'd ever fully understand.

His bright light was a warm and basking glow that anyone in their right mind gravitated toward immediately. Protecting something precious like that was important above all else.

"Hey, how about this," he suggested. "I'll talk Avery out of suing you if you come back to my place to take care of me."

"You're blackmailing him?" Silas drawled.

"It's *not* blackmail. It's an *offer*."

"Spoken like a true finance scumbag, bro."

"*Wow*."

The funny thing was Marlow didn't even have to *try* and blackmail me. I'd go willingly, wherever he asked. No questions beyond whatever information he wanted to give me. I'd done the same when I'd teased him with the idea of joining him up at the peak and packed my things the second he'd given me the green light to go to him.

"Don't you have a manservant to take care of you?" Silas asked. "Oh, sorry. *Butler.*"

"He's on vacay. I sent him to Cancun since I was going to be in Wakefield for six weeks. I can't call him back now when it's only been two weeks."

"Speaking of which, you owe me."

"Uh, no. Try again. I lasted way longer than a week. *You* owe *me.*"

"The bet was—"

"That I lasted a week," Marlow finished. "Which I did. I lasted *almost* two. It's not my fault it was cut short."

"I'm sure it was much easier to occupy your time when someone was warming your bed. To me, that seems like cheating."

"No way. I won, fair and square. Now fork over the savings account."

"Fuck off."

Lifting my head up from Marlow's chest, I quickly swiped my hand under my eyes before looking at him. "You... actually want me to go home with you?"

His eyes snapped back to me, lighting up immediately. "*Yes.*"

How easy it was for him to be so honest. To

want things and ask for them with no regard as to how painful a potential rejection might be. That was a quality I heavily admired in Marlow, one I found myself lacking most of the time.

To be wanted by someone like him... what did that mean for my future?

How easily could I start to forget about my responsibilities and allow myself to fall into his spell like I so desperately wanted to?

Back at camp, it seemed straightforward and uncomplicated to deny wanting anything outside of sex and getting off with him. I had so much to do that it gave me little time to reflect on my own feelings when they came to Marlow.

Cradling his broken body while Talos frantically called for an SOS, and now here, seeing the aftermath of his life being saved, was putting so much into perspective for me that it was getting harder and harder to ignore what was blatantly right in front of me.

I *wanted* Marlow in more ways than just sex.

Believing he'd died had destroyed me. My heart only shakily putting back the pieces once his lungs drew in that first gasping breath in my arms, hope blooming for the first time since I'd unclipped myself from the belay and stumbled through the brush after him.

Why chance fate when it was clearly giving me a second offering?

My granddad, Talos, my staff, the kids, they could forgive me eventually for spending the rest of the season with Marlow.

"Okay," I breathed out.

Marlow's grin was blinding. "*Excellent. Blake, you're going to* love *my house. I have an indoor pool.*"

I tilted my head back to press my ear to his chest again, closing my eyes while the healthy thumps of his heart beat back at me.

Marlow's alive.

CHAPTER 24

Blake

FIVE DAYS LATER, and with another intense cornering from Silas under my belt, I was taking Marlow back home to what I could only describe as his ridiculously luxurious mansion in Ellington Heights.

Having only driven through this small town twice in my life as a kid, and being blown away both times at how opulent everything seemed, doing so as a fully grown adult was giving me much more of a flabbergasted feeling than when Marlow had told me he gave little shit's as to how much money he'd ended up wasting on his wrong package deal.

The gated community leading up to his house, along with the hand on my thigh that squeezed every so often while Marlow hummed along to the radio, continued to toss me between nervous and pure contentment.

The car ride from the hospital was quiet but not awkward. No tension left hanging over us outside of my occasional heavy bouts of remorse.

For now, I'd focus on helping Marlow heal and push back whatever else swam inside of my brain, clogging it up from allowing happiness to creep back in. It was the least I could do after everything.

"*This* is where you live?" The words were out of my mouth the second the GPS was bringing us up the long drive. Ahead was a large, Tudor style mansion with a well-kept lawn and tastefully done curb appeal that lined along the entire front of it.

"What, you not a fan of brick?" Marlow teased.

"It's so..." I shifted the car into park, staring through the windshield at it.

"Come on, the suspense is killing me." He tightened his hand on my thigh.

"It's beautiful, don't get me wrong. But I never expected you to live in something like this." When I turned my attention over to him, I found him squinting at me.

"What, you expected me to live in a dump?"

"No, just a frat house."

He slapped my thigh, sending pleasant tingles racing to my dick. "Funny. That was college."

"I knew you came across as a fan of keg stands."

He grinned. "Careful, Blake. I may just talk you into getting drunk with me. We'll see how far my hands wander. I'm told I'm quite the flirt."

"Can't imagine what you're like with loose inhibitions." If that was even possible. A part of me suspected he was more the type to get *others* wasted than let himself get too hammered to not be in control.

"Guess you'll have to find out."

Shaking my head, I slipped my hand under the handle of the door to pop it open, stretching once I was out in the fresh air. Silas had been weirdly nice enough to retrieve Marlow's car for me early this morning, literally throwing the keys at me on his way in for his shift.

'Don't crash it or Avery really will *sue you'* was the only thing he'd said to me before disappearing beyond the staff doors.

I had yet to meet Marlow's other friend officially, but from the sound of it, the man was just as terrifying as Silas was. Maybe even more so with the amount of money and resources he apparently had.

Shoving my door closed, I came around to the other side where Marlow was already trying to struggle his way out of the car, completely ignoring the crutches that were tucked into the backseat.

I shoved him back into the car, smiling a little at the grunt I received in return as I opened the back door.

"I don't want those things," he complained.

"I'd love to carry you but you weigh too much for me to properly balance you." The rubber stoppers on the bottom slammed against the side of the door as I pulled them out, forcing me to hold back a wince while slamming it shut.

What were the chances Avery did an inspection on Marlow's car to make sure I wasn't fucking it up in other ways outside of crashing it?

He gasped dramatically. "Blake, are you calling me *fat*? What the hell, I thought you were supposed to be all about body positivity."

"Nice try." I shoved the crutches into his hand. "You want help standing up?"

"No."

I eyed him carefully. "You sure?"

He seemed to think about it for a second, moving the crutches to his sides while measuring how exactly he was going to get himself from sitting half tucked inside of his car to rolling up onto his feet and fitting each pad under his arm.

Silas had forced him to practice a few times while still in the hospital but now he was all on his own.

Thankfully, the only thing that had actually come out broken was his leg that had needed to be reset surgically. Pins and screws were holding it together while it slowly healed, carefully protected under his cast, which reached all the way up to above his knee.

A miracle, really, that the rest of him had only been badly bruised and sprained, and by now, was on its way to healing completely.

If that wasn't sheer luck, I couldn't fathom what was.

"Okay," Marlow mumbled, finally tugging himself out from the car.

I stood back to give him room, keeping my arms out to catch him if he ended up tipping over from the weird displacement of weight. The way his cast was fitting around him had his leg permanently bent at a slightly odd angle, remnants of how truly bad his fall had been.

According to his x-rays, his leg had taken the brunt of the impact, saving him from completely shattering his ribcage and arms on the way down. He'd be in a cast for at least three months, with the possibility of having permanent screws in his leg for the rest of his life afterward.

At the time, he'd joked about being half robotic, his spirits barely taking a hit when he'd been given a close-up view of his x-rays after Silas had personally brought them to his room to show him the work he'd done.

That was all to say that despite the seemingly giant setbacks, Marlow was barely letting it slow him down.

"Got it?" I asked.

He hobbled slightly before getting a good

balance going. "Better watch out, Blake. I'm going to be faster than you with these things."

I smiled, even with my heavy heart. "Let's see how well you do with stairs and then we can talk."

"You're on."

SETTLING into Marlow's home was weirdly easier than I expected.

Upon first glance of the outside of it, it felt more structured and rigid, not at all fitting the man who lived inside of it. However, the second the front door was opened and that deep scent of *Marlow* hit me, things began to feel strangely like *home.*

His decor was, while tasteful, still uniquely him. The bold colors and over-the-top design quality spoke of a man who wasn't afraid to think outside the box and live life to the fullest extent, bleeding that same mindset into the rest of whatever he touched.

I liked being here more than I missed being back home.

What did that say about me?

I had the sense in me to be wary of how easily I was falling into a routine only hours into arriving. Giving in to the want and desire of molding myself into his life was natural enough for me to forget all about it, until the stark reminder that I'd need to go back to Wakefield eventually hit me the second I'd caught my own reflection in one of the passing mirrors.

Maybe it was a bad idea to agree to any of this, to kid myself into thinking taking care of Marlow would be a simple thing and not end with me giving myself yet *another* existential crisis.

My granddad had already given me the green light to take as much time as I needed, and the rest of my staff were simply relieved to hear of Marlow's harrowing survival to be upset that I was taking time off during the busiest season we were open.

I only wished I could've finished out seeing the end of my youth group's tournament. From Talos's recount, it had gone on without a single hitch—an impressive feat I wasn't so sure I could claim responsibility for even after his heavy insistence.

Nonetheless, I hoped next year we'd have an even better turn out.

Warm lips ghosted along the column of my neck. "Here I thought I'd find you cooking lunch, only to catch you overthinking the pasta to death."

I winced.

How the hell was he able to sneak up on me with those damn crutches?

I wasn't *that* lost in thought... was I?

He trailed his mouth up to my jaw, nipping slightly at the skin there before moving up to the spot right below my ear. "Camp got you worried?"

A damn open book. I had to get better at that. It wasn't fair that I had all my cards out on the table so readily available to him.

Where was the mystery? The hint of intrigue?

"Sort of. I talked to Talos this morning before we left the hospital. He said everything was fine. I just..." My voice trailed off.

"Next year, Blake," Marlow murmured, reading me instantly. "Maybe you can even get a few sponsors to host your event to make it even bigger than this year's. That would be cool."

I wanted to melt back into him. Let him pamper me like he'd promised to do when he'd told me to leave my worries and my control at the door. Stepping into that dynamic again, allowing myself to give everything over to a man as capable of taking care of me as Marlow had proven in the past to be capable of, felt so damn right it hurt.

"Aren't I supposed to be taking care of you?" I mumbled.

He snickered. "Two-way street, hm? I think that's fair. Plus, this was just my bribe to get you to come home with me."

"You didn't need to do all of that."

"How else was I going to get you to come see me again?"

I turned to look over my shoulder at him, surprised. "You thought I was going to ghost you?"

He shrugged, a playful smile teasing his lips. His eyes were telling a different story, though, one that was tinged with uncertainty and worry for whatever rejection he was expecting to come.

Had I been so damn avoidant that he'd believed I'd do something like that? Even after all of *this?*

'Friday was really rough for me'. He'd told me that much over the radio.

How deeply had I hurt this man after running away?

Turning away from the stove, I reached forward to slip my fingers into his hair, bringing him down to kiss me. His lips fit against mine perfectly, his head tilting to the side just enough to deepen it and send a shiver racing up my spine.

Whatever these next three months brought, I'd do whatever I could to make things up to Marlow. He meant too much to me to let me see him suffer, even due to my own insecurities and self-preservation.

I hoped I could make things right.

Even if it was only until he got better and moved on to big and brighter things after me.

CHAPTER 25

MARLOW

"I'M FINE, MA."

The phone's speaker rattled against my ear as she let out a long, labored sigh on the other end of it, the tell-tale cue for the beginning of a lecture being wound up for the proverbial batter making their way up to the plate to crack the home run hitter over the grandstands.

To think I once believed I was in the clear of being my mother's problem child after I graduated. Naive, apparently, considering my track record. Turns out, I'd only just been getting started on sending her to an early grave with the chronic stress of being out of her house and running wild out in the world to my heart's content.

Being a free bird sometimes meant consequences for not just me, but everyone else who loved and supported me, too.

A rather sobering thought, now that it was all sinking in.

"Marlow Alexander..." I winced at her tone. "I don't care how well those pain meds are working. I am coming over there to take care of you until you get that damn cast off. And that's final."

Yeesh. Talk about a mother's undying love.

Under any other circumstance, I would've loved to invite her over to wait on me hand and foot, just like any other spoiled only child in my position. The promise of home cooked meals on the regular, complete and undivided attention from my first and only caretaker just like I had when I was a child, and an overwhelming amount of praise over simple things like lifting a single finger to do something, was incredibly tempting.

Who wouldn't want to take up an offer like that?

It was every mama's boy's wet dream.

The problem was that I had a grand plan already in the midst of enacting that I wasn't going to let anyone, not even my own dear mother, fuck up. And that was to convince Blake to stay here with me in Ellington Heights forever.

"I'm really okay, Ma. I swear. I've already got someone here to help me."

She huffed. "I thought you said you sent Niles to Cancun?"

"Someone *else*."

My body twanged with a dull shot of pain, rolling up from the base of my spine to settle where my bruised rib was. Forcing myself to breathe through it while straightening back up from where I'd hunched myself over trying to retrieve a sock from the floor that I'd accidentally dropped on my way to getting myself dressed took way more effort than I was expecting.

Goddamn, that kills.

This is what I get for being stubborn and not letting Blake help me.

Silas insisted my ribcage hadn't been cracked in half during and even after being airlifted to his hospital, telling me several times over that it was all in my head before I'd been discharged, despite me ragging on him to check again.

How the hell did he know there was nothing wrong without actually opening me up to see if there was some kind of hairline fracture just sitting there?

Of course, every time I'd brought it up to him, he'd slapped me with a curt, *'I'm not slicing you open to prove your delusional ass wrong.'*

X-rays could only show so much and if it was a thin enough fracture to not be picked up on after a third pass of my imaging, then who was he to tell me it was all in my head with every bout of dizziness that came with bending over

I'd seen it plenty of times on Grey's Anatomy. You were either dying or soon to be dead once the room-spinnies started.

Now, it wasn't my place to allege malpractice... but if the cookie crumbled...

Maybe I'll get Avery to sue him instead.

"Who?" My mom asked.

"No one you know. A friend."

While I wasn't exactly gatekeeping Blake from her, my plan was contingent on not freaking him out too soon by throwing him into the middle of my life and compressing him with it on all sides. My family, my friends, hell even my job, were all incredibly substantial parts of my life. No matter how delicately I was going to be in trying to integrate him into those aspects of it, it was going to end up devolving into some kind of shitshow.

All I could do was try and mitigate the worst of it.

He'd survived Silas so far—one could argue was one of the bigger obstacles in this entire ordeal to overcome—and next would be my mom.

Avery?

Could go either way.

He was still caught up in Brandon most days, which hopefully meant he'd soon forget about the threat of that lawsuit.

"Avery?" she wagered.

"No. Someone from that camp I attended."

She huffed again. "That camp. They're lucky we haven't gone to the media with their negligence. Did anyone ever reach out to you about what happened? I can't believe you didn't at least receive someone stopping by your hospital room to check on you."

"Yeah." Choosing my words carefully in

order to skirt around telling her the truth was a bit harder than I anticipated. "The director actually offered his sincerest apologies."

Not entirely untrue. If anything, he'd been over the top in how sorry he was. Ridiculous, considering none of this was his fault in the first place.

Blake's teary eyes flashed in my mind, along with the dark circles that seemed permanently stamped into his tanned skin.

He'd been staying here with me a week and he still had yet to get rid of them, no matter how many times I coaxed him into taking a nap with me. With my meds making me dog-tired by the time night fell, it was hard to keep track of how often he was actually falling asleep while he brushed his hands through my hair, lulling me into my own dreams.

His wariness and overall edge toward touching me outside of helping me dress or get around the house when my arms ached too much to keep using the crutches was also concerning and the last thing I wanted happening.

This was supposed to be our excuse to get closer without the threat of camp looming over us both. Not putting more distance between us, no matter how often he tried to smother those worried frowns with forced smiles that never quite reached his eyes.

I wanted him to stay. Not out of obligation but because he also couldn't stand the thought of leaving my side just like I couldn't imagine leaving his.

"Really?" My mom sounded surprised.

"Yup. So stop trying to encourage Avery in finding a law firm."

"Did they give you anything? Your money back? Flowers, at least?"

Honestly, if I asked, Blake would no doubt give me the literal shirt off his damn back, let alone all of my money I'd paid and then some. He'd probably erect some kind of memorial bench by the lakefront, complete with my name on a plaque and everything, if I so much as hinted at the idea.

"Something like that," I replied.

"Why don't I at least come over for dinner tonight. I can make you and your... guest? Something to eat."

Giving Blake the night off was enticing.

The subsequent interrogation that dinner

conversation would lead to the second she found out who he was?

Not so much. I needed to at least get through the month, really let him settle into his life here, to let that subject be breached.

Plus, it gave my mom plenty of time to cool off before trying to verbally slice and dice my poor, hopefully, future boyfriend.

Boyfriend.

Damn, did I like the sound of that.

Never in my life did I ever think I'd find someone I'd want to give that title to. Then again, I never thought I'd find my literal soulmate casually managing a million dollar business in the middle of the fucking mountains only an hour away from me either.

What was that saying?

That all red strings of fate eventually met when you least expected?

"Actually, I'm pretty tired today. Rain check?"

She sighed again, though it was much softer than the one before it. "All right. Fine. I can take a hint."

I grinned. "Love you, ma. Make sure to call

me tomorrow, okay? I'll tell you all about my weird drugged-up dreams."

Her laugh released the tension that had been building up in my shoulders over the past ten minutes. "Hope it's not another zombie one."

"You and me both."

"Bye, honey, I love you. Tell your...um, friend? I said hello."

"I will. Love you, too."

Ending the call, I tossed my phone onto the bed and leaned back until I was flat against the mattress. As annoying as it was to be stuck in my house with limited mobility, I had to say, watching the people in my life come out in droves to check on me and offer whatever help I was willing to take from them was heartwarming.

Not that there were ever any doubts in their care for me, but seeing it firsthand really put a lot into perspective. Especially, with how fortunate I was to have such a close-knit safety net.

One I desperately wanted Blake to join.

Taking him away from the camp was selfish, I'd admit that in a damn heartbeat if pressed. And while I did feel pangs of guilt here and there for pulling him away so soon into the season, I was also glad at how willing he was to come home with me.

That had to mean I wasn't the only one feeling this. That we were meant for so much more than a few hookups.

The longer I spent with him, the more I was beginning to understand Avery's obsession with Brandon. How deep that need went in keeping that person who held your heart close to your side. How tender and delicate this stage was before things were finally settled.

Back then, I was of the mindset of losing the freedom to come and go as you pleased was worse than death.

What kind of life was it to be trapped in a relationship, tied to one single person for the rest of your life?

Naively, I'd been blind to the fact that I, too, had someone that was perfect out there for me. I was stupid to think otherwise—to think I was above love and having someone to call mine.

That hubris within me had gotten slapped hard with reality with my near-death experience finally opening my eyes.

"You okay?"

Turning my head, I spotted him just shy of

the doorframe. He had his hands in front of him, fingers twisted together tightly while he wrung them in an apprehensive way.

My poor Blake. Such a worrywart.

Holding out my hand, I gestured for him to come closer. Obediently, he walked into my room, his steps careful and cautious. Breaking him out of seeing me as fragile would be difficult. My still-healing body, a constant reminder of how he found me, wasn't doing either of us any favors.

Whatever Blake's hangups were, whatever was preventing him from falling back into those easy laughs and poignant jabs, needed to be taken care of before we could move on to an actual fruitful future.

If he wanted one with me, that is.

"Your leg hurt?" he asked the moment his hand found mine.

I tugged him forward. "Come here."

His brows knitted together but he still allowed me to pull him up onto the bed, swinging a leg over my waist when I curled my free hand under the backside of his knee and tugged. He was mindful with settling himself down onto my hips, keeping most of his weight pressed forward into the mattress by leaning onto his knees.

We were at an awkward angle with how I had one leg, my good one, dangling off the edge of the bed while the other was slightly hiked up onto it, my hip popped out at an angle to keep my leg from cramping inside of my cast. The damn thing was, thankfully, not up to my thigh, a threat Silas had made damn sure to pass onto me if he caught wind of me misbehaving and not using my crutches.

Still, having Blake sitting on me made up for the slight twinge in my back.

"Much better." I grinned.

He huffed out a short laugh. "I don't think we should be doing this. Weren't you just complaining about your ribs yesterday?"

"Nonsense. Silas said thirty minutes of exercise a day is good for me."

"I think he meant walking around your house."

"If he did, he should've been more specific."

Blake simply shook his head, leaning away as if to get up again.

I clamped my hands down on his thighs,

keeping him pinned against me. "And where do you think you're going?"

His eyes went wide. "Marlow."

His shirt was easy to slip my hands under, his body jumping at the sudden contact. He was warm and pliable under my touch. Leaning into it without meaning to while he let himself go for a split second before his mind caught up to him and told him no. His lips parted as I reached his waist, moving my hands up to his chest and flattening both palms there.

He grabbed at my wrists, keeping them in a tight hold. "We... shouldn't."

As he spoke, he rolled his hips against mine, drawing a moan out of both of us.

"I won't break, Blake. If that fall didn't kill me, this definitely won't."

Whatever I said seemed to break the spell immediately. Gloom returned to his eyes while the corners of his lashes grew wet with tears. My heart squeezed, watching the pinch between his brows become more pronounced by the second. He slid my hands out from under his shirt, pushing them back toward my body in an effort to untangle himself from me.

"No." I grabbed at him again, snatching his

arm before he could fully pull away from me. "We're not doing this."

"Please," was all he said.

"I'm not letting you push me away. Not this time."

His breath hitched. "I'm not trying to."

"You are if you keep acting like I'm still in that damn hospital bed."

He bowed his head, shame causing his shoulders to sink. Reaching up slowly, I traced my thumb along his temple to his cheek, cupping my other fingers around his jaw to keep him from moving again. The small and dejected sigh that came tumbling from his mouth only served to make me tighten my hold on him.

"Listen," I spoke softly. "I know you feel bad. I hate to see you continuing to kick yourself over something you had no control over. I'm *okay*. Better, actually, with you staying here with me. I only wish you could give yourself some grace."

His watery eyes met mine. "When I found you... I didn't—I thought..." He swallowed thickly. "It follows me in my dreams."

Oh, Blake.

That explained the poor sleep.

"I'm sorry you were the one to find me." No

one should ever have to stumble upon a sight like that, trained or not.

"I'm not." His hand was tight where he grabbed my wrist. "I got to make sure I was the one who kept you still breathing. There was no other person I would've trusted to do it over me."

Yes, and shouldering all of the responsibility along the way, I almost retorted with. As per usual, Blake's overwhelming responsibility with holding everything together, even in the face of a potential tragedy, was ever present. I had no doubt Talos helped as much as he could but there was no way Blake hadn't kept my care solely up to him.

How hard had he fought to keep himself levelheaded while Talos called for help?

How many times did he pray for me to open my eyes to make sure I was actually still in there and not long gone while my body fought to continue going?

None of it seemed fair for him to harbor that amount of culpability. If anything, he was a damn hero in my eyes. The moment I'd realized he was there with me was the moment all felt right in the world.

He breathed out slowly. "I'm just... I'm glad I started out earlier on that hike than I planned. I got to the peak a little after you fell. Something was telling me to go before the sun was up, so I did."

Using my hold on him, I forced him into bending forward, curling my other arm around his waist from behind to help flatten him against my body. His cheek was slightly damp against my bare chest, a slow exhale shuddering out of him the moment I locked my arm in place. His hair was soft as I threaded my fingers through the tangled lengths, cupping the side of his face to keep him there.

"Hear it?" I asked. "My heart beats because of you. I'm *alive* because of you."

As soon as he started to shake his head, I tightened my hand to stop him.

"I mean it."

His body stiffened. "Do you... you actually like me being here with you?"

"Absolutely." There was no hesitation in my voice, nor in how swiftly the confirmation fell from my mouth. "If falling off a fucking cliff is what got you to come home with me, then I'd do it all over again."

He scoffed. "That's morbid."

"And true."

I felt a shiver move under his skin the moment I slipped my hand under his shirt again, tracing the dimples etched into his lower back. I loved touching him. I loved the small twitches and faint sighs he made from something so simple as me tracing a nonsensical pattern wherever I pleased. I loved his hidden masochism and how fucked up he liked to get as I made a mess of him. I loved those bright smiles and the way his eyes sparkled when the sun hit them just right.

Everything about this man, I wanted to keep all for myself. I wouldn't be letting him go so easily, not when I was right on the precipice of this, *hopefully,* being a permanent thing. There would be no one after him—no one could compare.

I wanted to memorize every goddamn inch of him. To be able to conjure him even in my dreams. I wanted to know every little thing that made him tick and everything that made him come undone. There would be nothing left hidden from me by the time I was done.

"No more adventure sports," he muttered.

"Can't stop me from trespassing onto your

property." Technically, he could, but I'd gotten my way around plenty of figurative and actual fences in my time.

"Should I be scared I ended up saving a stalker?"

The light teasing in his voice made me breathe out a sigh of relief.

Was he finally coming back to me?

"Can't stalk someone who likes it."

He forced his head up from my chest, a vague kind of smile playing on his lips. "You're trouble. You know that? I could just ban you from the property. Have police posted outside the entrance all summer."

"Is this a bad time to remind you I have a billionaire friend?"

He rolled his eyes, pinching my side lightly. "Yeah, let me know when that lawsuit is supposed to hit my desk. I want to have a fresh bottle of whiskey unsealed and ready to go."

"To party, I hope," I egged on. "It's not every day someone gets sued."

"Are you trying to say I'm special?"

"To me? Definitely."

His smile widened ever so slightly. "Maybe

I'll sue you right back for fucking up my ratings and scaring my whole staff with the airlift."

I gasped. "A countersuit. I'd be honored."

I hooked two of my fingers under the hem of his pants, teasing the spot right above one of his ass cheeks. The sudden levity in our conversation was tempting me too much to talk me out of sliding my hand down between his firm cheeks until I had both digits pressed against his hole. The resounding gasp when I finally reached my destination further encouraged me into circling around it slowly.

"Remember how you were naughty and kept those condoms from me?"

He groaned in response, hiking one leg up to give me better access.

Pulling my hand out from his pants briefly, I shoved my fingers into my mouth, coating them both in spit before replacing them right back where they belonged. A hard shiver shook Blake's entire body, his jaw dropping in time with his lashes fluttering closed.

"You're sure?" He shoved back against my hand, nearly penetrating himself. "I won't hurt you?"

"You could never."

He groaned once more the second I slipped a finger into him, his tight heat burning me. Rising slightly from where he'd been held against me, he shifted back just enough to push the finger deeper, clenching around it immediately.

Holy fuck.

This man got hotter and hotter as the days rolled on.

"Just imagine." My lungs were practically punching the air out of me. "How much better my cock is going to feel."

A small noise bubbled up from his chest, desperate and keening. One hand splayed over my chest, keeping away from where my bruised —*definitely broken*—rib was as he used it for leverage to ride my finger. My other nudged against his entrance when he rose again, just enough to slip another finger in beside the first as soon as he pushed back down.

"*Fuck.*" He shuddered again, losing himself.

My dick was throbbing in my sweats the longer I watched him getting off. The unfortunate part about wearing a leg cast was how fucking annoying it was going to be to try and wrestle myself out of these goddamn clothes. Thankfully, I was only halfway through getting dressed when my mom called and interrupted me.

"Blake." His eyes fluttered open, that beautiful flush already coloring his cheeks and the bridge of his nose. "Condoms and lube are in my dresser next to the bed."

His thighs squeezed my hips. "You're sure?"

I clapped my hand against his thigh, muffling the sound of it through his pants. "Go on. Strip while you're over there. I want to see every inch of you." I drew my fingers out slowly, letting him go.

He fell onto his side next to me, his leg popping up into the air briefly while he rolled off of the bed and to his feet.

Amused, I hooked my arm back behind me to prop me up, giving me a perfect view of him stripping off the layers from his beautifully sculpted body.

I found it ironic that for how athletic he was, he preferred to hide it under things two sizes too big. Lucky me, I got to see exactly what was being kept from everyone else.

He dug through my dresser, finding the items quickly before shoving the drawer closed and walking back over to me. His half-hard dick bounced slightly while he moved, making my own twitch in my pants.

He was such a fucking sight to see. I could stare at him all day if he'd let me.

The bottle was tossed perfectly next to me in an impressive show of marksmanship, the condom following right after. Just as my mouth opened to hit him with a smart-ass comment, he dropped to his knees in front of me.

The tenderness in his touch in carefully tugging the cuff of my sweats down over my good ankle sent my stomach rolling with butter-flies. So used to being on the opposite side of things, it was strangely sensual to have someone taking care of me with even the simple things. So far, Blake had fallen into the role of housekeeper, cook, and occasional bathroom attendant.

And yet *this* was far more intimate.

He eased it down slowly, no rush to his movements as he switched to the other side once he had that cuff over my foot. My toes tingled at the brush of his palm against where they were exposed, covered briefly to match the other side as he pulled the cuff free from where it was trapped around my cast.

Arching myself up, I lifted my ass from the

mattress long enough to help him tug my waistband down over my hips and thighs, exposing me. I had the sense to stop wearing boxers since coming home from the hospital, the annoyance in getting them on and off over my cast far outweighing proper etiquette at this point.

Plus, who cared? It was just me and Blake.

As soon as I was free, I kicked up my good leg to help me scoot farther back onto the bed, dragging the other one with me.

Blake followed close behind, his movements mindful to not knock against my bad side while throwing his leg back over me to straddle my hips once more.

"Perfect. Just where I wanted you," I said, curving my hands around his thighs.

His smile was radiant. "But how will you restrain me?"

"Oh, I'm quite creative." I'd proven that much in his office.

He toyed his bottom lip between his teeth while reaching over to grab what he'd tossed onto the bed, holding up the bottle of lube first. "You want me to do the honors?"

"Nope." I snatched it from his hand

instantly. "You're going to behave yourself. I'm in control, remember?"

"He said as the one being sat on."

Satisfaction rolled through me the second my hard slap against his thigh drew out a surprised gasp. He quickly leaned forward, both hands finding their way to rest on either side of my head while propping his ass up in the air for me.

"Good boy," I teased.

All jokes aside, he really was. One might say *perfect*, in fact.

Who in their right mind would argue otherwise?

He buried his face against my neck the moment I snapped the bottle open and drizzled some of it all over my fingers, coating them generously. Tossing the bottle next to me again, I reached around to find that perfect little hole of his, already waiting to bear down on my fingers the second I ghosted over it.

Spearing two fingers into him, I worked him until he was breathing hard against my neck, using each panted breath to guide me toward exactly where I wanted and soon finding it, reveling in the moment he choked around another moan. I brushed over that sensitive spot a few times, driving him into shoving back onto my fingers, and feeding him another digit to open him up. My dick ached to replace them all.

Watching him fuck himself like this was hot and almost just enough to get me off without actually having to wrap a hand around myself at all.

"Need it..." he whispered so sweetly in my ear.

"Sit back."

In seconds, he was pushing away from me to follow my direction. His hole tightened as my fingers retreated, a small shove of his hips catching the digits for a few seconds longer while he struggled with letting them go.

Already dick-drunk and I hadn't even begun to fuck him yet.

I gave his ass a hard swat and then reached up to twist one of his nipples between my knuckles. "So greedy. Aren't you supposed to be behaving?"

His back arched. "*Want.*"

Amusement flitted through me. "Impatient thing, aren't you."

He nodded quickly, eyes slowly growing hazy with lust. They tracked me as I swiped the condom up off the bed, teething it to rip the wrapper open and spitting out the piece left behind tucked between my lips. I kept a tight hold of his nipple to prevent him from moving again, a light sheen of sweat breaking out across his chest, giving him a slight glow.

"That's it," I murmured the moment he lifted himself up for me. Just enough to give me room to fit the condom over my tip.

A little tricky to roll it down with only one hand, but I soon had myself covered and ready to sink into what was hovering right over me. Gripping myself around the base, I lined up against him, precum already whiting the inside of the condom.

Honestly, I'd be lucky to get two strokes in before I blew. He was too hot not to let myself get carried away, especially with him riding me.

We'd have to do this slow, though. Not just to keep my raging hard on from blowing this all too soon, but to prevent me from hurting him in the process. The last thing I wanted was for him to walk away with from this hurting.

He slapped a hand down against my chest, almost as if to prevent me from sliding past that tight ring and getting myself right where I wanted. I froze on instinct, not at all expecting him to slam down onto me until his ass clapped against my hips. My dick spasmed inside of him, practically suffocating from how hard he tightened around it.

He winced visibly, pain causing his body to stiffen.

"*Blake—*" Holy *fuck*.

"So big," he moaned, rocking slightly.

I forgot I was dealing with a fucking masochist.

"You're going to make yourself bleed."

"Promise?" His face was so flushed he looked practically sunburned.

God, he was fucking hot as hell.

Fuck it.

He wanted it rough, that's exactly what he was going to get. I wasn't in the business to deny him anything, especially pleasure-wise.

My hand fit around his neck perfectly, his pupils blowing wide when I squeezed. "Go on, then. Take what you want."

There was absolutely no pain that radiated through me as Blake lifted himself up and then slammed back down onto my hips, practically bruising us both in the process. I was sure that by tomorrow morning, after the adrenaline from this, along with whatever bonding chemicals were racing through my veins, finally dissipated, I'd feel every little muscle twinge in agony.

It would all be worth it. Every little ache and pain I'd feel for the next few days would be a stark reminder as to how good fucking Blake felt. How *finally* I had him right where I wanted him. Where I needed to *keep* him.

His neck flexed under my hand as he swallowed and moaned, making it easy for me to readjust just enough to find his pulse point and drive my thumb into it. His skin burned against mine, a fire boiling to the surface.

Seeing him finally out of his funk from the past week nearly brought tears to my eyes. *This* was the Blake I knew and cared for—who I'd fallen for. The man I wanted as mine for as long as he'd let me keep him. I didn't want him to fall back into that sad and depressive state and would do fucking anything to prevent that from ever happening again.

Cum drooled from his tip, wetting my belly with each thrust. His rhythm stuttered when I clapped my hand against his ass cheek, hard enough to sting me right back. More cum leaked out of him, pooling on my skin.

"*Oh.*" Tears were wetting his lashes again, but this time for a much better reason than regret.

I pressed my thumb against his pulse point, cutting it off just enough to send that rush of endorphins racing through his body before letting up. He gasped and grabbed onto my wrist, steadying himself.

I bucked my hips up into him, drawing my good leg up to plant into the mattress to help me drive my dick deeper inside his tight heat.

So, so fucking good.

With each pass of my tip gliding along the inside of him and hitting his prostate, he quivered in my hold. He met me with each thrust, driving himself down until all that was separating us was a thin piece of latex that felt like it was barely able to keep up with us. Wetness gathered between our bodies, whether from sweat, lube, or blood, I couldn't tell and I was much too preoccupied with the blissed-out expression on Blake's face to care.

I slapped his wandering hand away the second it began to reach down to fist around his weeping cock. "No."

He whined back.

"Mine." I teased his pulse point with my thumb once more. "Behave."

He was so damn lovely this fucked up on my cock. Out of his mind with nothing but the burning need for me to keep fucking him until he was too far gone to even remember his name. I couldn't wait to explore all of it with him, his kinks, what got him off the quickest, how long I could torture him until he begged for mercy. We had so much damn time for it all.

He exploded in my hand the moment I got it wrapped around him, his hips jerking while cum painted us both. I squeezed his neck until his mouth dropped open and his eyes rolled into the back of his head, letting up right before he passed out on me completely.

The second his body swayed forward, I lowered him right back down to curl against my chest, tucking his face against my neck and keeping my hand cupped around the back of his head while spreading his cheeks with my other.

"*Marlow.*" My name whimpered like that had me ramming into him, jostling the bed under us until it knocked into the wall. "More. Feels so, so good..."

Ah, fuck.

My spine tingled from the praise, spoken so sweetly it was like a prayer.

"So good," he whispered in my ear, his lips brushing along the shell of it.

Two strokes and I was done for, coming so hard inside of it that I wouldn't be surprised if the condom split in two. My back arched, two places popping right above my tailbone that relieved whatever pressure had been building there instantly. Blake held onto me for dear life, a soft sigh leaving him the moment I relaxed back into the mattress.

He was perfect. *All of this* was perfect. Sex only solidified my resolve from earlier in convincing him to stay with me permanently.

How in the world could I give any of this up after three months?

How could I let him walk out of my life once I was healed and better?

The short answer was that I couldn't.

I wouldn't.

"Tell me that half-used bottle of lube was old and you just never bothered to throw it away."

I glided my hand up his spine, tracing the lines and dips under his skin in a languid motion.

I think I'm in love.

"What happens if I say I bought it like a month ago?"

Was that possible?

After only having known someone less than two months?

Avery certainly would say it was.

"Seriously?" was his not so satisfied-sounding reply.

I tightened my other hand in his hair, drawing a soft moan from his lips. "You aren't the only one who's had a healthy sex life."

"You're getting a new mattress," he muttered against my neck.

A laugh burst out of me. "So possessive. Does that mean I need all new sheets, too?"

He clamped his teeth down on my skin for a brief moment before saying, "*Yes.*"

"I'll agree to that under one condition."

"Is this more blackmail?"

"Nah." My pulse began to quicken again, a surge of anxiety rushing through me.

Rejection was never a subject I found myself afraid of. In fact, I took it as a challenge most days and used it to find whatever work around I could come up with to turn that *no* into a resounding *yes.*

This, though, opening myself up to Blake not wanting me in the way I wanted him, was fucking scary as shit.

"Stay with me." I pressed the words into his shoulder.

He shifted back just enough to lift his head and look at me. "For how long?"

"Forever." He had to feel how hard my heart was beating. "We'll figure out the camp thing. I'll buy a house up in Wakefield for the summer. What's your schedule like in the winter? Can't imagine there's too much to do up there after it snows? Unless you do winter activities... Fuck, you probably do. Snowshoeing and shit—?"

He cut me off with a chaste kiss. "Depends on the year. Depends on who signs up, really. Some years, we get a lot of interest; others, we coast on through a few reservations until spring hits."

He pursed his lips against mine, following the outline of my mouth until he reached the opposite corner and kissed there, too.

Not telling me no.
That's a good sign, right?

"You're not buying a second house," he finally said.

"Technically, it would be a third."

"Oh my god, Marlow."

"It's fine. It's not like I'd be hurting with another mortgage."

Did he want a nice little bungalow?

Where did he live in the off-seasons?

Obviously in Wakefield, but was it in one of those cute little apartments above one of the shops?

Or out in the suburbs with a white picket fence and a few nosey neighbors?

"I'm actually going to hit you if you keep talking."

Smirking, I gave his ass a nice little love tap in response, my expression widening when his body jerked. "Think you're the one that likes those, actually."

"Millionaire, he says. Just a simple millionaire with the means to buy multiple houses."

"Hey, I'm ethical. Unlike Avery who hoards the wealth. He's the one percent we need to eat. Not me, I'm innocent."

"And Silas?"

I shrugged. "Don't know. He won't let me

near his funds. Isn't that so rude? Like I'd gamble it all away on some failing stock. You know what, since I won our bet, I'm going to invest half of it in one of those scam bitcoins. That'll show him to try and go back on our deal."

Blake laughed. "You know, I'd like to keep you around for a little longer than next week. Why don't you table playing around with Silas's money for a bit."

"Oh? He wants to keep me around..."

His expression softened. "As long as you're okay with going back and forth... I know it's only an hour, but traveling can get annoying."

Relief flooded through me. "I don't care. Most of my clients are done remotely. Give me an Internet connection and I'm good."

"Off-season, I tend to not go on the property as much. Stopping by once or twice a week, at most. Summer is when I need to be there all the time."

"I can take summers off."

"Marlow—"

"Blake, I want this. I want *you*."

He reached up to brush his fingers along my cheek in the same way he had when he found me. A gentle caress to chase away whatever worries and troubles clouded my mind. Turning my head, I caught the pads with my lips, kissing them until a smile worked its way back onto his face.

"I want you, too," he whispered.

"Then stay. We'll figure it out."

He leaned over to rest his forehead against mine, his slow exhale ticking my face.

What was that saying?

About one person falling first and the other one falling harder?

I think I counted as both.

"I'd love to," he murmured and then kissed me.

CHAPTER 26

BLAKE

WATCHING Marlow's chest rise and fall in a steady motion nearly lulled me to sleep until the sound of his front door alarm disengaging hauled me right back into reality. Rubbing my eyes, I slowly untangled myself from his arms to sit up.

He hadn't told me he was expecting anyone later today. Then again, I'd caught him in the middle of talking with his mother and trying to convince her not to come over for dinner, so there was a strong possibility she'd gone against his wishes and come over anyway.

I had a hunch that him avoiding her was

because of me. Hopefully, that only extended into the realm of this being a new relationship and not wanting to jinx it by telling people too soon and not falling into *'I'm worried my mom is going to hate you'* territory.

I'd never come back from that, no matter how well I treated her son. Silas had made it damn clear to warn me.

Since my dating life was abysmal and non-existent before this, I had no experience impressing parents regardless of whether or not their preconceived opinions of me were positive or not. My own were an odd sort who played by their own set of traditions and values, not caring to follow the norm in anything they did.

I'd always appreciate that about them. Growing up in a 'free' household gave me plenty to be thankful for.

Rolling out of bed, I held back a wince as I stood, checking over my shoulder to make sure Marlow was still fast asleep. My body was sore from the sex, way more than I thought it would be, in the best way. It wouldn't surprise me if I tore something, but honestly, I didn't really care. That was hands down the best orgasm I'd ever had in my entire life.

Slowly hobbling to Marlow's bathroom, I slipped his robe off the back of his door and wrapped it around my body, covering up the marks imprinted into my skin by his hands. Feeling them with every movement of my body sent a twinge of delight tickling under my skin. They made me feel owned, belonged to.

Asking me to stay was the last thing I expected, yet somehow made so much sense even if it slapped me hard in the face with surprise.

Marlow was right. We'd figure out the logistics once he was all better and able to move on his own again. Until that time came, I simply wanted to stay in whatever this moment was.

"Marlow," someone called toward the front of the house. A man's voice.

Not his mother.

Silas, maybe?

Heading down the hall, I stopped short at seeing not the doctor toeing off his shoes, but Marlow's other friend I'd spotted waiting for him at the hospital. The taller one who'd spent the majority of his time there comforting Marlow's mother.

Avery.

Fuck me.

His eyes narrowed on me immediately. "You."

His dark blond hair was tied back in a half knot, the rest of the wavy lengths brushing his shoulders. While his clothes were casual, they were made with impeccable tailoring, displaying his wealth rather prominently without having to say a damn word.

In his hands was some kind of dish, the top of which was wrapped in tinfoil.

Nodding to it, I said, "You want me to take that?"

His shoulders stiffened. "Why are you wearing his things?"

Ugh, I really didn't want to get into this.

Especially, since my skin was still slightly crusted with our mixed fluids. I had no idea what the fuck I had going on between my legs, and at this point, I was far too sore to bend down to look.

Avery advanced toward me, his scowl deep as I remained quiet. "Does he know you're stealing his things?"

"I... don't think he would care?" Stealing was a rather harsh word. This was more like borrowing.

Though, to a protective friend, I doubted that mattered.

"I was going to put it back."

Avery shook his head. "Where is he?"

"Napping."

"So, you take advantage of a man who's too drugged up on meds to notice?" He leaned forward suddenly, forcing me to take a step back. "What's wrong with you? Wasn't it enough he got hurt under *your* watch? Now you think it's fair to steal from him, too?"

Oh god.

How the hell did I turn this around?

At least Silas gave me a little benefit of the doubt to prove I wasn't a total scumbag. Then again, the jury was still out on his formal opinion of me, though if I had to take a guess, it was probably mirroring this one.

"Avery, knock it off," Marlow's voice chimed in from behind me.

Whipping around, I spotted him slowly making his way over to us, his crutches stamping on the floor with each swing of his body. How he was able to move so quietly through the house with those things, I still had yet to figure out. It seemed whenever he wanted to remain stealthy, he had the uncanny ability to essentially make himself nearly inaudible to pick up on.

Now, though, he wasn't bothering to remain all that quiet. "You're such a bully."

Avery's mouth dropped open at the sight of him. "You're kidding."

Marlow had thrown on a matching robe, making this situation all the more obvious. If Avery hadn't picked up on what was going on before, he sure did now.

"You're *sleeping* with him?"

Marlow grinned. "Yup."

My hand conveniently found my face to sigh into. Leave it to him to not at all sugarcoat things.

What did I expect, though?

This man was honest to a fault sometimes.

"I can't help it. Look how cute he is." A kiss was pressed against my temple, drawing me out from under my hand.

"*Cute?* Marlow, he almost got you *killed.*" Concern was taking over the anger in Avery's voice, shifting it from a pointed and aggressive tone and turning it into one that was close to almost begging.

As if he were trying to plead with his friend

to open up his damn eyes and see the truth for what it really was: that he was taking a liability to bed.

Too bad we were both too far down in the trenches to care.

"It'll be a fun story to tell our kids," was all Marlow followed up with.

Wryly, I glanced at him. "Kids, huh?"

He shrugged, grinning again. "Maybe a dog, too. I'm thinking a lab. They like the water. Perfect for the lake."

Or a golden retriever, my mind helpfully supplied.

All right, I didn't hate that idea, but that was getting far too ahead of ourselves. Letting my mind wander to the fantasy wasn't helping with the fact that we had a very angry man in the house who was looking close to throwing whatever casserole dish he had in his hand right at my head.

Turning back to Avery, I said, "I'm sorry we are meeting like this. If I knew you were coming over, I would've fixed you up a drink first."

That had him blinking in surprise.

An arm was thrown around my shoulders.

"Blake here is the caretaker type. Kinda like your Brandon."

The other man's face pinched suddenly, his fingers lightly tapping the sides of the dish. Whoever Brandon was, most likely the other man who came with him to the hospital, he had a deep and profound effect on Avery. Enough to cool him down almost immediately.

"Silas said you're the director of *Austin Adventures*." His words were slow as he spoke them. "Don't you think it's highly unethical to be sleeping with your clients? Do you do that often?"

"Wow, way to make me feel like a dime-a-dozen, Av," Marlow said.

Right as Avery was opening his mouth to retort, I cut in. "I've never slept with a client. Nor entertained the idea before this."

"So why do so now?" he asked.

Turning my attention back to the man attached to the arm around my shoulders, I held his gaze for what felt like eons. The fork in the road was giving me two choices: deflect and try to make this all seem like a happy accident that simply turned into a relationship that neither of us were expecting to blossom.

Or, the second choice, and the much harder one: be vulnerable. Open up to Marlow's friend and show him that this wasn't a one-off deal, that I wasn't going to grow bored in a month and skip out before my duties were officially done and save myself from facing any kind of accountability.

Being in it for the long haul meant putting myself in positions where the need to be honest about my true feelings was paramount. For all of Silas's harsh bites and Avery's callous words, they were simply trying to protect their friend from some bozo coming in and wrecking their friend emotionally again.

They'd seen firsthand how hard Marlow had taken me running away the first time and I doubted that was giving them a stellar first impression of me to work with. If I were in their shoes, I'd want me to prove myself, too.

Pulling in a deep breath, I said, "I never planned on it. I've always had a strict rule about never crossing any boundaries with clients, no matter how flirty they try to get. Truthfully, there was never anyone that even remotely interested me. I thought... for a long time, I was broken somehow."

"You aren't, Blake." Marlow squeezed my shoulders.

"I was until you came around." A smile broke out on my face. "You lured me right in. Like one of those fishermen with the really shiny baits."

"Hope it was one of those expensive silver ones."

I laughed. "Definitely."

Looking back at Avery, I was surprised to see how much his expression had softened. Clearly, whatever I'd said resonated with him in some way, tempering down the anger he felt for me for the moment.

"I was scared about my feelings. How intense and real they were. But the more I tried to run away from them, the worse it felt to put distance between us. I don't want to go back to that ever again."

Marlow pressed another kiss to my temple. "Me either. Let's not."

I could get behind that. "Deal."

Avery's gaze flitted between us. His fingers drumming against the dish while lost in thought. When he finally spoke, he asked, "You're sure about this?"

With a first nod, Marlow replied, "More than I've been about anything in my life."

"He lives out in Wakefield, Mar. You remember that, right?"

"I'm gonna buy a summer home out that way."

I dug my elbow right into his ribs. "Knock it off."

His only response to that was to lift his arm from my shoulders and swing it around to clamp a hand against one of my ass cheeks, squeezing the sore muscle hard enough to make me jump. He threw his head back to laugh, a devious glint to his eyes.

He was lucky we had company.

Avery sighed. "Well, we might as well all eat together. Brandon made it for me to bring over since he knew you wouldn't be doing any cooking. But could you both go shower first? You reek like sweat and sex. It's making me nauseous."

"Say less," Marlow winked. "Any excuse to see Blake naked again is fine with me."

Grabbing his shoulders, I used them to spin him around, coaxing him back toward his bedroom. Avery merely shook his head at us before walking to the kitchen, throwing a quick '*don't take too long*' over his shoulder before disappearing beyond the doorway.

"Come on, grandpa," I said, gently nudging him forward.

"You into that, Blake? I know we're pretty far apart in age but I didn't think you were into the major age gaps."

Feeling ballsy, I slapped his ass. "Guess you'll have to find out."

The grin he turned to throw over his shoulder at me was all the more promising. "Oh, I intend to find out every little thing about you. Don't you worry."

Oh man, did I love the sound of that promise.

EPILOGUE

Blake

Pulling up the short drive, I sat back in the driver's seat and threw the car into park.

The lights on the porch were on, along with a very festive set of Christmas lights, still strung up along the porch from last year that had yet to be taken down despite it being well past the season by a long shot. Next to me, my companion shifted in his seat, still deathly quiet from our trip over here.

Which... wasn't at all helping with my damn nerves. If anything, I would've preferred the mindless chatter to keep me distracted from the rolling nerves in my stomach.

"Cute place," Marlow observed.

"Thanks." Though why I was taking credit for it was beyond me. I supposed that's what you kind of did when it was the place you grew up in all your life and regarded as a safe landing pad in times of trouble.

Beyond the porch light was another one coming in from the front door's window. The small chandelier my mother had inherited from my grandma before she passed just out of view. Thankfully, no one was rushing out of the house to come drag us inside yet.

Though, it was only a matter of time before that happened.

"How's your leg?" I asked, turning my attention away from my childhood home.

Marlow slowly looked down, slapping his hands around his thigh and drawing it up from where it was tucked under the dash. He rotated his ankle a few times, finally free from the cast that had been confining it for the past three and a half months.

In the grand scheme of things, that was a blink of an eye compared to the years that were left down the road. But for someone as active as Marlow, it might as well have been torture.

"Oh my god," he murmured. "It's... alive!"

The joke cracked through the anxious cloud hovering over me. "Oh no. What does it hunger for?"

A horrified look crossed his face. "It... it's... hungry for blood!"

He jerked it around the small leg space, noises that sounded close to cats being strangled tumbling past his lips. Amused, I patted his shoulder a few times before popping my door open, letting the fresh autumn air hit me.

I never minded the changing seasons.

Going from spending all day under a hot sun to a nice, crisp fall evening gave me the kind of reset I was looking for after the busy summer months that felt never-ending at points. Things slowed down this time of year, giving us all a much-needed reprieve.

The passenger door popped open, Marlow's familiar figure coming into view. He ducked behind to the back seat to grab what he had deemed his 'humble offerings', gathering the *very* expensive bottles of wine along with the large king-size boxes of candy into his arms.

"Want help?"

"Nope." He hip checked the door closed behind him. "You just get that pretty little butt of yours up the front steps and open the door for me."

"Yes, sir."

Even in the dark, I could tell his eyes instantly flashed with interest. "Careful, Austin. There's still time to drag you into that back seat."

A shiver rolled up my spine. "Don't tempt me."

Fucking in my parent's driveway. Now that would certainly be a first for me.

If this wasn't Marlow's first time meeting my entire family, I'd take him up on the offer. If only to check it off on our bucket list.

Keeping close to him and a wary eye on his newly free leg, we headed up to the front door. It was already unlocked when I tried the handle, a good sign that everyone was already here ahead of us.

While my two younger brothers were still teenagers and lived at home, my two older sisters had long since moved on to greener pastures, coming around for the festivities whenever the option was presented in the family group chat.

Loud voices hit my ear immediately. The familiar sounds of a game night going very poorly telling me all I needed to know about what the hell we were walking into.

Oh, boy.

"Rowdy bunch," Marlow said, amusement dripping from his tone.

"You have no idea." Toeing off my shoes, I took both wine bottles from him while he squatted to unlace his. "Remember how much you said you loved being an only child because it was nice and quiet and you got all the undivided attention from both parents?"

"Look, that was the old me. The *new* me loves big, loud, obnoxious family gatherings."

"Famous last words."

He grinned, standing up to snatch the wine bottles from me. "Are we making a bet? Please say yes, I'm dying for the dopamine hit."

"You literally just closed a giant portfolio last week."

He pecked me on my lips. "Old me, babe. This week is the *new* me. New leg, new screws and plates, new everything."

"Right," I drawled, not being able to help the smile crawling across my face.

"Do I hear my favorite at the door?" My mother's voice cut through the arguing.

Marlow nudged my side. "She's talking about me."

Her stomps moved from the living room and down the hall toward us. Her wild and curly dark hair was pushed back with one of those plastic headbands found at the dollar store, her glasses tucked up on top of it.

She was in a matching set of clothes, plum colored corduroy pants and a satin blouse with a bow tied at the neck. Her beaded jewelry was in the form of earrings today, hanging down and just brushing her shoulders as she walked.

She lit up the moment she spotted me, her arms jutting out to pull me into a tight hug. "Blake!"

I hugged her back just as firmly. "It's nice to see you. I missed you a lot."

"Oh, stop it." She ripped me back from her. "You're going to make me cry."

She glanced next to me, her eyes going wide the second she remembered who was behind me.

"You must be Marlow."

"Guilty."

She laughed. "Come on in! We've got Jenga

set up in the family room. What's all that you brought with you? Oh, Blake. I told you we didn't need anything."

Shrugging, I replied, "He insisted."

Marlow leaned into me from behind, holding up a wine-filled hand as he stage-whispered at my mom. "It's my way of trying to butter you up so that you like me enough to not turn me down when I ask you for your permission to marry your son."

I choked. "*What?!*"

Her face lit up immediately, taking one of the wine bottles offered to her. "How exciting! Blake, you didn't tell me you two were getting so serious!"

My face was on fire, tongue too tied-up with disbelief to answer her.

Was he kidding?

He had to be. We'd only been dating three months. That was way too soon for him to want to get hitched, right?

He...

Did he really...

When has he ever lied?

"Of course." With his hand now free, he wrapped it around me to pull me against his chest, a soft kiss finding its way to my forehead. "I love him with all my heart."

My jaw dropped.

Love.

Marlow loved me.

"You do?" I choked out.

"Till my last dying breath… and probably a little bit after that, too." His eyes twinkled with mischief. "Let's be honest, I'll definitely be haunting you in the afterlife."

"I'm flattered to be haunted by my dead boyfriend for all eternity."

"Don't worry, I'll chase off any prospects that try and make a move on you."

I let out a small laugh. "Poltergeist style, huh."

"Complete with the spooky notes on a foggy mirror after a hot shower and everything."

Oh, how I loved this man.

Really, *really* loved him.

"You can't go first. That's not fair. You already tried that, remember?"

"Too true." He cupped my jaw. "What a poor choice in trying to get your attention."

"Seriously."

My mom clapped a hand over her mouth, a small sob nearly escaping. "Oh, you two!"

Slipping the other bottle from Marlow's grasp, I passed it over to her before the water works could start. Not that I minded them, but once she started, she was going to get me going, too. This sudden and profound love confession was already making me dizzy with emotions as it was.

"Want to go pop those open? I'm sure Cassie and Carly will be happy to snag a glass."

She quickly nodded her head, holding both to her chest like precious cargo. "Yes, absolutely. Oh, I'm so happy. Marlow, please come on in. We don't bite."

"Can't say the same for myself," he teased.

She let out a delighted sound. "You're funny. I like you. You're going to fit right in." Pivoting on her heel, she stomped down the hall, toward the kitchen, calling out for my father. "Mark! Blake's here!"

The moment she disappeared around the corner, I turned back to Marlow. "You meant what you said?"

"Every damn word," came his easy reply.

I couldn't help but sag into him, letting my arms wrap around his waist. "Me too."

He gasped. "You bite? Since when?"

The moment he cupped my face to tilt it up toward his again, I smiled. "I love you, too, Marlow."

His smile was incandescent, deepening his dimples in the most charming way, sending my heart fluttering. He slotted his mouth over mine, kissing me until my entire body tingled.

"I love you, Blake... forever."

Not being able to help myself, I replied, "I hope you remember that when we're five rounds deep into Jenga."

"That's what the wine's for."

Touché.

"Come on," snagging his hand, I tugged him down the hall. "My family awaits your anticipated presence."

He squeezed my hand in return. "Can't wait."

∽

TERRAN

. . .

A KNIFE THUNKED into the side of the wall right by my shoulder, missing me by a mere two inches. Attached to the handle was a white-knuckled hand that strained to pull it out, the soft grunting of someone close to me sending chills racing down my spine.

Holy shit—

I brought my arm up to block the fist thrown at me, surprisingly with a good amount of force behind the swing. The knife was dislodged a single second later and swiped at my face, a breeze ghosting over my cheek and narrowly missed me for a second time.

Less than twelve fucking steps from the door and this jackass decided to attack us now.

Another tone chimed in my ear, muffled by my heart hammering in my chest, a familiar voice coming over the radio—dispatch? Another unit arriving? I couldn't tell. Not with my focus pinpointing directly on the man trying to stab me.

I caught him by the shoulder before he could swing back around again, shoving him hard in the opposite direction and toward the wall on the other side of the hallway. His body snapped back the second he hit it, his head slamming hard enough to force a wince out of me. To my surprise, he didn't crumble to the ground like I was expecting, keeping himself upright with one hand splayed out next to him and the other with the knife still clutched tight between his fingers.

His long hair obscured his features, stringy from sweat and slightly curling at the ends. He swayed slightly on his feet.

I reached for my gun again. "Don't."

If this fucker even thought about—

He lunged forward, slamming his entire body weight into me and taking us both down to the floor. My shoulder connected with the ground first, radiating pain up my entire spine and shooting right to the base of my skull from the force, leaving me with little room to breathe through the pain while his weight shifted on top of me.

Pinned at an awkward angle like this made it fucking impossible to reach for my gun strapped to my right hip. Mere seconds into this fight and I was already losing, getting my ass handed to me by a goddamn junkie.

One of his hands fisted in my hair and held me down while the other rose above us, metal glinting out of the corner of my eye.

Oh, fuck.

The snap decision to ram my fist into his side and knock him sideways was the only thing that saved that knife from connecting directly with my skull at the last second. His pained grunt telling me when to twist and flip us both over, upending things in my favor for once. The moment his head thumped against the floor, I reached for my handcuffs, fisting my free hand against his shirt to pin him down.

"You're under arrest."

The one thing I neglected to remember, was securing the weapon above anything else. A training module from my first weeks at the academy flashing in my mind mere milliseconds before I felt the dull sensation of something colliding with my stomach.

There were a million things to remember on this job, ranging from reading off rights to making sure a crime scene was properly taped off in the event of a crisis. So many, in fact, that they often had me waking up in cold sweats at night, the recited words from those practice exams still lingering on my tongue.

How ironic that of all times, this is when I forgot the most important step.

My body froze out of sheer shock, my eyes glancing down to where the man's fist was pressed up against my stomach, the knife buried deep enough into my body that only the hilt was still visible.

Gruesome and yet impressive. The kind of strength it took to actually force your way through clothing *and* skin like that was actually a lot harder than many people knew. Our bodies were made to survive the worst conditions, sharp knives included.

"Terran!"

My vision swam the second I registered TJ's voice.

Blood coated the perp's hand, thick trickles that grew worse the second he twisted the handle and then forced it out of me, taking my entire lung capacity with him.

There wasn't much that scared me these days when I was constantly putting myself into dangerous situations for a job. Dealing with people that could suddenly turn on you in an instant was always a risk and one I'd whole-heartedly signed up for the moment I graduated from the academy.

Plenty of times in the past, I'd come face to

face with a situation that had the potential to result in death, but somehow with my luck, it'd never seemed to come to pass.

Until now, apparently.

.

CLICK NOW TO READ *SILAS*, the next book in the Billionaire Bad Boys & Blue Collar Men series.

DEAR READER

Dear Reader,

Thank you for reading Marlow, book two in the Billionaire Bad Boys & Blue Collar Men series.

If you enjoyed this book, then please let me know. You can simply return to the online retailer where you made your purchase and leave me a short review.

Your thoughts may just encourage other readers to try my books, and help me continue writing the characters we all adore and root for.

Even a few words would mean the world to me.

~Love, Evie Riley

OTHER BOOKS BY EVIE

Other Books By Evie

My action-filled, romantic suspense, and darker-themed books:

Rock Hard Mountain Men
Magnus
Brody
Creed

Federal Protection Agency
Mason
Rafe
Ryzen
Cooper
Noah
Damien
Sebastian
Gabe
Logan

Ruthless Empire
Courting Danger
Chasing Danger
Kissing Danger

Smokejumpers
Hawke

Cyrus
Jase
Gage
Jackson
Xavier

From The Edge
Shattered
Runaway
Jaded
Rescue
Hidden
Tormented

Gray Vale Pack
His Fated Mate
His Wounded Warrior
His Healing Heart

My more romance-themed books:

**Billionaire Bad Boys
& Blue Collar Men**
Avery
Marlow
Silas

Rock His World
Hollow Heart
Wild Stars
Grave Misgivings

Jasper Springs

OTHER BOOKS BY EVIE

Cade
Dawson
Drew
Grayson
Riley
Mitch

ABOUT THE AUTHOR

Evie Riley believes too much time spent at the beach is barely enough. She enjoys spending time puttering in the garden, cooking yummy things for her family, and has a quirky personality, described by her partner as ranging from cute to deadly, depending on her blood-chocolate levels.

Evie crafts steamy gay male romance filled with all the edgy angst, or dark and gritty romantic suspense where her men must overcome difficult obstacles and may find love along the way while dishing out their own brand of justice.

Evie spends her nights writing bad boys in love, and her days wrangling the sweet boys she loves.

www.ingramcontent.com/pod-product-compliance
Lightning Source LLC
Chambersburg PA
CBHW070340170726
48291CB00001B/119